GLITZ. GLAMOUR. MURDER.

GLITZ. GLAMOUR. MURDER.

Hollywood Has It All

SONNY HUDSON

William K Hudson

*Any sufficiently advanced technology
is indistinguishable from magic.*

Arthur C. Clarke

PROLOGUE

Life was hard inside the Federal Correctional Institute (FCI) Medium 1 in Victorville, CA. A hard place for hard men. It was even harder at the high-security facility located on the same sprawling property; anyone who'd ever been in a maximum-security prison had the attitude that medium security facilities were country clubs. Still, with 1800-plus men crammed into a crowded, violent hellhole, it's not exactly a day at Disneyland. Located between San Bernardino and Barstow, CA, the prison felt like it was a million miles from anywhere. That was surely part of the appeal from the Bureau of Prisons' perspective: cheap land, wide open spaces that make it hard for people to disappear, and a less-than-affluent area where the locals are eager to invite in almost any kind of industry that brings jobs to the area. If that industry dropped thousands of the worst members of society right into your backyard? Well, you have to take the good with the bad. And remember to lock your doors.

Brookes Williamson had only been at Victorville for a few months following his conviction as a co-conspirator in the infamous 'Murder Game' case for being an active and frequent bettor and for evading taxes on his winnings. Even his family's considerable wealth and influence, and his Beverly Hills legal team, couldn't keep Brookes out of prison. At his attorneys' urging, almost insistence, he had taken the plea deal offered by the US Attorney rather than going to trial. While he considered any sentence that included prison time a travesty of justice, not to mention a colossal waste of money for his high-priced attorneys, 18 months in a federal prison with 5 months suspended for 'time served' in the County jail, was lighter than most other Murder Game co-conspirators received. Everyone told him that his sentence would likely be much longer if he went to trial, but his narcissistic mind couldn't wrap itself around a scenario where he couldn't talk himself out of trouble and be found not guilty.

Williamson shared a cell with John Westbrook, an inmate serving a 15-year sentence for armed robbery and a repeat 'resident' of Victorville. Other inmates referred to them as 'The Odd Couple' because they were polar opposites: Williamson was on the thin side at 5'11" and 175 pounds, and his idea of physical activity was a bike ride around his neighborhood or hanging out at the beach. Westbrook, on the other hand, was 6'7" and nearly 300 pounds of rock-solid muscle, and he worked out daily to keep himself in top physical shape – not to mention, intimidating as hell to most of the other inmates. They were also vastly different when it came to education and intellect. Westbrook had dropped out of school in 10th grade, while Williamson had a B.A. and M.A. from the University of Virginia. Strangely, though, they got along well, and Westbrook took on the role of Williamson's protector inside the prison walls, and while there were whispers that Williamson was his 'bitch', that line had never been crossed, not even approached.

They stood together in the exercise yard out of earshot of the other prisoners and the guards. People were always listening, trying to catch some snippet of gossip or information that they could use as leverage over others or as 'currency' to be traded with the guards or prison administration. Everyone knows that prisoners need to develop eyes in the back of their head to survive, but the reality is that they also need to develop a sixth sense of when others are snooping on their conversation. Of course, that doesn't always help when prisoners are more than happy to make up conversations and overheard jailhouse confessions if it will serve their own selfish ends, but you control what you can control.

"Everything still a 'go' for this afternoon?" Brookes looked directly at John and kept his voice low, but his eyes never stopped scanning the other inmates scattered around the yard. Attacks could happen anywhere in the prison – and they do – but the yard is often the go-to spot.

"Yeah, everything is in place. I was able to confirm that today's laundry pickup and delivery is scheduled for 3:30, and that aligns perfectly with the scheduled shift change for the guards. The inmates assigned to the laundry will be ending their shifts at the same time, so a lot of confusion and moving pieces. I think it's our best window." Westbrook was assigned to the prison laundry in a role best described as shift foreman. It was a hot, muggy environment even on the coldest winter days, but it was his detailed knowledge of that huge facility, including operational details about contractor scheduling, guard shift changes, and inmate assignments, that was invaluable.

"And you've confirmed my assignment to the laundry?"

"Yes. You'll work your usual shift in the library up until 2:00pm, and then you'll be escorted to the laundry to start your orientation and training. I'll be showing you around, and when it's time to slip away, you'll just stick close to me."

Ask any inmate, and they'll all claim to have a fool-proof escape plan that they plan to execute at some point in the future. Some are convinced they can tunnel their way out, while others think they can crawl through a ventilation shaft and make their way to freedom. Some just plan to go old-school and overpower the guards, and if necessary, shoot their way out. The reality is that few inmates ever attempt an escape, and for those that do try, nearly 100% of the attempts fail. When they fail it's usually because of a lack of careful planning, making the plan overly complicated, or involving and trusting too many people. *Loose lips sink ships*, and that's never truer than in prison. The few escapes that are successful tend to be relatively simple and straightforward, like the inmate that escapes while being transported for a court hearing by overpowering a few guards and hauling-ass. Of course, escaping is just the first step; you've got to figure out where to go, how to get there, and how to avoid being captured. You're escaping with pretty much nothing but the prison uniform on your back: no money, no 'civilian' clothes, nothing that would let you live off the land for days or weeks at a time. Very few manage to stay on the run for long since the police, and especially the US Marshals, are very good at their job. It's usually just a matter of time, a *very* short matter of time, before they're back in custody. Or dead. Brookes Williamson didn't plan to be either.

It was almost 2:30 before Brookes and his escort made it to the prison laundry, but once there he was checked-in by the assigned guards and handed over to Westbrook. Over the next hour the two of them went through the motions of mentor and trainee as Brookes was shown around all areas of the facility, how to operate the machinery, and how to fold laundry per regulations. As 3:30 approached, Brookes was led to a storage room where the laundry carts were kept awaiting pickup.

"OK, the two carts closest to the exit door are the ones that I modified with false bottoms that we're going to use. It won't be comfortable, but even when the cart is stacked with laundry bags, we should still have plenty of air for at least 30 minutes. We need to move quickly; we've got maybe 10 minutes before the laundry service guys get here and start rolling these out."

Brookes was not a fan of tight spaces, but he knew this was his one shot at escape. The whole thing had been his idea and he and John had talked through the plan for more than a month. John provided the labor and the know-how when it came to building things. The idea of using a simple piece of plywood that was braced around the perimeter of the cart with small pieces of 2"x4" was elegantly simple. The plywood 'floor' would be about 18" above the real bottom and had dozens of holes drilled through it for ventilation. They'd even gone the extra step and measured the average weight of the laundry bags so that the people moving them wouldn't notice that they were especially heavy or light: that meant that in John's case, they had to compensate by loading fewer laundry bags on top.

"One thing I'm still not clear on is how we get in and out of the carts once we've loaded the laundry bags on top of the false floor," John had wondered during their early design discussions.

He's not the sharpest knife in the drawer. "It's simple, really. You take a knife and cut out a hatch in the canvas on each end of the cart that's big enough for us to crawl through, and then you secure that fabric back to the cart with Velcro or double-side tape; I'm sure you've got something like that around the laundry. That way we can sneak into the cart during the confusion of the shift change and crawl back out once we're outside the prison walls."

The trickiest part was going to be getting out of the carts while in the back of the truck without being noticed by the driver and his helper. At most, they probably had about 15 minutes before someone noticed that they were gone, and after that, maybe another 5-10 minutes before the alarm was raised when they couldn't be found anywhere within the prison. That meant that they had to get out of the carts and start making their way out of the area with no time to waste. Luckily, Brookes had already thought about that.

"You've been able to confirm that we're the laundry service's first stop, right? And that they've got several stops on their route?"

John nodded. "Yeah, I confirmed that. They leave here and then hit a couple of restaurants and the hospital before heading back to their facility. We should plan to make our way out of the truck and away from the area at their first stop."

"Definitely. The longer we're in that truck the more likely it is that someone will notice that we're missing. Hopefully we can make our way out of the truck without being seen by anyone, especially the truck crew, but if they see us or try to stop us, we need to be ready to take them out."

"That's not a problem. I'd rather avoid that because it just increases our risk of exposure, but if that's what it takes, that's what we'll do."

"And you've already loaded our street clothes in the carts?"

"Yeah, in each of our carts. I put the stuff in a small laundry bag with a red tag on it to make it easy to find."

"Excellent. And we'll stick to the plan: as soon as we're clear of the truck, we'll split-up and go our separate ways." Brookes had insisted on this point because the two of them together would be easier to spot than either one of them alone. Plus, Brookes knew that John was such a big guy that he stood out from the crowd, to put it mildly. Being near him just increased his chances of getting caught, and he wasn't about to risk that. Every man for himself.

Finally, it was time. The laundry service truck arrived as scheduled, and John greeted the crew, as usual, and led them to the storage room. "We've just got these six carts today, guys, so if you want to start taking them out, I'll go ahead and sign the paperwork now so you can be ready to roll."

As the driver and his helper rolled the first two carts out, Brookes and John checked to make sure that no guards or other inmates were nearby and, seeing that all was clear, crawled into the modified carts. They were in the last ones to be taken out, but that would be only a few minutes. It wasn't long before they were being wheeled out the door and loaded into the truck and the door being closed, and after a cursory inspection at the prison gates, they were on their way. So far, so good.

The truck's first stop was barely five minutes away at a chain casual dining restaurant. As soon as the crew exited the truck, Brookes and John slipped out of their carts and quickly slipped into the clothes they had stashed. Not perfect, not exactly stylish, but at least they were out of their orange prison jumpsuits. Seeing that things were all clear, they stepped casually down and away from the truck and started walking east.

"Change of plans, big guy. I see a chance for us to get away faster than we'd planned." He nodded his head towards a car pulling into the parking lot not 50 feet away and, luckily, no one else around. "Let's jack this dude that just pulled into that parking space in the blue Lexus. I don't see anyone else around; let's grab his keys and the car and get the hell out of here."

John nodded his agreement and slowly started making his way in the direction of the Lexus. As the driver emerged, John hit him with a vicious right hand that knocked the man unconscious. It took just a few seconds to grab his keys and wallet and then roll the unconscious man under the large Ford F-250 pickup parked next to them.

John tossed the keys to Brookes. "Here, you drive. It's been too many years since I've been behind the wheel."

"Let's go. We'll head east towards Barstow, and then we can decide where we want to go from there. We'll probably have to dump this car in an hour, maybe less, so let's put some distance between us and this place."

As it turned out, they had more time than they realized. While the prison did note their absence within 30 minutes and raise the alarm, it was another hour before it was determined how they'd escaped. Worse, it was nearly two hours before they found the unconscious car owner, and only because the truck owner almost ran over him when leaving the restaurant. John had hit the man so hard that he had a concussion and was still unconscious, and because he had no ID on him, he was listed as a 'John Doe' at the hospital. It was another 90 minutes before someone put together the fact that he'd been carjacked, likely by the two escapees. By the time that Brookes and John were connected to the carjacking and an APB issued for the stolen Lexus, they'd already reached Barstow and left it in a parking lot with the keys still in it. Of course, they helped themselves to the contents of the wallet.

I

MONDAY, MAY 8

"Uggghhhh!! How is it possible that I have spent my entire adult life writing hundreds of articles, on surely hundreds of different topics, but I can't even string two coherent sentences together on this godforsaken screenplay? Especially when I'm writing about something that I lived through and know in intimate detail?" Kristyn's frustration was boiling over, and not for the first time since she and JJ joined the team of writers developing the screenplay for their first feature film.

JJ giggled at Kristyn's outburst. They had both had a lot of them over the past few weeks. "How do you think I feel? At least you know *how* to write and have experience doing it! I haven't written anything more exciting than an FBI report since I was in high school English class."

"I don't know about you, but I could definitely use a break. My brain has had it. You feel like taking a walk on the beach? My doctors are still saying that I shouldn't sit for more than a couple of hours at a time and that I need to keep moving and stretching." She knew that JJ was always up for a walk on the beach or just sitting by the ocean, no real excuse or rationale needed. Kristyn was already up from her chair and reaching for her jacket.

"You don't have to twist my arm," JJ giggled. "I'd love to go for a walk." JJ knew that Kristyn needed to keep herself active to help speed her recovery from the horrific injuries she'd suffered just over three months ago during the Murder Game investigation. While the head wound had been superficial and healed quickly, the gunshot to the shoulder was much more debilitating. She'd already had two surgeries and months of physical therapy, but she still had quite a way to go. The shoulder tended to stiffen up if she sat at her computer for too long or skipped any of her exercise sessions. JJ was like a mother hen in that respect: she 'reminded' Kristyn several times a day to take a break and do her exercises. Fortunately, her own injuries, a couple of broken ribs suffered when Jamarcus Hicks shot her with a high-powered sniper rifle, had healed pretty quickly. If she wasn't already a believer in ballistic vests, she certainly was now. Without the one she'd been wearing that day in Dallas, she'd be dead.

The two of them had been inseparable since Kristyn was released from the hospital. JJ moved into her house to take care of her, or at least that was the story she told herself. It was really about being head over heels in love, and unless she misread the signals – and admittedly, she was known to do that when it came to matters of the heart – Kristyn felt the same way. After JJ resigned from the FBI, it was good for her to have a shoulder to cry on, albeit Kristyn only had one good shoulder to serve that purpose. While JJ had been brave and stoic, and maybe even a little bit cocky, during her FBI disciplinary hearing and when she resigned, the truth was that she needed some time to recover and get her head back on straight. The FBI had been her whole life, really all that she had known, for years. Walking away from that was scary and debilitating. Taking care of Kristyn and helping her heal and recover from her wounds, both physical and mental, was a huge help.

Neither of them were used to sitting around doing nothing and dwelling on their pain and problems, so it was a godsend when the deal was finalized for them to join the talented team of writers that was developing the screenplay based on the famous – and infamous – Murder Game case. Perhaps the most exciting part, though, was their agent negotiating spots for them as producers and helping them set up their own production company, Supersleuth Productions. They hoped to soak up all the knowledge they could on this production and then find projects of their own to develop and produce from start to finish in the future. Nothing like an exciting new project or goal in life to help you get over the past.

Now they'd moved their relationship to the next level and moved their lives to California, ready to dive headfirst into a new adventure. They'd rented out both of their homes in Dallas and made the leap. They'd gotten lucky and found a long-term rental right on the beach in Santa Monica, and it was far from a little beach cottage. Just a few steps off Ocean Avenue, it was 6500 square feet of luxury: 4 bedrooms, 5.5 bathrooms, a wine cellar, two offices, a beautiful pool, and a 3-bedroom, 2-bathroom guest house. Best of all, their agent had made a great deal where the studio covered the not-insignificant monthly rent as part of JJ and Kristyn's salary.

It was a beautiful day for a walk on the beach, with temperatures in the mid-60's and plenty of sunshine. They'd fallen completely in love with their new life and location. "I heard that they were having freezing temperatures and ice storms back in Dallas today. I really don't miss that kind of weather," said JJ.

"Me either. I should feel bad for them, but I don't. I guess I'm just getting old and jaded. And spoiled as hell by this beautiful place."

"Me, too. And even though we've only been here a few months, I can't imagine ever wanting to live anywhere else."

"You mean you're not absolutely dying to move back to Dallas?" Kristyn couldn't help but smile when she posed this question to JJ.

"Oh God, no. There's nothing for me back there. I realize that it's different for you because you have family back in Texas, and if you ever wanted or needed us to go back there, I'll be right there with you. But if it's a choice, I'd take California in a heartbeat."

"Right there with ya on that one. By the way, speaking of Texas, have you talked to Isaksen lately?" Kristyn was referring to JJ's former boss, the Special Agent in Charge (SAC) of the FBI's Dallas Field Office. JJ had resigned from the FBI when she was being investigated by the Office of Professional Responsibility (OPR) after the Murder Game case was wrapped up. It was obvious that the OPR wanted to force her out because she'd played a bit fast and loose with the rules, not the least of which was allowing Kristyn to be involved in the case and almost getting her killed. As a condition of her resigning, JJ had made it abundantly clear that the OPR had to back off of their hidden agenda to try to force Isaksen out at the same time or else she would drag the whole affair out in the courts and in the press.

"I actually have a call with him this afternoon to catch up on things, especially the ongoing investigation and indictments of the online players. The US Attorneys around the country are going for the jugular with these guys, not that I blame them. Hopefully they won't need me for any more in-person interviews or, God forbid, being called to testify."

"Will US Attorney Maria Dasher be on the call, too? I haven't heard you mention her name much lately." JJ had worked closely with Maria Dasher during the Murder Game investigation and would have been the key witness in the trials of Jamarcus Hicks, Mark Saxe, Calvin Mitchell, and Graham Robbins, collectively known as the Slayers, had they survived long enough to be arrested and stand trial.

"There's a good reason for that. Since all of the Slayers are dead, the high-profile trial that she'd hoped for, complete with live Court TV coverage, is never going to happen. And since the majority of the online bettors are a bunch of unknowns, they're not nearly high profile enough for her to take the lead. There are a few exceptions, including a few judges, a high-profile televangelist, and a smattering of congressmen and senators, but I'm guessing they'll all cop a plea. She always looks for the cases that are a slam-dunk win and front-page news; she's a great prosecutor, but she's always looking for those cases that raise her profile and help her climb the ladder."

"I guess it's a major disappointment for her; I know that she'd hoped to ride this case all the way to a state Senate run. For that matter, I wouldn't have been shocked to see her go for a Congressional seat in the next election. Too bad for her that you did your job so well and all the bad guys are dead, leaving her no one to prosecute. Then again, maybe she'll decide to come after you for some kind of trumped-up charges of excessive force or violating their civil rights."

"I would say that that's the craziest, most ludicrous thing I've ever heard, but then my jaded mind realizes that one can never be too certain when it comes to politics and what some people will do to get what they want. Let's just hope that she's got better sense than to go down that route. I can't imagine that being a popular case with the public. Or maybe I'm kidding myself."

Kristyn giggled. "Please, you did the people – hell, the taxpayers – a huge favor, and they know it. You saved them the hassle and expense of trials and God knows how many years of the Slayers sitting on death row and going through forever-appeals. They'd probably give you a ticker tape parade and vote for you for Congress."

"Oh, God, don't say that! Can you imagine the field day they'd have dragging my sordid past through the mud? I'd make Nixon and Trump look like veritable choir boys." JJ was already too embarrassed by all of the details of her life that had been dragged out and publicized even when she was being hailed as a hero; she couldn't imagine how vicious things would be if she were crazy enough to jump into politics.

Realizing that the dredging up of her past had caused JJ unneeded embarrassment, stress and anxiety over the past few months, Kristyn quickly changed the subject. "I know what would make both of our days. Let's walk down to the pier and grab an ice cream cone! I could use the break, and the walk would do us both good. What do you say?"

Thinking it through didn't take but a few seconds. JJ was always a sucker for a sweet treat. "I think that sounds like a great idea. I could use a couple of scoops. And the long walk would offset the calories. At least in theory." She smiled at Kristyn and took her hand.

"You know that eventually we will have to head back to the house and get back to work on the screenplay, right?"

"Yeah, but the key word is 'eventually'. Right now, my focus is on figuring out which flavors of ice cream I want, or if I want a sundae instead of a double-dip cone. For the time being let's focus on this beautiful day, this beautiful place, and each other. And let's just be thankful that this whole Murder Game insanity is behind us. And may they all rest in hell."

2

TUESDAY, MAY 9

It was 10am when everyone finally gathered in the conference room at Highline Studios in Hollywood, the studio that had secured the rights to produce a film based on the Murder Game case. While the studio had agreed to put up a significant percentage of the money directly, they had enlisted one of the top Hollywood power players, Jackson Taylor, to serve as Executive Producer on the film. Taylor, as was his practice, agreed to put up a generous portion of the budget himself and worked with other high-rollers and financiers to secure the rest. With a budget of $52.5 million, this was not slated to be a low-budget, straight-to-pay-per-view kind of movie. True, it didn't have the huge budget of a Marvel superhero film or one with tons of expensive locales, CGI, and other things that blow through money like it's going out of style. Still, $52.5 million was not exactly pocket change.

Pre-production had been going on for almost eight weeks, and with the budget already secured, it was Taylors's job as Executive Producer to identify the lead actors, hire the production team, and set the budget for each aspect of the production. Hiring the producers was the simplest task since he'd worked with all of them on past projects, with the exception of JJ and Kristyn. Admittedly, he was never a fan of having to work with 'trophy producers' that get attached to films because they wrote the book that's being adapted for the screen or had a hand in the 'real life' events that led to the film project. Oftentimes these 'producers' added little or no value while sucking up valuable time and budget dollars, but he was pleasantly surprised by JJ and Kristyn: they'd added great ideas and perspective and been like sponges trying to listen and learn the business.

JJ and Kristyn had come into this project knowing that they had a lot to learn but fully intending to prove themselves. The other producers, all of whom had tons of awards for their work on other Hollywood projects, including Oscars, Emmys, and Golden Globes, were not going to be impressed by their business cards identifying them as the owners of Supersleuth Productions, a company with zero projects, credits, or awards to its name. Luckily, the team welcomed them with open arms and were very patient in mentoring them and helping them better understand the business and their roles as producers.

"So, Jackson, where are we regarding locking down the actors to play JJ and Kristyn?" This from Kelli Markowitz, who along with her partner, Miles Carpenter, had produced more than a half dozen films that grossed at least $100 million in her career. "And are we losing any of the backers since Jennifer Lawrence pulled out of the project after you'd promised her as one of the leads?"

"Losing Jennifer is definitely a blow, but fortunately the backers are hanging tight for now because I've gone out on a limb and promised them that I'm close to a commitment from another A-list actress....."

"And who's that?" asked Devin Wiseman, another superstar producer, which he would have to be to have the stones to interrupt Jackson Taylor in the middle of his answer.

"Truthfully, I have no idea at this point. I've got a few people in mind, and I'm open to ideas from everyone in the room, but right now I'm basically stalling for time while keeping everything else moving forward. And let's not forget, we also need to find someone to play Kristyn's character."

Rob Davis, who along with his partner Rich Goodman was one half of RD/RG Productions, added, "Well, at least we have all the other high-profile characters locked down and signed. Are there any concerns that we'll have salary cap issues when you try to hire the two leads?"

"Fortunately, no, but I will personally commit to another $10 million if that becomes necessary. I don't think it will, but the fact that we have that cushion takes some of the pressure off."

Kristyn looked at JJ and her eyes got wide in disbelief that someone could so casually commit to throwing another $10 million on the pile. JJ read her mind and fought to suppress a smile. The fact that they were contributing nothing towards the production costs but collecting a salary and percentage as producers and screenwriters didn't escape either of them. And they were sure it hadn't escaped any of the other producers, either, though in truth, they had all seen this happen many times before and didn't seem to hold any animosity towards them.

"Let me throw this out to JJ and Kristyn: if you could have your choice of any actor in Hollywood, who would you choose to play you in the movie? Bonus points, obviously, if they're someone who can actually 'open' a movie." Jackson put the ball in their court, knowing that it's surely a topic they'd thought about since the project first started; it's human nature.

JJ felt extremely self-conscious. If she named some drop-dead beautiful actor, would she seem conceited or someone having *way* too high of an opinion of herself? Did it need to be someone who was comfortable playing someone as ordinary – *and damaged* – as she? "I guess in my fantasy world I've always imagined two different actors that would be great in this role. The first would be Emily Blunt. She's a great actress, definitely an A-list star, and she can handle herself in rough and tumble, action-oriented films; she was excellent in *Sicario* where she played an FBI Special Agent and member of a drug task force trying to apprehend a Sonoran drug lord. Feels eerily similar."

"Wow, that's a really good observation and suggestion," said Angela Stephenson, another seasoned producer of countless movies and television series. "And based on her roles in recent movies like *The Girl on the Train* and *The Quiet Place*, I think she's bankable."

Rob Davis asked, "Who's the second possibility that you mentioned?"

JJ shifted in her chair, uncomfortable with everyone's gaze on her and the weight of their expectations. "I had thought of Katherine Winnick, the star of the series *Vikings*. While she's not quite as high profile as Emily Blunt, she's done a couple of dozen movies and TV shows where she's cast as a really strong, capable female. And I just think she's a badass. Beautiful, but a total badass."

"I like her," offered Miles. "And I agree with your statement about her being both beautiful and a total badass. And not to mention, she'd probably cost us a few million dollars less than Emily Blunt or Jennifer Lawrence. I guess the question becomes, is she someone that can 'open' a movie?"

"On that point I definitely have to defer to the rest of you in this room. You have the experience and expertise, and I'm just here trying to learn and help create a good screenplay."

Jackson withheld any comment, but asked, "How about you Kristyn? Any thoughts on who could play your role?"

Kristyn had been mulling that over but now felt like a student called on by their teacher when they didn't know the answer. "Luckily, I don't think my character has to be as strong and badass as JJ's; if you look back at the Murder Game case, you'll see that all I did was basically write some articles, bawl like a little baby, and get shot. I'm guessing any actress can pull that off." That drew laughter from everyone in the room.

"You know that you're really selling yourself short there, right?" JJ asked. "That case couldn't have succeeded without you, and you did a helluva lot more than sitting around blubbering. Don't be shy: tell them the names that you've been thinking about ever since this project started." JJ reached out and held Kristyn's hand in a show of love and support.

Everyone in the room looked at Kristyn expectedly. "OK, so it's true. I have had two names in mind that I thought would be perfect for my character. They're both A-list actresses, for sure, and I think they come across as smart and articulate in addition to being brave enough – or maybe crazy enough – to insert themselves into this kind of investigation. The first is Kristen Bell, and the other is Natalie Portman. But like JJ said, I totally defer to the brain trust in this room."

Jackson was the first to speak. "I have to say, for first time producers, and totally new to the movie game, you guys really seem to get it. Unless anyone has objections, I'll start making inquiries with their respective agents about their interest and availability. In the interim, if anyone has any other ideas for possible leads, don't hesitate to share them with the group. I'd like to have this locked down within the next 3-4 weeks so we can continue with all the other million-and-one steps in the pre-production."

The meeting continued for another 90 minutes and touched on what seemed like those million-and-one steps that Jackson had referred to. JJ and Kristyn were still amazed at the huge sums of money that were being talked about. Not just for the big-name actors, or even the dozens of co-stars, but for everything imaginable: the dozens of film crew members, craft services, sound and lighting technicians, licensing and fees for shooting locations, marketing, and on and on. Jackson had told them, when they'd first met, that they were going to be absolutely shocked when they realized how many people it took to make a movie today compared to the 1970's and 1980's, for example, or even the early 2000's. To prove his point, he showed them the movie trailer from *The Godfather* and then compared it to the 2022 release of *Top Gun: Maverick*. The difference was startling, with the new movie's credits running for almost four minutes longer, and the cost difference, even when normalized for inflation, was huge.

As they walked together after the meeting ended, JJ turned to Kristyn and said, "I still feel like I'm drinking from the proverbial fire hose trying to learn this business, don't you? Thank goodness that the others are patient and kind enough to help us get up to speed."

"Yeah, it's definitely been baptism by fire, but I feel like we've really learned a lot in a short time. It feels like we're in one of those fast-track MBA programs, and every day feels like exam day."

"On the other hand, at least we've been able to go a few months without anyone trying to kill us, so that's something." JJ smiled and giggled as she said this; California had been good for her stress and anxiety. "And what's the worst that can happen if the movie bombs?

We don't make a lot of money., but at least I don't think any of the producers or studio bigwigs will be gunning for us."

"Let's hope not. I'd be happy to never see another gun, and certainly not another dead body, for as long as I live. But like you said, what's the worst that can happen?"

I hope you haven't jinxed us!

3

WEDNESDAY, MAY 10

"So let me see if I've got this right," JJ responded to Bill Astin, Deputy Director of the US Marshals Service in California. "One of the people convicted as a co-conspirator in the Murder Game case, who was sent to Victorville, escaped from custody and is on the run, along with another convict. And they carjacked a guy just a few miles away and left him with a major concussion, and no sighting of them since. Is that about right?"

"Yeah, that pretty well sums it up. They escaped in a laundry truck during the confusion of a shift change and then jacked this guy barely five or ten minutes later. Obviously, the escape in the laundry truck was planned, but the carjacking appears to be just dumb luck. Especially for the poor guy that they jacked; he was lucky to survive."

"This Brookes Williamson guy, do you think he was the one that assaulted and injured the car owner?"

"Definitely not. Williamson is an average-sized guy, and not known to be violent. The other guy, John Westbrook, he's a different story. Guy is freakin' huge, built like an NFL lineman, and he definitely has a violent streak. He's been in and out of trouble for pretty much his whole life, and he's not adverse to beating the shit out of people. In fact, I think hurting people is his favorite pastime."

"How did Williamson and Westbrook connect while inside? They don't sound like they'd be BFF's, to put it mildly."

20

"They're cellmates. Williamson has only been at Victorville for a few months, and according to the officials there, everyone is surprised that he survived this long. Usually some little disagreement or perceived slight sets Westbrook off. He's put several men in the hospital over the past couple of years and is suspected in at least two inmate deaths. And like you said, I wouldn't have expected the two of them to become BFF's. At least from what we've learned, and others have observed, they couldn't be more different."

"Think maybe Williamson has been paying Westbrook to be his protection from all the other miscreants in there?"

"Anything is possible. Maybe he was Westbrook's 'girlfriend'. Who knows? The one thing we know for sure is that Williamson had to be the brains behind this escape. Westbrook has been in Victorville for years without any escape attempts, and the same goes for every other prison he's been in. I'd say that it's a virtual certainty that Williamson is the brains and Westbrook is the muscle."

"Even though it was Westbrook that worked in the laundry, and that's where they escaped from?"

"Yeah. There was a lot of planning and creativity that went into this, and that's just not Westbrook's forte. He did take care of virtually all the hands-on work, though, to make the escape possible. For example, he's the one that did the modification to the laundry carts that gave them a place to hide until they were outside the prison walls. There's even some indication that the carts were loaded with just the right amount of laundry bags to ensure that their weight didn't arouse suspicion with the drivers. That is, there were significantly fewer laundry bags in the cart that held Westbrook to accommodate his nearly 300 pounds, while Williamson's cart held almost twice as many laundry bags since he weighs about 125 pounds less. That's too sophisticated for Westbrook to pull off; he's street smart, but he's a long way from book smart."

JJ pondered this situation for a few moments. "I have to admit, you've really piqued my interest. So how can I help the Marshal Service? Since I'm no longer with the FBI it's not like I have access to their people and tools and labs."

"Trust me, I have zero interest in working with the FBI. It's you that I'm interested in. Nothing against FBI agents; they're damn good at what they do, excellent investigators. But their jobs are totally different from the US Marshals, and personally, I don't think most of them could find their ass with two hands and a GPS."

That made JJ laugh. "Oh, and you think I can?"

"Yeah, I do. Without a doubt. You've got incredible instincts, and that's what counts when it comes to tracking criminals, especially those that have escaped from custody; they're desperate and impulsive and willing to go down swinging. Or shooting. Plus, I think every cop in the country is familiar with how the FBI fucked you over. Pardon my French. But after you cracked the biggest case in decades, maybe ever, and then they drum you out of the Bureau? Screw 'em. We'll take whatever assistance you can provide, and I'll make damn sure that you are kept in the loop and treated – *and compensated* – as a consultant on this case."

"I appreciate that, and I'll be glad to consult with the Marshals service on this. I don't like the thought of having any of these sick puppies that were part of the Murder Game case out walking the streets. That goes double for any of them that were already sentenced and sent to prison. That tends to make them even more dangerous. But then, look who I'm telling. You live this shit every day."

"Don't I know it. I can forward all the information we have so far so you can review it, then maybe we touch base tomorrow to get your initial thoughts?"

"That works for me. I'll check my schedule for tomorrow and get back to you; this whole Hollywood scene and being involved with this movie is a lot more work than I would have thought. I'm not complaining, mind you, I'm just surprised how much goes into these things. But catching this Williamson guy, as well as Westbrook, is critical. We don't need these guys out on the street, that's for sure."

"True, but based on Westbrook's history, I wouldn't be surprised if he kills Williamson and goes it alone. Now that he's on the outside, I don't think he has any need for him anymore."

"That could be, but I can envision a scenario where it goes down quite differently. Admittedly, I'm probably too far out over my skis at this stage, having just come into this and not even reviewed the files yet, but I wouldn't be shocked if the exact opposite happened. Williamson doesn't need Westbrook anymore, so he might try to take him out and go it alone. Plus, as you pointed out, they look like the Odd Couple out there, so Williamson has a better chance of blending in by himself. And even though we assume that the courts found and confiscated all his accounts, his homes, his passports, and everything else that people on the run usually need, we can't be certain."

"Interesting. Since Williamson has no reported history of violence, I hadn't really thought along those lines."

"Well, you know how it is: just because someone has no record of violence or arrests doesn't mean they haven't done bad things. It sometimes means they just haven't been caught."

"True...."

"One other thing: I think it would be a good idea if we focused a bit on why Williamson wanted to escape. I mean, nobody really *wants* to be in prison, but maybe he's got some unfinished business or a score to settle. We need to dig into his world and figure out what that may be."

"I see your point, but that whole 'score to settle' might involve you. Even though you weren't directly involved in his arrest, it was the work that you and Kristyn Reynolds did that brought his whole world crumbling down. You might want to keep your eyes open."

"Trust me: that's the only way I know how to live my life at this point."

4

WEDNESDAY, MAY 10

"It sounds like the information that this Marshal Astin shared has you more than a bit concerned. Do you think we might be in danger? Again?" Kristyn had listened to JJ's story about Brookes Williamson and his escape from Victorville prison and didn't think it was anything that should rise to the level of panic. At least not yet. Hopefully never.

"No. Or at least I don't think so. I mean, there were literally hundreds of these online bettors that were arrested for their role in the Murder Game case, and I have to imagine that, by and large, they're a bunch of incels or cyber-geeks that live in their mother's basement. I never really thought of them as being dangerous, per se."

"Do you even remember this Brookes Williamson guy? I don't."

"Me either. Truthfully, there are only a very small handful that I do recall, and that's because they were charged with additional offenses like resisting arrest, obstruction of justice, or threatening a witness. I never heard of this guy until today."

"What kind of promise did you make to Marshal Astin as far as helping on this case? And do you think you can afford to devote any time to an investigation when we're committed to helping produce and write this movie?" Kristyn realized that the question came out with a little bit more edginess, a little more attitude, than she had intended. Was that because she was really more concerned about this guy escaping than she had realized or admitted? She knew that she had not fully recovered, mentally, from the terror and trauma that she went through just a few short months ago. No way could she face that again, not now and probably not ever.

Kristyn's tone of voice wasn't lost on JJ. "Not to worry. Truly. I didn't make any commitments at all, other than that I'd try to help. That means I'm going to review the reports they have so far, including the prison files on both Williamson and Westbrook, to try to develop some ideas about where they might go next, if they'll stay together or split up, what resources they have to fall back on while they're on the run, that kind of thing."

"I'm sorry, I didn't mean that to come off as bitchy or controlling. I just don't want you to exhaust yourself with too much work and stress. You're still recovering, too, whether or not you like to admit it." Kristyn gave a weak smile. "But I know that you want to keep one toe in the water when it comes to police work and investigations. It's who you are, definitely something that's in your blood and always will be."

"It's true, I do want to continue to be involved in police work, at least in some limited fashion. Not just because I love it, or because I think I'm some super-cop. The selfish side of me wants to continue working cases – a limited number of cases that I pick and choose -- because I think it might inspire some great stories for Supersleuth Productions. Maybe it's solving cold cases, or maybe it's catching criminals that are on the run. Whatever. There are *so many* potential stories out there. I just need to be positioned to be aware of them."

"Well, I can't argue with that. Too bad simple, safe stories like finding a lost pet or tracking down some porch-pirate stealing Amazon deliveries aren't exciting enough to be the basis for a blockbuster. That would definitely be less stressful. Then again, from what I've seen so far, making any kind of movie is its own kind of stress."

"Based on how restless you've been every night the past few weeks, I'd have to say that's true. Legs kicking, moaning, tossing and turning. I don't think you've had a good night's sleep, really restful sleep, in a while." JJ gave a little flirty smile and added, "Not that I haven't done my best to try to make sure that you go to sleep exhausted and with a satisfied smile on your face."

Kristyn smiled. "Well, you've certainly gone above and beyond on that front, so whatever my sleep issues are, it's definitely not from being sexually frustrated."

"That's good to know." They both giggled as the tension eased. "Maybe we should shut it down for the rest of the day and take a drive along the coast, stop somewhere for drinks and dinner. Somewhere with a great ocean view."

"Ooooh, that sounds great. Probably just what the doctor ordered. Maybe we drive down the coast to Long Beach, find a nice waterfront place to kick back and relax for a few hours?"

"Sound perfect. Better yet, let's pack a bag and stay the night. We can be at the studio by mid-morning, even with the dreaded L.A. traffic, and still have time to meet with the team as scheduled."

"I like the way you think. Give me an hour to get ready; I need a shower after working out earlier, and I need to pack. OK?"

"Definitely. I'll go online and find us a hotel on the beach and a good place for dinner. I'll be ready when you are." JJ knew from experience that Kristyn's promised one hour would likely turn into at least 90 minutes, but she didn't mind. Actually, she was counting on it.

It took her less than 10 minutes to book the hotel and restaurant, then instead of 'shutting it down' as she'd promised, she dove-in to the files that Marshal Astin had sent to her. She wasn't scared, not yet, but she also didn't take the situation lightly. Would Williamson, with or without Westbrook, actually have a vendetta against her and Kristyn? No way to know, but she intended to look at every angle, every possibility, every bit of information available on these two to make sure that she was keeping them safe.

Like Kristyn, JJ had no desire for more violence and terror in her life, but she knew that to keep them safe she had to be prepared and ever vigilant. And, just as importantly, she had to do everything possible to shield Kristyn from the ugliness. She couldn't bear to bring another minute of stress or danger into her world. Without question,

Kristyn was the love of her life, and she would do anything and everything in her power to protect her. And sometimes protecting and shielding others means putting your own safety – *and sanity* – on the line. So be it.

As they got on the road, the L.A. traffic was its usual miserable slog as they headed south, even at this time of day. Then again, there's really no such thing as a 'good time of day' when it comes to traffic there, just varying degrees of shitty. While it was only about 35 miles to their destination, they expected it to take more than 1.5 hours. Luckily, they were in no real hurry since their dinner reservation at a lovely oceanfront restaurant was not until 6:30pm. That left them plenty of time to get there, check into their hotel, and walk around the waterfront and town.

Conversation on the long drive down had been pleasant and focused mainly on the movie production and plans for the coming weekend. Any discussion of JJ's involvement in the hunt for Brookes Williamson and John Westbrook never came up, or, more likely, was intentionally avoided.

After checking in and making their way to their ocean view room, JJ pulled a surprise – actually two surprises – from the small overnight bag that she'd packed in addition to her suitcase. "As the saying goes, *'it's 5 o'clock somewhere'*, so that means it's Happy Hour! I thought we could start the evening off by treating ourselves to a glass of wine. Maybe two."

"Oh, great idea! What did you bring? Let me see!"

JJ pulled a bottle of their favorite Napa Cabernet, a Vice Versa from the Beckstoffer Las Piedras vineyard, and Kristyn's face lit up. "Ohhh, my favorite! Great call."

"I thought we could sit out on the balcony and enjoy the view and a nice glass of Cab before we head down to the waterfront and dinner. Sound good?"

"Absolutely. It sounds fantastic! What wine did you bring for dinner? I'm sure it's something equally awesome."

"Since we're going to a seafood restaurant, and since it's still relatively warm outside, I thought a nice white wine might be in order. I brought a bottle of Brilliant Mistake Sauvignon Blanc. This is the last bottle of the case we bought early in the summer, so we'll have to savor it."

"And buy some more. Definitely. Let's put that in the mini fridge for now to keep it cold before we go to dinner."

JJ opened the Cabernet and retrieved two glasses from her bag. She poured the wine and handed a glass to Kristyn, then they made their way out to the balcony. The view of the Pacific was spectacular. "This is heaven. Or damn close to it. Beautiful weather. Beautiful view. Fantastic wine, and spending quality time with you. Cheers!" They clinked glasses to toast their blessings and their love for each other.

Kristyn hesitated to ask something that had been on her mind but thought this was a good time to broach the subject. Certainly, their relationship had grown to the point where they could have deep, even uncomfortable, conversations. "I hope this doesn't make you uncomfortable, but I realize that this is only the second or third time you've had a glass of wine in the past few months. Are you starting to have concerns about your drinking?" JJ had shared with her, soon after they met, that she'd spent time in rehab for alcohol early in her career.

JJ squirmed, obviously uncomfortable. "Honestly, it's not the drinking that got me concerned. It was the narcotics that I was prescribed after being shot coupled with the stress of losing my job, seeing you nearly killed, and a million and one other things, had me worried that I could fall back into old habits."

"But you didn't even fill the prescription for the pain killers. You were just taking Advil, which I still find incredible. I imagine the pain was off the charts."

"It was, admittedly, but I couldn't risk taking Oxy or other pain killers. I know that I have a weakness, a predilection, if you will, to addictive behavior so I have to fight that constantly. I never want to be in that situation again."

"And you're having the same concerns regarding alcohol?"

"No, not really, but I don't want to turn a blind eye to the risks, either. I want to continue to enjoy a glass or two of wine with you in the evening, or when we're out to dinner. I just don't want to use it as a crutch when I'm stressed or upset or pissed at the world. Does that make sense?"

"Totally. I mean, it may not be how AA would do things, but we'll call this the *'AA according to JJ rules'* since it's worked well for you all of these years." Kristyn smiled and reached out to touch JJ's hand. "I support you 100%, so don't' ever feel the need to drink just because I order a drink or feel like you have to explain if you want water, or tea, or a Coke, instead of alcohol. I admire your self-awareness and resolve."

Minutes passed by in silence as they savored the wine, the scenery, and each other's company, and seemingly nothing could ruin this idyllic getaway. Tomorrow? Next week? They could worry about that later, not now. This little getaway was all about relaxing and reconnecting, and great food, wine, and scenery were the catalysts for both.

Of course, sometimes what you don't know *can* hurt you, totally turn your world on its head. You may not know when those wheels start in motion, but once they get rolling, once inertia takes over, it can be like a runaway train ready to roll over anything and everything in its path. *And that includes JJ and Kristyn. Again.*

5

"Alright, well thanks for keeping me in the loop, Marshal Astin. I'm disappointed that there's been no sighting of Williamson and Westbrook since their escape. I had hoped that by now they'd be back in custody."

"You and me both. Other than finding the stolen car about an hour or so away, we really haven't uncovered a single piece of useful information or clues. And the car didn't really give us anything to speak of, other than their prints all over the place. Not much help when we already knew that they stole the car and left the owner laying half-dead on the ground."

"And not even any indication if they're still together or went their separate ways. That's especially frustrating. Though if I were a betting woman, I'd still put my money on them splitting up. Or Westbrook being dead."

Astin chuckled. "You're still hanging onto that theory that Williamson, the guy with no record of violence and that probably looked to Westbrook as his protector, managed to kill one of the biggest, meanest, most dangerous men in Victorville? If that's the case, I would have loved to have been a spectator for that."

"I'm not saying that I'm right, but I still say that Williamson doesn't need Westbrook anymore, and he probably doesn't trust him to keep his mouth shut and not throw him under the bus if he were caught. Like you said, Westbrook is a bad man and a career criminal, and he'd sell-out his own mother if it cut even a few hours off of his sentence. I'm sure he'd give up Williamson in a heartbeat. Probably even try to convince the cops that it was Williamson that caved in that guy's skull when stealing the car."

"True enough. Alright, I've got to get back to it, and I'll keep you posted if we hear or see anything. If you come up with any other angles or ideas, don't hesitate to call."

"Will do. I need to get back at it, too. You can't believe how much is involved in making a movie! I had no idea, that's for sure. Makes my FBI days seem downright mundane sometimes."

After several months of working at the studio and focusing on all the myriad details of movie pre-production, JJ and Kristyn were both well past the point of believing that being a producer was a glamorous, chic job. While they had never had any illusions that it would be easy, they had let their imaginations run wild with fantasies of hours spent over fabulous 'business lunches' with high-power Hollywood players, including tons of 'A' list stars. The reality was not so glamorous, and any thoughts that TMZ or *People* magazine would be following them around and creating salacious headlines about their hedonistic Hollywood life-style were way off-base. It wasn't drudgery, per se, and they definitely felt blessed to be involved in creating a Hollywood blockbuster instead of living their old mundane lives. Plus, no one was shooting at them like back in Dallas not too long ago, so there was that benefit.

At least they could take solace in the fact that they didn't have to be involved in all of the minutiae the way the rest of the production team did since they were also deeply involved in developing the screenplay. Writing could be stressful, frustrating, and soul crushing, especially since they were part of a team of six writers. While they had grown close to the team and respected the hell out of them and their collective experience, they sometimes grew frustrated when others took liberties with real-life events – *their real-life near-death experiences* – to create a different or more dramatic vibe. As if the reality wasn't dramatic enough.

The writing team consisted of five women and one man, and all of them, except, of course, JJ and Kristyn, had been nominated and/or won multiple Emmys and Oscars over the years. The team was led by Catherine Comrie, a 50-something industry veteran with a resume that would be the envy of most of Hollywood. Samantha Downes and Ian Breton were a married couple that had worked together on multiple projects over the years, including a couple of Best Picture of the Year winners, not to mention dozens of projects before they were a couple. They were also veterans of multiple action thrillers, including three of the *Jason Bourne* franchise hits. The other writer was Paige Madison, and while barely into her 30's, she was already considered the best of the best when it came to writing action scenes that drew the audience in and left them on the edge of their seat. If the movie had gunfire, explosions, car chases, terrorist attacks, police rescues, pretty much anything involving elements that drive tension and danger for the characters, Paige is the first person that every Hollywood director wants on their team.

The writing team meets most mornings around 10am to review progress, talk about the next scenes, and to pick Kristyn's and JJ's brain for details. The whole writing process was a collaborative effort, and even once the meeting broke-up, they tended to spend more time working together than alone. That suited JJ and Kristyn fine: they viewed the whole process of creating the screenplay – and God knows it's more of a process than they'd realized – as a learning experience. Even though they often felt that they were there as 'inside sources' and merely adding 'color' to the dialogue and scenes created by others, they couldn't complain. So far, they'd been embraced as part of the team and their opinions and insights respected. You couldn't ask for much more than that.

About 45 minutes into the meeting, there was a knock on the door and Jackson Taylor, stuck his head into the room. "Morning folks. Sorry to interrupt you, but I need to borrow JJ and Kristyn for just a bit. That OK with you all?"

"Of course, not a problem." Catherine nodded towards JJ and Kristyn and added, "We'll catch up with you guys after lunch then. I think by then we'll have the first few pages from the scenes where you were at Columbia University and talking to the Registrar and the professor that was in cahoots with the Slayers." Looking towards Jackson, she added, "We're using JJ's notes and Kristyn's articles to help keep us on track and honest, but we'll want your input to see how it resonates with you."

"What's up Jackson?" asked Kristyn. "Are we being called to the principal's office?" She flashed that dazzling smile, but he didn't seem to notice.

"Let's talk in my office." JJ and Kristyn looked at each other. His tone, his demeanor, seemed much more intense than usual, and he was, by nature, a pretty intense guy to start with.

It had been a while since they'd been in his office, which was the largest and nicest on the whole studio lot. Nearly 1800 square feet, sumptuous furniture, private bathroom and shower, the obligatory well-stocked bar and wine cooler, and pictures of him posing with virtually every power player in Hollywood since the early 90's. If it were almost any other man it would have felt like their own personal testament to their greatness and vanity, but not so with Jackson. For him it was just a place to do business and a place to be comfortable during his typical 60–70-hour work weeks. If it gave him an advantage in impressing and landing a big star or a big investor, that was just icing on the cake.

As they walked in, he pointed to the couch and chairs along the wall. Normally Jackson was a thoughtful and gracious host and would at once offer his guests a drink or have some small snacks available, but all indications were that this was not a social gathering, or even a typical business meeting. Before closing his office door, he stuck his head out and asked his assistant to hold all calls. Now JJ and Kristyn felt certain that they'd been called to the principal's office. Had they done something wrong? Did he want to remove them from the movie for some reason? The tension was palpable for both.

"Sorry to pull you out of your meeting, but I have something that I need to bring to your attention, and for now I'd like to keep it just between the three of us. I don't want to create a panic among the crew."

That piqued JJ's cop-sense. "What's going on, Jackson? I take it this isn't something to do with production budgets or schedules?"

"No. If it were only that simple. I'd almost welcome it." He smiled weakly. "I guess that's not something that you'd ever expect an Executive Producer to say."

"That's for sure. But that makes me even more concerned about what you *do* have to say," JJ responded. She looked at Kristyn and saw the growing concern on her face.

"Over the past few weeks, I've started noticing some ugly, fairly aggressive social media posts about *The Murder Game* production. Threatening, but not overly so. At least not at first. They were pretty generic but seemed to disparage law enforcement, call into doubt the whole crime and how it was reported, and try to create a false narrative about how the Slayers and others died. Some posts even take the position that all the victims that were killed during the Murder Games were simply made up, nothing more than false flags."

Kristyn asked, "That sounds like the kind of bullshit that Infowars and their ilk like to spew. Does it appear that these social media posts all came from the same person?"

"I can't say for sure, because I don't know enough about the technology to know if one person could hide behind so many fake accounts, but I can say that the addresses attached to the postings were different. Many were repeated, but there were literally dozens of them."

"It could be multiple people, or it could be one person with control over dozens, even hundreds, of bots that create and send the messages. It would take serious forensic skills to uncover the user or users, much like Quantico did for us when digging into the Murder Game bettors to uncover their identities." JJ thought for a minute. "Even if it's one person doing this, it's a certainty that they're counting on others to glom onto their little conspiracy theories and have this take on a life of its own. That's generally the way that flat-earthers and QAnon faithful spread their craziness."

"Are these postings directly threatening the production, or threatening anyone in particular? Not that what you've mentioned so far isn't bad enough, but at least it doesn't rise to the level of direct threats of violence." Kristyn was hopeful that's as far as it had gone.

Jackson looked down at his shoes, avoiding their gaze while searching for the right words. "The social media posts on Instagram and Twitter have been only as I described. Nothing too bad. But I've received some direct messages that got more specific and more threatening."

"How did you receive those more threatening messages?" JJ didn't like where this was going.

"I've had DMs on my private Instagram and Twitter accounts, as well as emails into my private Gmail. There've been text messages on my mobile phone. That number, by the way, is probably only known to about a dozen people, including my family; I use another mobile phone for business and day-to-day stuff. Essentially every application I have seems to be compromised. I gotta tell you, I'm more than a little nervous at this point."

"What's the nature of the threats? Depending on what this is, we may need to call the police or FBI to investigate." JJ was already leaning that way.

"That's the thing. The threats started off focused on the production and the crew in general. They dropped a lot of crew names; normally that would concern me, but I know that it's easy to get a full list of the people working on the production from any number of sources, including union lists. They probably think it makes them look more connected or threatening."

Kristyn looked at Jackson with a look of deep and growing concern. "You said that the threatening messages started off focused on the production and crew. Did the focus of those messages change?"

"Yes." He swallowed hard, trying hard to stave off the panic. "The messages directly threatened you and JJ in very deep, dark, and disturbing terms and descriptions. I think whoever is behind this, whether it's one person or a whole group, has a serious grudge against you. And I'd say that they plan to do something about it."

JJ and Kristyn exchanged a look of concern, both having the same thought running through their minds: could this be connected to

Brookes Williamson, the inmate that just escaped from Victorville that Marshal Astin had warned JJ about?

Jackson's mobile phone rang, and as he answered it JJ took the opportunity to whisper to Kristyn, "I know what you're thinking. The same thing I'm thinking. But let's wait a bit before we share that and see what information Jackson can share with us."

Kristyn nodded her agreement, though she had hoped it might go a different direction.

I'm trusting your instincts on this, JJ.

6

∽

MONDAY, MAY 22

"That seems to be rapid escalation, from what you've described. Assuming it's the same person or persons, I wonder what drove that escalation? Did you respond to any of the messages, end up engaging someone in conversation?" JJ was concerned but tried hard not to show it.

"No, not a single message. I deleted the first few messages, figuring it was just the typical internet trolls. But as the volume of messages increased, especially across multiple accounts, I started saving all of them. I figured they'd ultimately be of interest to law enforcement if this kept on. You guys want to review them?"

Kristyn jumped in. "Yes, definitely. I want to see them all, starting at the beginning. I think the progression of the threat intensity is interesting, and possibly relevant. Scary, maybe, but interesting from a criminal perspective." She looked over at JJ and saw her nod in agreement.

They started by reviewing the early messages, and as Jackson had said, they seemed almost like run-of-the-mill conspiracy theory bullshit, but the fact that they sometimes got specific with their threats against a number of crew members – from production assistants to carpenters and electricians, to caterers – was unsettling. When they turned to a message that specifically mentioned two members of the screenwriting team, Paige Madison and Catherine Comrie, it sent a chill up their spines.

"Woah, that's hitting a little too close to home, wouldn't you say?" JJ looked over at Kristyn and saw her eyes wide. The fear was evident.

"No doubt, but it makes me wonder if this is all just smoke and mirrors, or a way to grab our attention, since Jackson said that the threats escalated and shifted to us. You think maybe this person, or persons, is trying to establish his bona fides by name-checking other people involved in the production? Especially Paige and Catherine?"

"That's a good thought, for sure. I'll hold judgement until I see the other messages, but at the very least I think we have someone, or some group, that wants to see this production shut down. Hopefully, it doesn't move past the threat stage, but my gut says that this is just the opening salvo."

"Do you think it could be someone that's only in it for some sort of financial gain, like maybe a rival studio trying to kill us off – sorry, bad choice of words – so as not to compete against a movie they're working on?" A not unreasonable question from Jackson.

JJ thought for a moment. "I supposed it could be, but I don't think that's the most likely scenario. If it were another studio, or some rival producer or director, I think they'd probably attack from more of a financial angle. That is, maybe they'd threaten, even blackmail, the people financing the picture. Pull the money, pull the plug. Just an opinion, for what it's worth."

"And Jackson, would you really expect another studio, or even an industry rival, to go to these lengths to shut you down? I know that this can be a cutthroat industry – whoops, there's my own poor choice of words – but doesn't this seem a bit extreme?"

"You're probably right, Kristyn. There are certainly some bad apples in the movie business, but I can't imagine someone taking it that far. Maybe I'm being naïve, but I'd like to believe that most of the people in this industry are better than that."

"Let's take a look at those other messages that get more aggressive and threatening towards Kristyn and me. Maybe we'll have a different opinion after reading through them."

"I'll warn you; they are extremely graphic and unsettling. You want to take a break for a bit before diving into them? Even what you've read through so far, the 'milder' messages, are bad enough. The others are the stuff that nightmares are made of."

JJ shook her head. "No, let's jump into them. The sooner we dive-in the sooner we can start to figure out what steps we need to take to ensure everyone's safety and keep this production on track."

"But maybe before we start, we can grab a drink? Something strong? I don't know about you guys, but I think a good stiff drink might help to settle my nerves. Or hopefully so."

"What can I offer you, Kristyn? I know you're a red wine lover."

"As JJ likes to say, this kind of day calls for whiskey, not wine. I'll take a double Knob Creek, neat. And keep the bottle close by."

"I'll just have a Coke Zero. It's a little early for me." JJ knew that she could be excused having a drink this early in the day under the circumstances, but she was serious about not letting alcohol become a crutch for dealing with all the bad things that life throws at you.

Jackson added, "As I like to say, on days like this, fuck the clock."

7

MONDAY, MAY 22

Jackson grabbed two matching crystal highball glasses and gave himself and Kristyn each a healthy pour, then handed JJ her can of soda. Not usually a heavy drinker, especially in the middle of the day, he threw half of his glass down in one swallow. It was obvious that the tension and the stress were weighing heavily on him.

For the next 45 minutes they read through every message from every platform, and they were immediately struck by the vile, vitriolic tone of the postings. They were called pretty much every possible name in the book, and the references to their parentage, ancestry, personal mating habits, and proclivity for social diseases were constant and reminiscent of high-school locker room talk.

"I can see that somebody never had their mouth washed out with soap by their mother, that's for sure," said JJ. "Pretty juvenile stuff, though I have to admit I really admire his use of the phrase 'feckless cunts' when describing us. Maybe I'll get us matching T-shirts, or maybe bumper stickers, with that lovely phrase. He, or they, certainly have a way with words."

Kristyn was not taking it quite so well. "I guess I'm not seeing the same humor in it that you are. I find it quite unsettling and scary, to say the least."

Jackson added, "I agree with Kristyn. This is very disturbing."

"Look, I'm not denying that it's disturbing, and we haven't even talked about the actual threats yet, only the nasty comments about us and the investigation. But one thing jumps out at me: I think all these messages came from the same person. I can't prove it, of course, and I will absolutely consult with specialists and defer to their expertise, but just reading through this stuff and comparing the choice of words, the tone, the sentence structure, even the places where the progression of the responses almost feels like a script, I'd almost bet on it. They're trying to cover their tracks with the multiple screen names and platforms that they're using, but I think that's just someone trying to stay hidden."

"If that's the case, this must be one sick puppy, don't you think?"

"Definitely, but at the same time it might help us understand where he's coming from, why he has a major hard-on for us, and if he's likely to take things further."

Jackson asked, "If you bring in the police or the FBI, do you think they'll be able to identify the person, or at least where these messages are coming from? Like if it's someone local, which makes them even more of a threat, versus someone halfway across the country or around the world?"

"It's possible, depending on how sophisticated and smart this guy is at covering his digital tracks."

"Are we going to ignore the elephant in the room, the actual death threats directed at the two of you?"

"Definitely not," answered JJ. "We'll coordinate with the LAPD on this and make sure we're considering all angles to protect everyone associated with this movie. But before we go there, there's something we need you to be aware of. I promise that we weren't holding out on you, but we just became aware of this very recently and, until hearing and seeing all the information that you just shared, we weren't certain that it was related."

Jackson listened as JJ told him everything she knew about Brookes Williamson, his involvement as a bettor and co-conspirator in the Murder Game, and how he'd recently escaped prison. The concern, even dread, was evident on his face. He looked like he might get sick at any moment. JJ poured him another drink. "You look like you could use another."

"I think that's an understatement. Make it a double. At least."

Kristyn had recovered a bit from the earlier shock of reading through the threats, and her analytical mind was back in action. "If I can make a suggestion, for right now let's not say with certainty that Brookes Williamson is the person behind this and focus on him to the exclusion of all other potential suspects."

Seeing Jackson's look of confusion, she quickly added, "Admittedly, it's very likely that he's our guy, but if we, and the police, put all our focus on this one guy we may overlook important clues. We can't afford to have tunnel vision on this."

"That's a good point. And we've seen dozens of examples of defense attorneys getting their clients off by convincing juries that the cops were myopic and so focused on their client that they didn't even consider evidence pointing to others." JJ liked Kristyn's perspective.

"I think we need to consider this person's motives in all of this. They could be someone who just wants to halt the production on the movie because they're fanboys of the Slayers and looking for revenge. Or maybe they're someone who was involved in the games and lost a lot of money, or their friends, or their jobs and place in society when they were arrested and the whole thing crumbled."

"I agree," said JJ. "Although I think I can see the possibility of overlap in those two views. That is, maybe killing the two of us as revenge for what happened to the Slayers and the people that played the game is the ultimate goal, but he may want to prolong this and make us suffer. Worrying about when the next shoe is going to drop is almost as bad and debilitating as the actual violence. What I mean is, maybe he will do anything he can to disrupt this production, possibly up to and including hurting other people involved in the movie, just to watch us twist in the wind. Killing us, in his mind, is probably the grand finale."

"Do you think that other people, and the studio itself, are in danger? Believe me, the last thing I want to do is pull the plug or delay this production, but I also don't want to put everyone here at risk." Jackson had valid concerns with both options, but ultimately it was his decision, at least up until the point that the studio took that decision away from him.

"I honestly don't know, Jackson. My gut says that we don't need to do that yet, but we need to be prepared for the possibility. But we do need to step up our security and vigilance here at the studio, at the very least. Keep the number of visitors on the lot and on our set to a minimum, hire additional security, that kind of thing. I would suggest that you also hire security for some of the more high-profile players on the team, like Steven Carter, all the key producers, and probably the writers, too."

"It's going to be hard to keep this quiet, isn't it? I was hoping that we could keep this just between us three, but as the Executive Producer I feel a responsibility to keep everyone safe and secure. And that's in addition to being very protective of the huge investments that our investors have provided; shutdowns and delays, to say nothing of cancellation, could be financially devastating."

"You're right, but I think it's something that we need to share with the whole crew. We can ask them to keep it to themselves, but I don't know how well that will work; I'd give it no more than 24-48 hours before TMZ or other media are reporting on it. But let's try to communicate, at least for now, that the threats are non-specific and focused more on the production itself, like someone who seems to have a grievance about the whole Murder Game case and how it's going to be presented. Nothing about Kristyn and me, or anyone else, being specifically called-out or targeted at this point."

Kristyn finished the rest of her glass of Knob Creek. "I think I'm going to need another double, Jackson. It's not every day I get to read messages from someone threatening to rape me, eviscerate me, and burn my body in the middle of the street. That kind of talk can give a girl a complex."

"To say nothing of nightmares for the rest of your life." JJ smiled at Kristyn and added, "I don't know why both of us aren't sitting in therapy every damn day at this point."

"I'll go you one better: I don't know why both of us aren't sitting in Fiji or the Seychelles or the Maldives enjoying life on the beach and curled up with a good book and a beautiful tropical cocktail with one of those little umbrellas. What I wouldn't give to be thousands of miles away from this craziness."

"Amen to that."

8

WEDNESDAY, MAY 24

Brookes Williamson admired his fashionable new clothes in the store mirror. He'd been on several shopping sprees since escaping Victorville, thanks to his old friend Curtis Mays. Curtis had also been caught-up in the Murder Game online wagering scandal but was let off with a fine and slap on the wrist, and when Brookes had reached out and asked him to retrieve his hidden stash of fake ID's, passports, credit cards, and cash he was happy to oblige. Growing up together in the tony Brentwood area of Los Angeles, they'd both managed to stay one step ahead of legal problems their whole lives. Rich parents ready to swoop in and rescue them from the system, whether by donating to the right politicians, funding a new building at their kids' overpriced prep schools, or paying their high-priced attorneys, certainly helped. Now that they were adults and getting involved in riskier behavior, their parents had all but washed their hands of them. That would never need to be a concern for Curtis' parents again, though: Brookes had left Curtis dead on the kitchen floor of his apartment just off Sunset Boulevard, having practically severed his head from his body by using a garotte constructed of piano wire and wood handles.

Brookes was thrilled to be back in L.A., even if he was on the run. He loved the city. The beautiful weather, the beautiful people, even the conspicuous consumption of the pampered masses. It also didn't hurt that he knew the trendiest places to hang out, the best restaurants and bars, the best beaches, and the best places to lie low. Luckily for him, having access to almost unlimited funds made the idea of hiding out a bit easier to take. If he kept moving every couple of days, he was confident that they would never track him down. His money afforded him the option of staying in 5-star hotels and the best Airbnb and VRBO properties on the beach. It *sure beats the hell out of Victorville.*

Whenever people met Brookes, they were never surprised to learn that he came from money. Even his name screamed upper-crust, WASPY rich kid. His parents were both from wealthy families in the Greenwich, CT area, and they, of course, had been educated in the finest boarding schools and the top Ivy League universities. Brookes had the brains to get into any of those colleges, but, as his parents often said, he had a 'misspent youth'. Vandalism. Stealing cars. Shoplifting. Assault. Breaking and entering. A whole Chinese menu of offenses. Daddy's money kept him out of jail and under the radar, for the most part, but even in his 20's he still hadn't grown out of his juvenile delinquent phase. Most people expected him to either end up dead or in prison before he hit 30, and the things that Mama and Daddy didn't know about would have curled their perfectly straight and coiffed hair: the arson, the animal torture, the times that he threw acid on homeless men and women. He was a sociopath of the highest order, though no psychologist or psychiatrist had ever given that clinical diagnosis. Mama and Daddy could not let their problem child and his mental illness interfere with their social standing in the community.

As happy as he was to be out of prison, flush with cash, and enjoying his shopping spree at the Galleria Mall, he had to constantly push down the rage that was eating at his soul and his tortured mind. It was almost like vomit trying to force its way up. He raged at the pain and humiliation of having to sit through his trial and the time spent in the L.A. County Jail and Victorville. He raged at the FBI for shutting down the Murder Game and costing him hundreds of thousands of dollars. But mostly he raged against the FBI for shutting down the game that had become his true passion, his reason for living, albeit vicariously, and how they had killed the men that he looked up to, practically worshipped: the Slayers.

Before John Westbrook he had never killed anyone, but for the past few years his greatest fantasy, his greatest aspiration, was to gain the same skills and abilities that the Slayers exhibited and find a way to become part of the game. He wanted to go beyond his passive role of wagering on the games and being an armchair observer. He wanted to be an active participant, one of the elites that executed the chosen targets, to feel the rush of taking someone's life. Whether from an up-close attack with a knife, a garrote, or a handgun, he was adamant that he had the balls to pull it off. He'd even spent hours at a shooting range getting comfortable with various types of rifles, and, after a year of lessons and practice, he felt confident that he could take out a target at 350 yards. Maybe not yet Slayer-class, admittedly, but he was driven to improve.

Unfortunately, despite his drive, determination, and hours of practice, he was no closer to being one of the actual Slayers than he was when he started. Even as one of their online bettors for more than three years, he was no closer to understanding how to reach out to them and ask for an 'interview' and a chance to prove himself. Messages and queries via their website did not even receive a response or acknowledgement of receipt, much less an invitation to meet them and show them just how skilled he was.

Of course, now the point was moot: the Slayers were all dead. The Murder Game had been shut down, and all the intellectual property and programs created by the Slayers was beyond his reach, not to mention his technical capabilities. Not that he was lacking in technical acumen, he just wasn't a technology god like the Slayers. No matter. Even with the game now consigned to history, and his heroes all dead, he was ready to move forward. It would no longer be a game, no longer reliant on servers and bits and bytes and artificial intelligence to choose the victims and how they would be dispatched. He would make those decisions. He would decide who would die, when they would die, and how they would die. Though he already knew who his final victims were going to be, but only after making their lives a living hell by unleashing unimaginable chaos, terror, and panic: former FBI agent Jessica Jansen and Kristyn Reynolds.

***

"It looks like you were right, JJ. I guess I was crazy for doubting you." US Marshal Astin was reaching out with an update on the manhunt for Williamson and Westbrook.

"What was I right about? I'd like to think that there's a lot of things, but I'm guessing that you're calling with something in particular."

"You were right about Williamson getting rid of Westbrook and not the other way around. We just found Westbrook's body, or what we assume is his body, pending final identification, near Barstow. His body was found inside a burned-out car that was abandoned in an industrial warehouse area."

"Any idea how long he's been dead and how he was killed yet?"

"We're waiting for the medical examiner to complete his work, but best guess is 7-10 days, maybe more. As I said, he hasn't been positively identified yet, but based on his size, tattoos, and clothes, I don't think there's any doubt. As far as cause of death, the ME might come up with something more, but our preliminary investigation points to blunt force trauma. His skull appears to be crushed, I'm guessing by something like a heavy bat or rock."

"So, I guess Williamson lulled him into trusting their friendship and partnership, and then at the first opportunity, he gets the drop on Westbrook and caves his head in. If that's the case, it appears that our Mr. Williamson is not the soft, sweet, and innocent player that we'd assumed. If he took out a hard ass like Westbrook, and then went the extra step to burn the body, there's no telling what he might do. Or who he might try to do it to."

"I think you and Kristyn would do well to keep your eyes open. There's no indication that he's targeting you, but I think chances are better than even that he heads to L.A. since that's home and where he's got friends and family. I'd hate to see him use that L.A. proximity as a reason to come after you guys."

"If he wants us badly enough, I don't think proximity is that big a factor. Think about the Slayers: they were so intent on killing us that they traveled from all corners of the country to hunt us. And they almost succeeded. If Williamson decides to target us, he'll do the same thing. But to your point, if he's already here, it's just that much easier for him and gives us less time to prepare and react."

"Exactly. One last thing: my next step is having my bosses get a court order to have Williamson's juvenile record unsealed. I want to know more about this asshole."

"I think that's a great move. From what we read in the initial re-ports, it sounded like he was just a naughty schoolboy, not a hardened criminal. But now, having masterminded a prison escape and killed his partner – in a very gruesome manner, I might add – I think there's more to this guy than meets the eye. And none of it's good."

"I'll be back to you ASAP, and I'll forward you copies of whatever we get from the courts. Fingers crossed that it's something to help us track him down."

As JJ hung up, she started to consider how much of this to share with Kristyn. They didn't keep secrets from each other, but she still wanted to shield her from as much of the craziness as possible. Kristyn had been through enough terror, enough physical and mental pain, that JJ's nascent motherly instincts had been awakened. Maybe it was selfish of her, maybe she shouldn't try to protect her from every little thing. Not that this was a little thing. This could be another life-threatening situation. Just what they *don't* need.

9

THURSDAY, MAY 25

The day started off badly, courtesy of a bad car accident that had the already hellish L.A. traffic backed up for miles, and it went downhill from there. Whoever expected a two-hour commute to be the highpoint of their day? Jackson Taylor had called while JJ and Kristyn were stuck in traffic, and the concern in his voice was evident. He told them that he was calling a meeting for the producers and screenwriters at noon, allowing time for several people, in addition to the two of them, to make it to the studio. Obviously, they weren't the only ones caught in this nightmare traffic.

As they approached the studio gates, they noticed an increased number of security guards present and it took almost twice as long as usual to make their way onto the lot. While they were usually waived through with no problem, this time their IDs were checked and their cars given the once-over, including with a long-handled mirror that was used to check underneath the car. JJ and Kristyn knew enough and had seen enough over the years to know that this was not a good sign.

As they approached their office and soundstage area, the indications of increased security became even more evident and ominous. There were several police cars there, yellow crime scene tape surrounding several parked vehicles, and a contingent of cops, studio security, and studio honchos. Nobody looked happy about what they were seeing. JJ was directed to park about fifty yards beyond their offices and their usual parking spots, but she didn't mind that. At least the cops weren't refusing them access to the building.

As they made their way into the building, they noticed that there were far fewer people than usual, and instead of the typical buzz of activity and noise it was eerily quiet. JJ turned to Kristyn and said, "This doesn't bode well for whatever Jackson wants to talk about. This place is like a damn ghost town; there's more cops and studio security outside than people in here working."

"You're right. It's almost noon now, so why don't we head straight to the conference room? I hope he planned ahead and ordered some catering. I missed breakfast this morning," she said as she gave JJ a smirk, "because someone was feeling more than a little bit amorous this morning. And insatiable."

"I'm not sure if you're talking about me or both of us. It does take two to tango, you know. But I agree: I could definitely go down on something, too." She saw Kristyn suppressing a laugh. "Get your mind out of the gutter, you nasty girl! You know what I meant!" JJ fought it hard, but she couldn't suppress her own smile and giggling. It was nice that they'd lightened the mood, if only for a few moments. The rest of the day would be anything but something to smile about.

When they walked into the conference room, they saw that they were the last two to arrive. Anyone coming into the studio from the south or the east had arrived at their normal times after their normal, shitty commutes. It was the people coming in from the north or from the Malibu and Santa Monica areas – meaning, more than half of those in attendance – that had been delayed. Jackson was the last to enter the room, though not because he'd run into traffic; he'd been at the studio since about 2:30am after being roused by the police, security, and studio honchos.

Jackson stuck his head into the room. "Hey guys, I need about 15 more minutes and then I'll be in. Sorry for the delay, but it can't be helped. Why don't you grab something to eat – I ordered tons of food and drinks, which are setup in the back of the room – and I'll be back as quickly as I can. We might be here a few hours, so if you haven't already, I'd cancel any plans you have for lunch or meetings."

The tension in the room was palpable. Several people were almost pale with fear and anxiety, and they hadn't even heard Jackson's message yet. Seeing the police presence but not knowing the facts made things worse as their imaginations got the best of them. Nobody spoke out loud about their suspicions or concerns, but it was clear from the whispering and the looks on their faces that they were uneasy.

It took about 20 minutes before Jackson returned, and the studio head of security, Carlos Hernandez, was with him. He didn't bother with the lunch spread, but he did grab two cans of Coke Zero Sugar and moved to the head of the conference table. It was obvious that he'd been practically mainlining caffeine all night, whether from coffee, Red Bull, or Coke Zero. His face was flushed, and his speech and mannerisms were practically at warp speed compared to normal. "Thanks everyone for coming in. As I'm sure you noticed as you arrived this morning -- *and how could you not?* – we've had some issues on the set overnight."

"What kind of issues? Kelli Markowitz was the first to ask what was on everyone's mind.

"Let me let Carlos kick this off. I assume that you all know Carlos, the head of studio security. Carlos, why don't you give everyone an overview."

"Thanks, Jackson. Last night some members of the crew and production assistants were working late, and when they came out, they found several cars vandalized. It was mostly just flattened tires and some spray-painted graffiti, nothing too serious. What I mean is, no one had their car set on fire or anything stolen, no broken windows or damage to the car itself."

"Maybe whoever did this wanted to be sure that they didn't make any noise and call attention to themselves?" offered Ian Breton.

"That's the theory we're working under," admitted Carlos.

"Did security cameras capture the person doing this? I mean, there must be hundreds of cameras around the studio property." This from Devin Wiseman.

"Cameras did capture someone, so we at least have the exact time that these acts occurred. Unfortunately, we're not able to see the suspect's face or tell too much about him. Appears to be a white guy, probably around six feet tall, average build. Can't see his hair or face since he's wearing a hoodie and a face mask. Still, we're glad to have the little bit that we have on video in case we ever do identify any suspects."

"Did the police find any useful evidence, like maybe a discarded can of spray paint that can be checked for fingerprints?" JJ knew it was a waste of time to even ask about touch DNA since there was no way the cops were going to go to that much trouble and expense for simple vandalism.

"No, we've had no luck there. From what we can see on the security feeds, the suspect appears to be wearing latex gloves. No real surprise."

"If I may, it seems like an awful big police and studio security presence for a few vandalized cars. Was there other damage in addition to the cars?" A reasonable question from Kristyn.

Jackson answered. "Yes, there was. There was also vandalism on one of our sets. Someone destroyed the set that we had just completed for the scene where JJ and her boss were meeting with the US Attorney in Dallas. We'd spent hundreds of manhours, not to mention considerable dollars, constructing that set, and now we have to start from scratch to rebuild it."

"What will that mean to the production schedule?" asked Miles Carpenter.

"That's still to be determined, and on that point, I will defer to Steven Carter, as Director, and his team. They may be able to shift their shooting schedule around depending on the cast's availability. Fortunately, it's a couple months out before we'd start shooting that scene, so I'm hoping that he can shift things around if needed. At this point it may be more of a nuisance, and a hit to our wallets, than anything."

JJ leaned over close to Kristyn and whispered, "This may be more of an opening salvo from whoever has been posting those threats on social media. Like maybe they're starting to take things to the next level."

"I'm wondering the same thing. Do you think Jackson is ready to share that? I think it's time, don't you?" Seeing JJ nod in the affirmative, Kristyn thought about how to broach the subject if Jackson didn't do it himself. Could the whole production, not to mention the entire staff and crew, be in danger? She didn't think it was worth the risk.

There was a knock on the door, and then Jackson's assistant stuck her head in the door. That was highly unusual: Jackson didn't tolerate interruptions, whether of his meetings or just general conversation. "Sorry to bother you, sir, but you're needed. Urgently. I have some people waiting in your office and they need to speak to you and Carlos right away."

Jackson's face went from red with anger at the interruption to white with panic in seconds. "What people? We're in the middle of something here, and it's also incredibly important."

"It's detectives from the LA Sheriff's department, and some others that may be FBI, sir. I was so nervous that I missed their names and who they're with."

"Everyone, take a break and hopefully I'll be back shortly. Carlos, you're with me." Jackson stood up and quickly made his way to the door. Everyone in the room was momentarily shocked into silence, but that lasted mere seconds before the cacophony of voices became as indecipherable as a multi-nation meeting at the UN.

"What new, fresh hell is this?" JJ whispered to Kristyn.

"I'm scared to find out, but I don't think they interrupted the meeting to share good news about capturing someone who vandalized a few cars and a movie set."

"I wish that were the case, but I'm afraid you're right."

10

THURSDAY, MAY 25

It was nearly a half hour before Jackson and Carlos made it back to the conference room. To say that they both looked shocked, and pale would be an understatement. That was understandable in Jackson's case if they'd received disturbing news, but Carlos was not only the head of studio security, he was also an ex-Army Ranger and ex-LAPD. He'd seen things, bad things. Apparently, whatever he just heard had shaken him deeply, too. He didn't look much better than Jackson.

Everyone's eyes were glued to Jackson and Carlos, but nobody spoke a word. They quickly made their way back to their seats. It was Angela Stephenson who finally broke the silence. "I can tell by looking at you that something terrible must have happened. What is it? If it concerns this production, or the people involved with it, we need to know. We have a right to know."

Jackson was staring straight ahead, his speech quiet and almost robotic. To most people, it appeared that he was in shock. Finally, he spoke. "Last night, one of our production assistants, Laura McIntosh, was murdered in her home near Griffith Park." Before he could say another word, everyone started talking, practically yelling over top of each other, to be heard. "Please, please. Let me finish and tell you what I know, or at least what was relayed to me by the detectives."

"Sorry, Jackson. Please go ahead." This from Catherine Comrie.

"Laura worked late last night, as did several other crew members and PA's. She left at the same time as the others, and when they came out, they saw the vandalized cars. Hers wasn't one of them because she happened to have parked in a different area, but she stayed with her friends until the police came. She even gave one of the other PA's, Danny Mattox, a ride home. He was the last one to see her alive, and that was about 1am."

"I assume the police have already questioned him and ruled him out?" asked JJ. She knew the likely answer but wanted the others to hear it, too, before any speculation or rumors got out of hand. She knew that the police would question Danny right away since they were last seen together.

"Yes, and his wife confirmed that he arrived home around 1:15 and was home the rest of the night. Turns out that his in-laws are staying with them for a few weeks, too, and they also confirmed that Danny arrived home and was there the rest of the night."

"How was she killed?" asked Kelli Markowitz.

Carlos jumped in to answer that question. "We weren't given all the details, which is typical, because the cops want to hold some details back so as not to compromise their investigation. That is, they don't want a million crackpots making false confessions based on what they heard on the news, and when they think they have their real killer sitting across the table from them in interrogation, they want to see if that person knows details that only the real killer could know."

"So, what can you share with us?" Kelli asked as follow-up.

Carlos glanced at Taylor as if asking permission to share. Taylor gave him a small, almost imperceptible nod to have him continue. "She was stabbed to death. Not just a couple of times, but dozens of times. Speculation is that at least a dozen of the stab wounds were post-mortem. They're waiting on the ME to give them an exact count. From what we were told, it was especially bloody and gruesome, and the very definition of overkill."

"Obviously, the killer had a lot of rage. The question is, was Laura the target of all that rage or just a crime of opportunity." JJ collected her thoughts for a moment. "Were there indications that the crime had any sexual components?"

"Why in the world does that matter?" yelled Rich Goodman. "A young woman is dead, brutally murdered, and that's the bottom line."

JJ remained calm, understanding that everyone was scared and beyond stressed. "I don't disagree, Rich, but if there is a sexual component to this crime, it might mean that others are in danger. And I'm sure that the cops are looking at this angle, too, because it can help them create a more accurate profile of the killer, maybe even a list of suspects that have been involved in similar crimes."

"I don't have the details regarding the stab wounds and if there was a sexual component to how and where he cut her; we'll have to wait to see if the police share that with us, and right now they're not saying anything until the ME makes his report. They did share one detail, but before I share it with you, let me make one thing crystal clear: this information *cannot* leave this room. I probably shouldn't share it, but I think it's only fair that you be aware. If you leak this to anyone, I'll fire you from this picture immediately. Got it?" Jackson looked at every person in the room to make sure that there was no mistaking how serious he was.

Jackson had to take a breath to calm himself before he could speak again. "There is evidence that Laura was raped and sodomized before she was killed. According to the cops' preliminary report, it was beyond brutal and may have gone on for hours. And the object that he sodomized her with? He left that still in her, even after she was dead. They wouldn't tell me what the object was, surely for reasons that Carlos mentioned, but it was gruesome. Whoever did this is obviously very sick and very depraved."

"And very angry and full of rage, which is quite an understatement in this case." Kristyn could barely hold back her tears. JJ patted her arm and reached out to hold her hand to comfort her.

"May we take a short break before we continue? I don't know about the rest of you, but I could use a drink and a bit of fresh air." JJ looked at Jackson and let her eyes linger on him for just a bit, hoping that he'd somehow read her mind.

"I think that's a great idea, actually. Let's take 15 minutes, step away from this nastiness for a few moments and clear our minds." Jackson stood up from the table and turned to leave, but JJ reached out and took his arm with hers, as if she was leaning on him for support. She looked back at Kristyn and nodded her head in the direction where she was walking with Jackson.

Once the three of them were away from the others, JJ told Jackson what was on her mind. "I think we need to share with them about the social media postings and threats that you've been getting. There's no way to know if it's related to Laura's murder, but my gut says that it probably is. I think it's only right that we make them aware of all that's going on."

"You know that the whole group is going to totally lose their shit, right? No matter what we say or how we rationalize it, they're going to fucking lose it. Can't really say that I blame them. I know that we had the best intentions, but they won't see it that way."

"Maybe if JJ and I tell them rather than you? We can explain how some people involved with the Murder Game case are still pissed at us, but we all agreed that the social media threats felt more like someone wanting to sabotage or delay the movie. Like you said, Jackson, no matter what we say they're going to lose their shit, but better to have them direct their anger at JJ and me instead of you. Directing it at you could harm this production, and that's the last thing we want. Well, next to not being raped or killed, but keeping the production going is a close second."

They talked a bit longer, and Jackson reluctantly agreed. He didn't want them getting thrown under the bus, but he agreed that they could take the lead in the discussion. "Before you start, there's one point I want to make to the team before you guys fall on your sword in there. I'm going to shut down production for the rest of this week and all of next week. Next Monday is Memorial Day so there's already a lot of people taking extra days off. Plus, closing down for the week will give the cops unfettered studio access for their investigation and allow the crew to decompress and, hopefully, re-energize. Agree?"

"I think that's a great idea. I know that we both need it about now."
JJ looked at Kristyn, who smiled and nodded in agreement.

As predicted, everyone in the meeting totally lost it when JJ and
Kristyn told them about the earlier social media postings and threats.
Jackson remained mostly quiet, and as predicted, the team's venom was
directed almost entirely at JJ and Kristyn. There was screaming. There
was name calling. There were insults. There were even veiled threats. It
took almost 90 minutes, but finally everyone was spent. Voices lowered,
and tempers cooled. Mostly the mood changed to genuine concern for
JJ's and Kristyn's safety and their desire and willingness to continue
moving forward with the movie production. The team made it clear
that, as much as they wanted them to stay as part of the team, they
totally understood if they felt that they'd be better off walking away.

"We won't run. We won't hide. And we won't walk away. But we will
watch our backs, and we encourage all of you to do the same. Like they
say, "if you see something, say something". JJ smiled and saw that the
mood in the room had significantly lightened. Thankfully.

As the meeting broke up, there were hugs all around. More than
a few tears were shed that day, but in the end, they had managed to
weather the storm and agreed to continue working as the tight-knit
team that they were. Walking down the hall towards the exit, Jackson
stuck his head out of his office and signaled for them to join him.

They assumed that he wanted to tell them that he was happy with
the meeting outcome, but the look on Jackson's face, totally devoid of
color, told them that was not the case. "I just got this picture forwarded
to me from one of the detectives on Laura's murder." He plopped
down in his chair, looking like he might either throw up or pass out
any second.

JJ took the picture from him, and she and Kristyn looked at it
together. "Oh, shit."

11

FRIDAY, MAY 26

The flight from LAX to Houston was scheduled to take about three hours, but neither JJ nor Kristyn was able to sleep a wink on the plane. In fact, they had hardly slept the night before, with yesterday's events still too fresh in their minds. Kristyn was freaked out, while JJ was more pissed than concerned. Part of her wanted to stay in L.A. and work with the Marshals service to hunt down Brookes Williamson; while he was not yet an official suspect in Laura's murder, or the threats against the movie production, JJ was convinced that it was him. Call it a gut feeling. Call it women's intuition. Call it whatever you want, but JJ was certain that Williamson was behind this. Even if only a person of interest at this stage, JJ had already made the leap to *murderer* in her cop-mind. It was likely that his entire plan, from breaking out of prison, to killing his accomplice, to terrorizing everyone associated with the movie production was part of his grand plan for revenge against her and Kristyn. She'd have to work to prove it, but she knew that Marshal Astin would agree with her assessment. Williamson was already a fugitive, and technically, that's all the Marshals needed to get involved. If their fugitive was an ongoing threat to others? That made their job even more urgent and important.

Lying on the couch together last night, streaming a movie and drinking a glass of wine, JJ and Kristyn had both agreed that a change of scenery would do them good, especially since they had Memorial Day weekend and the rest of the week off. They settled on a week in Houston visiting Kristyn's sister, Stacey. Even though it was already past 10pm in Houston, Kristyn called her sister to see if she was up for company, and getting a quick and enthusiastic thumbs-up, plans were made in record time. Kristyn went online and booked them two first class flights while JJ booked a rental car at Houston Bush International airport.

After the flight attendant had cleared the breakfast trays and brought each of them another mimosa, Kristyn looked over at JJ and asked, "So do you think that this person that killed Laura and left that picture is a real threat to us?"

"First of all, let's stipulate that 'this person that killed Laura' is unquestionably Brookes Williamson, our favorite escapee from Victorville. I know that we don't have concrete proof yet, but based on the evidence we've already seen, I don't think there can be any doubt. And second, I have no doubt that he's serious. He killed the other prisoner that helped him escape, and now Laura; there might be others, but we at least know of these two. And you saw the pictures, and the threat."

"I don't know what's scarier, the fact that he had all those pictures of us, all taken within the last few days or week, or the sick things he said in the note. I don't think I've ever read anything so vile and disturbing."

The note didn't just say that he was going to kill them, as scary and disconcerting as that would be. It went into stark and vivid detail about how he was going to do it, how he was going to carve them up 'into a thousand pieces like a jigsaw puzzle' and the things he would use to rape and sodomize them. He also made no attempt to hide the reasons behind his fixation on them: he flat-out stated that they deserved everything that was about to happen to them and those around them because of what they'd done to bring down the Slayers and their online community of players. Was there a slim chance that there was another Slayer fanboy out there that wanted to kill them? Sure. But would any reasonable investigator believe that this was all a coincidence coming this soon after Williamson's escape from Victorville? Absolutely not.

JJ was mulling several key details in her mind, and then started verbalizing them aloud to get Kristyn's perspective. "One thing that I keep coming back to is his timeline. If we agree that we're his ultimate targets, and he knows that we're spending considerable time on the movie lot, likely living within reasonable proximity to work..... "

"Not to mention that he may have already followed us from the studio to our house...."

"Good point. He may very well already know where we live, what we have in the way of security. If so, is he ready to move on us now, or does he want to drag this out, hopefully scare the shit out of us for days or weeks or...."

"I would think sooner rather than later since the Marshals and police are hot on his trail, wouldn't you?" Kristyn assumed he'd want to hit hard and fast and then get out of the area as fast as possible.

"That might be right, but I think he imagines himself to be a lot smarter, a lot cagier, than anyone who's after him. Maybe he thinks he's smarter and cagier than anyone else, period. He'll likely balance those concerns as he makes plans, and if he's smart, he'll have prepared contingency plans in case things go south. One thing's for certain though: he'll move heaven and earth, put every other plan aside, to make sure he can take his shot at us. We're the end goal, and everything else is just his way to sow terror until he's ready to make his big move."

"Well, as far as I'm concerned, he's a fucking master at terrorizing people. Based on what we know about how he carved up Laura, coupled with the vivid description of what he wants to do to us, he's beyond sick."

JJ nodded her head. "Agreed. He seems to be totally off the rails; my guess is that he's probably a full-blown psychopath. I'd like to dig into his past to see if he's ever been diagnosed with any type of psychopathy, whether in prison or before he was arrested. I'm going to ask Marshal Astin to see if he can get a court order to access Williamson's medical records back to the day he was born. I find it hard to believe that someone this freakin' warped and violent has gone unnoticed and undiagnosed for all these years."

"You should probably ask him to request a court order to unseal any juvenile records, too. This guy was probably the proverbial bad seed growing up. No telling what he was into; I can imagine him being the type that tied firecrackers to a cat's tail."

"Astin already has that request in motion, but when I talk to him, I'll find out where things stand as far as getting court approval." JJ took the final sip of her mimosa. "But I think that's enough talk about this, it's too disturbing and exactly what we don't need while we're on vacation and spending time with Stacey. Let's agree that this will be the last time we talk about Brookes Williamson or Laura's murder or the threats against the production while we're in Houston, except for when I call Marshal Astin. I promise to update you on that discussion, but that's it. Agreed?"

"You're right. It will be tough, but I agree. Pinky-swear!"

Unfortunately, that pinky-swear lasted barely 30 minutes once the flight had landed.

12

“Oh my God, it's so great to see you guys,” Stacey squealed. She ran up and threw her arms around Kristyn's neck before she'd even climbed all the way out of the car. Kristyn hugged her back, tightly, relishing the comforting arms of her sister after several months apart.

“I've really missed you, too. Thanks for letting us crash with you for a few days, especially with just a few hours' notice.

“Of course,” said Stacey as she stopped hugging Kristyn and practically ran around to JJ's side of the car. Although they'd only met a handful of times, they'd immediately hit it off and become fast friends, practically family. Wrapping her in a big hug, she said, “JJ, so happy that you're here, too. You have no idea how excited I am to have you guys here, especially over the long holiday weekend!”

JJ embraced her tightly, feeling some of the stress melt away at last. “I think a little time in Texas is exactly what we need. Don't get me wrong, California is great, but it's nice to get some time away from La-La Land and back into the real world. Not to mention some great BBQ.”

“You're in luck! I'm taking you guys out for BBQ tomorrow night to celebrate. I hope you'll be hungry.”

“Well, you've seen us both eat, so I don't think that's something you have to worry about. We'll just make sure to eat a light lunch so we can really pig out at dinner - no pun intended. Not that Kristyn and I haven't enjoyed a lot of great meals in L.A., but they've got nothing on Texas when it comes to great BBQ.”

"Amen to that," added Kristyn. "Let's carry this stuff in and get settled. I wouldn't mind freshening up a little bit. Even after showering this morning, I still feel kinda gross from spending hours in the airport and on the plane."

The three of them carried the luggage up to the guestroom on the second floor, joking along the way that it looked like they'd packed for a month in Europe instead of a few days in Texas. "What would you guys like to do while you're here? I'm off all next week, and the kids are with their dad, so I'm at your disposal. We can stay around here, head down to Galveston Island, anything that ya'll want."

"Eat. Drink. Sleep. Lay by the pool. Maybe a little shopping. That's about all the excitement I need," said Kristyn. "And your house is like the perfect getaway spot, especially the pool. I've been thinking about that the whole way here."

"God, you're predictable," giggled Stacey. "What about you, JJ?"

"Not to sound like some boring old married couple, but I agree with Kristyn. Slow and relaxing seems like the perfect break to me."

"Alright but be warned that I *am* going to drag you guys out to some nice restaurants and some urban warfare level shopping. I need it, probably as much as you guys. There's been too much alone time."

"I was going to ask you about that, Stacey. How are things between you and John? Have things settled down since the divorce was finalized?" Kristyn worried about her big sister, especially since she was now halfway across the country from her instead of just a few hours away.

"I guess it's as good as one could expect after any divorce. There wasn't a ton of animosity to start with, and since it was just one of those situations where we'd grown apart rather than someone cheating, I guess it wasn't too bad. Of course, the lawyers, assholes on both sides, if you ask me, tried to make it more contentious when it came to dividing assets. It probably would have been much easier and cleaner if John and I had just worked out the property division on our own, to say nothing of less expensive. Anyway, it's all done now, and we've moved on. We're making the best of coparenting and getting along really well."

"I'm really sorry that you guys had to go through all of that. I wish that I'd had the chance to meet him; from what Kristyn has told me, he seemed like a decent guy and a great husband and father."

"That's true, JJ. No complaints there at all. I guess it's just one of those situations where we both realized, after 20-plus years and two kids, that our lives are going in different directions. It's nobody's fault, and there's no bad guy here, just two people that need to figure out where they're heading for the rest of their lives."

"That's a healthy way of thinking about it, Stacey. And I know you'll find love again if you want to put yourself out there and open yourself up to the possibilities. I mean, look at you! You're still young, not to mention gorgeous and in great shape, plus you have a great career and a beautiful home. When you're ready, I know you'll find love again. Or it will find you." Kristyn knew her sister well, and while Stacey was keeping up appearances, there was little doubt that she was still hurting. After less than a year since the divorce, that was understandable.

"I'd like to think so. I'm more open to the idea than I was six months ago, but I haven't been at all proactive about putting myself out there yet. I'm a 40-something woman, and I'm way out of practice when it comes to dating, so I'm not going to rush into anything."

"You'll know when the time is right. Or when it's the right person," JJ said with a smile.

Around noon the three of them made a light lunch of Caesar Salad with grilled chicken and iced tea and took it out by the pool. It was a beautiful day, with temperatures in the low 80's and a light breeze. After lunch JJ jumped in and swam laps for 15 minutes with barely a break. During her time with the FBI she'd let herself get lazy, sloppy, and out of shape, but now she made it a point to take long walks or runs on the beach almost daily and hit the gym at least four times per week. Once finished with her laps, she joined Kristyn on a big double raft where they floated for at least a half hour, the tension slowly ebbing away.

"God, this is heaven. I could stay here for hours," JJ said while looking at Kristyn through half-opened eyes.

"Totally. Although if we don't get out of the sun and back into the shade, we're going to be burned to a crisp. And I need a drink, I'm absolutely parched. Can I get you anything?"

"Maybe just some ice water for now, thanks."

Kristyn came back out with two large Yeti tumblers filled with ice water, and JJ climbed out of the pool to join her and Stacey at the table. "Stacey, this pool is just what the doctor ordered," said JJ. "The water temp is perfect, and the day really couldn't get much better for this time of year."

"I'm glad you're enjoying it. Sometimes I take for granted just how lucky I am to have the pool; too often I focus on how much work and expense it is, but I have to say, I think it's worth every penny and every hassle."

"I'll bet the kids love it, too."

"Oh yeah, and the best thing is, it keeps them out of trouble and close to home. We let them invite their friends over pretty much any-time they want, so we never have to worry about where they are or who they're hanging out with."

"Well, you have to admit that Amy and Austin are pretty good kids anyway. And I don't say that just because they're my niece and nephew." Kristyn smiled at Stacey.

"That's certainly true. As far as kids go, we definitely hit the jack-pot. I've seen the hell that many of the other parents at their schools and in our neighborhood go through, and I'm glad we've experienced little of that."

"Cheers to great kids and the great parents that raised them," said JJ as she raised her Yeti and clinked it with Kristyn's and Stacey's.

Stacey stared off in the distance for a moment, lost in her thoughts. Finally, she spoke up. "I do have one question I wanted to ask you two."

Oh God, here it comes, the inevitable question about when we're going to make it all legal and get married and start a family, thought JJ. *Even though we've been together less than six months!*

"Sure," said Kristyn, though she was feeling the same trepidation as JJ, and for the same reasons.

"When are you guys going to tell me why you're really here?" Stacey looked at each of them in turn, but they were stunned into silence.

13

❦

FRIDAY, MAY 26

"Wha...what do you mean?" said Kristyn, completely caught off-guard.

"You're my little sister, and I've known you and loved you your whole life. I know you as well or better than anyone, and I know that there's something worrying you, some reason why you felt the need to come to Houston. Don't get me wrong, I'm thrilled that you're here, whatever the reason. But something is bothering you, and if I don't miss my guess, I think it's bothering JJ, too."

Shit, why does she have to be so astute, so observant? She's just like Kristyn. JJ wasn't sure what to do, what to say. She thought it best to let Kristyn take the lead since it was her family. She and Kristyn looked at each other, and JJ nodded her head. "Go ahead, Kristyn."

For the next hour Kristyn and JJ explained all that had happened in L.A. and with Brookes Williamson escape from prison. Stacey was shocked and terrified – the reason why they hadn't wanted to share this with her in the first place – but at least she didn't panic. She fought back tears, sometimes with less success than others, and she peppered them with tons of questions.

Were they concerned about their safety? Yes, but they were taking every precaution, and working closely with the US Marshals.

Did they think this Williamson guy would track them here to Houston? No, they didn't think that at all, especially since coming here was literally a last-minute decision, and they hadn't told anyone.

69

Would they stay here in Houston indefinitely? No, they planned to be back in L.A. next week when production resumed.

Did they expect Williamson to be in custody by the time they got back to L.A.? Realistically, they had no way of knowing. JJ was in close contact with the US Marshals, but she'd seen no indication that they were close to finding him.

Were they scared to go back and resume their lives and work in L.A. if he hadn't been caught? Scared might be too strong a word, but they were concerned and cautious. They would take every precaution, including extra security at the studio and at home.

Stacey dabbed at her eyes. "How can you live with this, especially when it's not even been six months since both of you were almost killed by those sick bastards in Dallas? You were both lucky to come out of that alive." The tears started flowing more heavily.

"You're right, Stacey," said JJ. "No doubt that things could have turned out much differently, if not for Kristyn's incredible instincts and observation skills that let her escape the Slayers' ambush....."

"And to say nothing of JJ's brilliant planning and tactics that would give a West Point 5-Star General a run for their money...."

"But be that as it may, and to Stacey's point, we don't take anything for granted. Yes, this time we think we're facing one man, one very deranged man, but still better than the four assassins we were up against in Dallas. We have to keep our eyes open and continue working with the Marshals service. Plus, I plan to reach out to my old boss at the FBI to try to get them involved."

"Will people in the FBI still talk with you, still work with you? I know that you didn't get to leave there under the best circumstances, and they were probably a bit resentful of Kristyn since she was an outsider."

"Luckily I didn't burn all of those bridges," JJ said with a smile. "I'll call him at some point over the next few days, depending on what we hear from the Marshall service back in L.A."

"On a holiday weekend? You think your old FBI boss will take your call?"

"Well, to be honest, if I had to contact him on his office number and get past his bulldog admin assistant – she and I aren't exactly BFFs, to put it mildly – it might be an issue. But I have direct access to him via his FBI and personal mobile phones, so I don't expect any problems. But if things seem to be quiet, maybe I'll wait until next week. Let him enjoy his holiday."

It took some time, but Stacey finally relaxed a bit and was able to carry on the conversation without crying and shaking from fear and worry. Kristyn was holding up well, considering, but JJ knew that it was partly because she was becoming numb from the tension and terror and partly because she wanted to appear strong for Stacey. It was almost 4:30 by this time, and JJ tried to shift the conversation to a more pleasant topic. "I don't know about you guys, but I think it's about time to get ready for a night out on the town, maybe hit Happy Hour and a nice dinner. Maybe I'll head up in a moment and hit the shower and start getting ready?"

"Ummm, that sounds like a plan, and I could use a drink. Surprise, surprise! Maybe a margarita to start, then maybe some nice wine with dinner. What do you think, Stacey?"

"Perfect." The change of topic seemed to brighten her mood. "So, let me tell you what I was thinking for this evening. I made dinner reservations for 8pm at Mastro's Steakhouse, and if you've never eaten there, I promise you will love it!"

"We've never been to the one here in Houston, but we did eat at their Malibu location with the production team, and it was fabulous. Great choice!" said Kristyn.

"And there are plenty of bars close by if we want to start somewhere more casual, or if not, we can hit the bar at Mastro's. It's really nice, too."

"I love it. Good food, good drinks, great company. What more could a girl ask for?" said JJ.

"Well, how about good music? I got us tickets to the Last Concert Café for this evening, and one of my favorite bands, 'The Suffers', is playing. I think you guys will love them."

"It sounds like the perfect evening. Of course, now I can't imagine what you're going to have to do to top it for the rest of the days we're here." Kristyn smiled at Stacey and JJ. It did sound like the perfect holiday weekend evening.

Or it would be if she could only push down the fear and anxiety. She had her doubts.

I4

SATURDAY, MAY 27

Saturday was the perfect southern California day for kicking off the unofficial start of summer. The air was warm, but the light breeze coming off the cool Pacific waters kept it from getting too hot. Typical Southern California weather, one of the many reasons that locals and tourists alike consider it paradise. Tens of thousands of people flocked to the beaches, making the usual L.A. area traffic even more horrendous. Still, nothing was going to keep people away from the ocean, not on a beautiful Memorial Day weekend.

Paige Madison was one of the lucky ones. Beach traffic was never a concern since she lived in a gorgeous beachfront home in Malibu that she'd rented for several years. She started almost every day with a half-hour ocean swim followed by a long run on the beach. It was her stress reliever, and no matter what the project, she *needed* that stress relief. The days were long, there was the constant pressure of tight timelines, and more times than she'd care to remember, a lot of self-centered, narcissistic producers, writers, and directors. And don't even get her started on the actors.....

The fact that they'd had to shut down production due to the death of one of the production crew and the ongoing threats certainly didn't help her stress level, either. She was determined to decompress during the time off, especially during the holiday weekend. No travel, no work, no big plans, just going at her own pace and schedule. Maybe a little bit of shopping next week, possibly a dinner or two with a few close friends, but she was determined not to be her usual 'type A' self and schedule everything down to the minute. She would just play it loose and easy; her anxiety level needed the reset. She spent almost 90 minutes meditating and doing yoga on the deck overlooking the beach and followed that with a light breakfast of fresh fruit. Watching the people on the beach and in the water, listening to the rhythmic sounds of the waves crashing and the seagulls crying overhead, and feeling the warm sun on her face, pushed any thoughts of work out of her mind.

Around 11am she was ready to start her daily exercise regimen. For most people a one-mile swim, followed by a five-mile run, would not be their idea of 'exercise', it would be like the Bataan Death March. As someone who had been a standout cross-country runner in high school and a top NCAA swimmer at UCLA, not to mention someone who had competed in almost a dozen triathlons, she rarely missed a day of training. While she lived only about 10 minutes from the local high school and their well-maintained 400-meter track and indoor pool, she preferred to run on the beach and swim in the ocean. Fresh ocean breezes and beautiful scenery were preferable to the tedium of running in circles on a track; she'd done enough of that in high school and didn't care to ever set foot on one again.

She stepped back into the house just long enough to put on her red shorty wetsuit before heading out to the beach. The water was still cold enough that she probably should have worn a full wetsuit, but she always balked at the restrictive nature of those and only dug one out of her closet on the coldest days. Besides, she found the water temperature invigorating. Reaching the water's edge, she pulled on her swim goggles and walked out until the water was waist deep and then dove through the first breaking wave, punching through the other side, and immediately settled into her smooth, effortless freestyle stroke. She swam out about 100 yards, just beyond where the small swells started stacking up to form the 3' shore break and turned parallel to the beach. This was where she was most at peace, her true *Zen* place; just her and the ocean, no other sounds, no distractions, just the rhythm of her stroke and the sound of her own breathing.

***

Brookes Williamson was also enjoying the beautiful holiday weekend. He was relaxing, or, for him, what passed for relaxing, in a beach chair just down from Paige's house. He tried to watch her while remaining inconspicuous, which was not always an easy task when using binoculars on a crowded beach. When Paige started doing her yoga poses, Brookes nearly fell out of his chair. Her good looks, as well as her incredible flexibility, drove him to distraction.

When Paige came out of the house in her wetsuit, he couldn't help but appreciate how nicely it hugged her curves. Even with little or no makeup, he still found her attractive and desirable. Then again, after months in prison, he found almost any female desirable. He was finding it difficult to focus on his plan and almost considered shifting to a hastily conceived 'Plan B', namely, breaking into her house and waiting for her to get in from her swim. He could only imagine how nice it would be to take her while she's in the shower, force himself on her once, maybe twice, and then leave her bloody corpse sprawled on the shower floor, or maybe on the bed. Maybe he could just strangle her after he'd had his way with her. Or grab whatever sharp knife he could find in the kitchen and cut her to shreds. Killing such a pretty girl would be a waste, but he never allowed himself to focus on that point: she was part of the blasphemous movie that those cursed Hollywood pigs were making about his heroes, the Slayers, and they all deserved to die. Violently. *Eyes on the prize, Brookes.*

Once he saw that Paige was out past the breaking waves and turned parallel to the beach, Brookes grabbed his paddle board and headed for the water. He was soon up and paddling on a parallel course to her and quickly closed the distance. He kept one eye on her as she glided through the water, taking care to stay out of her line of sight. That meant that he was behind her and a few yards to her left since she turned her head to the right to breathe with every stroke. Brookes also kept an eye on the beach: did anyone seem to be focused on him? Or her? He knew that there was no way to be 100% certain, but he found the added risk exhilarating, even arousing. Again, despite his self-admonitions to focus on the prize, he was once again having lustful thoughts about her. Seeing her beautiful long legs and shapely ass moving through the water wasn't helping matters. *Focus, dammit!*

Finally, he judged that the time was right. Nobody on the beach seemed to be paying him any mind, and it was unlikely that they could see the swimmer in the water, even with her high-visibility red wetsuit. The plan was simple, though timing was everything. He wanted it to look like a simple drowning, so he resisted thoughts of smashing her in the head with his paddle or using the paddle board's ankle leash to strangle her. Besides, she was obviously athletic and in great shape, to say nothing of a great swimmer. He knew that his plan required stealth and overwhelming ferocity, and that's exactly what he intended.

He dug hard with two quick strokes of the paddle and was now practically touching her. Quickly setting the paddle on the board, he leapt out and crashed down right on top of Paige, grabbing her around the neck like a rodeo cowboy wrestling a calf to the ground. His momentum carried them several feet beneath the surface, but the surprise attack had the desired effect, totally catching her off-guard and sending her into a panic. She tried to scream, but only succeeded in swallowing a mouthful of water, and that exacerbated her panic. She fought and struggled mightily but couldn't overcome his strong grasp and pressure on her throat to make it back up to the surface. Brookes wasn't fairing much better as he felt his own first telltale signs of panic starting to creep in as he was running out of air, too. He knew that she'd be a fighter, but he hadn't counted on her being this strong and putting up such a struggle. *But God, how exhilarating!*

It took almost 30 seconds before he could choke her out, and as she went limp Brookes kicked his way back to the surface while still holding her by the hair. He greedily gulped air and coughed up water, feeling like his lungs were about to burst. Still, he managed to hold her head under water for the next couple of minutes, removing any lingering question about her survival.

He held onto the paddleboard, too tired to even consider treading water. Letting go of her hair, he watched her slowly drift towards the bottom some 20 feet away. She'd probably be discovered in a few hours, possibly rolled up on the beach by the waves. No matter, he'd be long gone. The police would assume it was a simple drowning, though the Medical Examiner would determine otherwise in minutes. Most importantly, he knew that this would send a message to Jessica Jansen and Kristyn Reynolds as well as the whole movie production crew. Even before the ME determined the cause of death, they'd suspect foul play. The notion that this would terrorize them even more brought a smile to his face.

He crawled back on the paddleboard and sprawled on his stomach, willing his heartbeat and breathing to return to normal. It took nearly 10 minutes for that to happen. He sat up on the board and looked around. He'd drifted a few hundred yards away from where he'd pounced on Paige, and as he surveyed the people on the beach, he didn't see anyone paying him the least bit of attention. That brought a satisfied smile to his face. Standing back up on the board, still on somewhat wobbly legs, he slowly made his way back to the beach. Another successful killing: he only wished that the Slayers were here to see, and hopefully praise, his handiwork. *And I'm just getting started.*

15

TUESDAY, MAY 30

It was early afternoon and JJ, Kristyn, and Stacey were just finishing lunch at a chic downtown restaurant when JJ's phone rang. She'd slowly felt her stress ebbing over the past couple of days, but as soon as she looked at the phone display and saw that it was Jackson Taylor calling, her stomach tightened into knots. She looked at Kristyn, who immediately picked up on her concern and tension.

"Who is it?" Kristyn asked. Seeing the look on JJ's face, she knew immediately that it was something concerning.

"It's Jackson. What new fresh hell is this?" JJ's hands were trembling as she answered.

Kristyn explained to Stacey that Jackson was the Executive Producer on their film, and they were expecting to have the entire week undisturbed since they'd shut down. Production. She couldn't begin to think of any *good* reasons why he'd be calling now, and that raised her fear level ten-fold.

As JJ stepped away to take the call, she tried to force down her own growing fear. She knew it wasn't rational to be afraid before she'd even answered the call, but for the last few weeks it seemed like all news was bad news. "Hi Jackson, I'm scared to ask why you're calling. Please tell me I'm just being paranoid."

Jackson hesitated. "I wish I could." He hesitated again, obviously having trouble finding the right words, or maybe he was just too upset to get the words out. "I received a call about an hour ago from the Malibu PD that Paige's body was found washed up on the beach in Malibu. According to the police, it appears to be an accidental drowning. "

JJ felt her legs get weak and it was all that she could do to remain standing. "Drowning? She's a goddamn triathlete, and she swims a mile or more damn near every day! How could she have drowned?" She rarely believed in coincidences, but with the events swirling around them recently it would take a lot to convince her that Paige's death was an accident. JJ was shaking, partly from the news that Jackson had just shared but also from the obvious implication that Brookes Williamson still considered anyone, or anything associated with the production as potential targets.

"I'm as shocked as you; I don't know how she could drown with her extensive training and experience. I don't want to see a boogeyman around every corner, but this feels too coincidental considering every-thing else that has happened. Maybe we're all paranoid."

"That may be, but this definitely merits a deep-dive investigation. For all our sakes. I'm going to grab the first flight out of here and head back to L.A. And as soon as we hang up, I'm going to reach out to US Marshal Astin to let him know about this. This may be a simple, unfor-tunate accident, but I think we need to consider every angle, including the possibility that Brookes Williamson was somehow involved. How, I don't know, but I consider him guilty until proven innocent for any-thing that happens involving this movie and the people working on it."

"Forget booking a flight. That could take forever. I'm going to arrange for a charter jet to pick you up in Houston. Give me a couple of hours to make the arrangements and I'll get back to you with the details."

JJ ended the call after promising Jackson that she'd reach out to him the second she touched down in L.A. She was getting ready to head back to the table where Kristyn and Stacey were waiting but decided to call Marshal Astin first. Better to have as many facts as possible and a clear plan of action before sharing with Kristyn. For the last couple of days, she'd seemed happier and much more herself, her stress level more under control. That was about to end abruptly.

She was able to reach Astin and explained what had happened and what she suspected. Astin admitted that he and his team were no further along in their investigation than when they'd last spoken, and he agreed that it would take a hell of a lot to convince him this was a coincidence. If anything, he piled on his own suspicions and made her feel even more certain that she was right. Before hanging up, she committed to connect with him when she got back to town. For Astin's part, he said that he'd reach out to the Chief Medical Examiner, Dr. Carlos Falla, and ask him to examine Paige's body with a fine-tooth comb. Better yet, if he could hold off his examination until he and JJ could be there in person, so much the better.

Now came the hardest part, namely, sharing the news with Kristyn. She wished more than anything that she could protect her from this, even on the slim chance that Paige's death turned out to be an unfortunate accident. It was not to be. Kristyn was waiting anxiously for JJ to return to the table, and the look on her face betrayed the mix of fear, tension, and anxiety that she was feeling.

JJ took her seat and dove right in, not even waiting for Kristyn to question her. Stacey looked almost as tense as Kristyn. "I'm not going to sugarcoat this, even if I knew how. This morning Paige Madison's body washed up on the beach in Malibu. At this point the police are only saying that they presume it's an accidental drowning, but the body has been sent to the ME for an autopsy. I have no real reason to be skeptical of the accidental drowning theory, but I am. Call it gut instinct. Jackson is of the same mind. For that matter, so is US Marshal Astin, who I just hung up with."

The tears were flowing for Kristyn, and Stacey held her tightly to offer comfort. "What are you going to do?" asked Stacey. She could tell by the look on JJ's face that the wheels were already turning as she formulated some sort of action plan.

"Jackson Taylor is arranging for a chartered jet to pick me up here, probably within the next few hours, and I'm heading back to L.A. With a little luck, and some persuasion from Marshal Astin, I'll make it in time to observe Paige's autopsy. The police assume it's an accident, but that's to be expected unless there are some obvious injuries. Otherwise, it's up to the ME to take a much closer look, find the things that aren't obvious to the casual observer."

"And if they determine it wasn't an accident?" Kristyn asked through her tears, almost scared to hear the answer.

"Then I'm going to step back from this movie and dedicate myself fulltime to catching this motherfucker and either put him away or put him in the ground. To be honest, I much prefer the latter. He's taken too much from everyone involved already, and I'm not going to sit by while he kills and terrorizes other people in some sort of retribution for us taking down his heroes. And I'm not going to let him even get close to either of us. It's time to end this asshole's reign of terror."

"How soon can we leave?" Kristyn asked. Her eyes were blood red, and her mascara was a mess. JJ felt nothing but love when she looked at her and wanted more than anything to keep her safe from this craziness.

"I was kind of hoping that you'd stay here with Stacey until this all blows over. I'd feel better knowing that you're 1,000 miles away from L.A., plus I'll be in and out at all hours working this case with the Marshals, and maybe the police and FBI. That wouldn't be fair to you."

"Nice try, but no way. No way in hell. If you're going back to L.A., then I'm going with you. And I want to help with the investigation. You can use me to focus on research and the millions of details that you won't have time for and don't like to work on anyway. And you know that I can add value; I proved that when we took down the Slayers and the Murder Game."

Stacey asked through her tears, "Can't you both let this go, let someone else run with this investigation? Haven't you been through enough? Haven't you risked enough? Let the real authorities take this over and you guys stay here, or else go wherever you'll be safe until this all is over. It scares the hell out of me for you two to risk your lives more than you already have."

"We can't do that, Stacey. As much as I'd like to run and hide, we can't. Too many people have already been hurt because of this asshole's vendetta against JJ and me. And until he's caught, I don't think he'll stop. He'll keep targeting members of the crew, vandalizing and destroying property to delay the production, and potentially shutting this whole movie down for good and costing a lot of people millions of dollars. I don't want all of that on my conscience. I want to help bring this to an end. Hopefully with him in a body bag."

JJ loved and admired how brave Kristyn was in the face of real danger. She was a reporter, not a cop, but she had a cop's instincts for investigation and one of the strongest moral compasses that she'd ever seen. "As much as I'd love for Kristyn to stay here, she's right. She and I need to be involved with this case; nobody knows more about the Slayers, the Murder Game, and their followers and fan boys than us. We'll let the cops take the lead and do the heavy lifting, take the real risks, but I'm going to be right there with them, and Kristyn is going to help dig into everything we can learn about Brookes Williamson and the other sickos that he may have collaborated with."

"So, when do we leave? We need to get back to Stacey's to pack."

JJ thought it through for a second. "I think it will be at least an hour or two before Jackson is able to take care of the jet charter. In the meantime, I'm going to call SAC Isaksen to loop him into this situation and ask for FBI assistance while we drive back to Stacey's. I don't think the Marshals, or the local police, will really object, but truthfully, I don't really give a shit. We need all hands on-deck here."

JJ always felt better once she had a plan and started putting the plan into action, and this time was no exception. Then why was her stomach still in knots? She knew that she'd never be truly free of this terror and anxiety until Williamson was either in jail or dead. And while she may later have to deny it if things ever ended up in front of a judge or jury, she very much wanted, needed, and intended it to be *dead*.

16

TUESDAY, MAY 30

FBI Special Agent in Charge (SAC) Ken Isaksen is the lead Federal officer for the northern district of Texas, the 12th largest field office in the US that covers an area bigger than most states. He was also JJ's former boss during her time with the FBI, and to say that their working relationship was strained or contentious would be somewhat of an understatement. There was no love lost between the two of them, at least not until the day that JJ walked out the door for the last time. While there was never a doubt that FBI leadership was going to force her out due to her flagrant disregard of FBI procedures during the Murder Game investigation, to say nothing of the way she left the Bureau exposed to incredible liability by bringing Kristyn, a civilian, into the case, JJ drew the line at dragging Isaksen down with her. He had never forgotten her sacrifice and her offer of friendship, and they had in fact remained friends and kept in touch since she left.

"Hi, JJ, and to what do I owe this pleasure?" he said by way of greeting.

"Hey boss. Sorry to come to you with a problem, but we've got a real situation on our hands, and I think it's time – probably past time – for the FBI to be brought in. The US Marshals Service is already involved and has the lead, and the L.A. and Malibu police are working the case, too. Still, I think there's a legitimate case to be made for the FBI to jump into the fray."

For the next few minutes JJ ran through the preliminary details of the case, starting with Brookes Williamson's association with the Murder Game, his escape from Victorville prison, his murder of John Westbrook, plus the vandalism and online threats against the movie production.

"Not to minimize the seriousness of what you've told me, but I don't think I've heard a strong case for FBI involvement in this investigation, at least not yet."

"You're right, sir, but it gets worse. We're pretty certain that Brookes Williamson is responsible for the rape and murder – *mutilation*, actually – of one of our production assistants, Laura McIntosh. And then just a few hours ago, one of our screenwriters, someone that Kristyn and I worked with daily, was found dead on the beach near her Malibu home. I'm heading back to L.A. later today and hope to be there when they do the autopsy; for now, the police are assuming it's an accidental drowning, but truthfully, none of us believe that to be the case. In the first place, she was a world-class swimmer and swam a mile or more in the ocean practically every day. Plus, admittedly, all of us are past believing in coincidence."

"Can't say as I blame you." Isaksen grew silent for a moment, thinking things through. "Tell you what, JJ. I've heard enough to convince me that the FBI should be involved. First, this Brookes Williamson guy was part of the whole Murder Game case, and we need to bring him in to find out if there's more to his story than was raised during the initial investigation or trial, like maybe additional conspirators. Second, while there's no evidence yet that his little crime spree has crossed state lines, I think we can use the fact that he's used the internet and possibly other methods of communication to transmit terrorist threats and extortion. I think that's enough to give us the green light, though I will run this past our legal team to make sure so that we don't jeopardize any future prosecution."

"I think that's smart, sir. What can I do to help get this moving from my side?"

Isaksen smiled to himself. *Still thinking like an agent, even though she's now a civilian.* "Normally I'd say that anything that you, or any civilian, might do at this point might be counterproductive, but knowing you as I do, I assume that you already have a good working relationship with the Marshals and others working the case?"

"Yes sir, that's for sure. Especially Marshal Astin, the lead investigator on the case. He and I have been in close touch, and he made my involvement official by bringing me on as a consultant. I've mostly been doing research and offering background, but that's about to change as soon as I get back to L.A."

"Perfect. You talk to this Marshal Astin and ask him to formally request FBI assistance, and be sure to let him know that the Marshals Service has the lead. I'll launch a call to the SAC in L.A. and let him know that a request may be forthcoming and that I'd like him to agree that the Dallas office should take the lead, with assistance from whatever manpower he can provide, since this appears to be a continuation of the Murder Game case. As far as the US Marshals, I'll make sure that L.A. FBI understands that the Marshals are in charge and we're just along to focus on the extortion and terrorist threats. Obviously, we'll offer whatever assistance we can on the other aspects of the case if the Marshals want or need us."

Isaksen was silent for a moment, then asked, "I feel like maybe there's something more here, JJ. Is there something you're holding back? Not that this hasn't been bad enough, but I have a feeling that you've glossed right over some other details. Like, maybe, you and Kristyn have been directly threatened?"

Damn! Nothing gets by him! "Guess I still can't slip anything past you, right sir?" JJ struggled to find the right words that would convey the seriousness of the threat without ending up on the receiving end of one of his lectures about staying safe and letting the 'real' authorities handle things. "Williamson has made some direct threats against Kristyn and me, basically threatening to carve us up like he did Laura McIntosh. Bottom line is that he blames us for the deaths of the Slayers and the end of their precious game."

"What precautions have you put in place to keep you both safe, other than bailing on L.A. for a few days and traveling to Houston?"

"We've hired additional security at the studio as well as outside of our house. The other writers and producers on the production have done the same."

"Good. I'm glad to hear it. But I don't suppose there's anything I can say that would convince you and Kristyn to stay here in Texas, or basically anywhere other than L.A., until this is over?"

JJ smiled. "I think you know the answer, sir. I understand and appreciate your concern, but I owe it to the people involved with this production to help keep them safe and to see this through to the end. I'm not going to allow Brookes Williamson, or anyone for that matter, to harm anyone else and derail this project. Too many people have too much riding on it."

Isaksen just sighed. It was worth a try, but he never expected JJ to listen to reason. Then again, he didn't blame her. He wouldn't either. "Of course. Stay safe and watch your six. Same goes for Kristyn."

"You got it, sir." She heard the words come out of her mouth, but she knew it was easier said than done.

17

Jackson Taylor had come through in a big way. In less than two hours JJ and Kristyn were boarding the chartered Falcon 900EX jet at Love Field. Unfortunately, as much as JJ wished that she could just click her heels three times and be immediately transported home, that was beyond her powers. Still, the pilot promised to do everything humanly possible to shave as much time as he could off the usual 3 hour and 20-minute flight time; he didn't mention that Jackson had promised him a sizable bonus if he could get there by 5pm Pacific Time. Luckily, with clear skies and light headwinds forecasted all the way to the CA coast, his chances of collecting the $10,000 bonus were favorable.

JJ talked to Marshal Astin, and he committed to reach out to the SAC for the FBI Field Office in L.A., and also relayed that the coroner had agreed to wait to start the autopsy once he and JJ were there. "Would you mind picking us up at Santa Monica Airport? We should land around 5pm local time. We left our car at LAX when we flew to Houston and I hate to waste time trekking all the way back there, especially when the coroner is kind enough to wait for us."

"No problem, and I'm happy to drop Kristyn off at your house on the way, unless she's going to join us at the ME's office."

JJ certainly didn't want Kristyn to be subjected to that. Viewing dead bodies was never pleasant, but drowning victims were particularly disturbing. "Thanks, but she wants to get back home and start researching Williamson and his life before he was involved with the Murder Game and his time in prison. We've even been talking about making a trip up to Victorville to see if we can interview the Warden, the prison shrink, and anyone else we can find that may have spent time with him."

"That sounds like a good idea. And I'll be glad to make some phone calls up to Victorville to try and make the arrangements so that you don't have people trying to give you the 'Heisman' and putting up a bunch of bureaucratic bullshit roadblocks."

"I'd appreciate that. I'll see you in a couple of hours when we land."

As she turned back towards Kristyn to share the update with her, she couldn't help but notice the tension evident by her body language as well as the look on her face. Her eyes were still red from the tears she'd shed from the fear, stress, and seemingly non-stop terror she'd been living with for the past eight months.

"Marshal Astin is going to meet us when we land and drop you back at home on our way to the ME's office. We'll figure out some way to get our car back from LAX over the next day or two. At least we have another car at home to use."

"I hope that's not too much trouble. I don't mind calling an Uber if that will save you guys some time."

"No, it's pretty much on the way, so it's no problem." Thinking that she needed to say something to make Kristyn feel safer, she added, "I'm going to call the security team and tell them to get back to our house and restart the 24-hour rotation immediately. I'd told them to just have a skeleton crew there while we were out of town and to check things 2-3 times per day, but now that we're home, I want them back in full force. I may even have them double the manpower."

"No objection here. Any idea what time you'll get home tonight?" It was evident that she felt much safer and in control when JJ was with her.

JJ realized that, as well. "I'm hoping no later than 10pm, but I'll call you. Most autopsies take 2-4 hours, as a rule. It may be days or weeks before the final report is completed, especially if they have to wait for toxicology reports, but I don't think that's germane here. Marshal Astin and I should be at the ME's office by 6pm, and I'm sure he'll be fully prepped and ready to go the minute we walk in there."

"When I get home, I'm going to dive into the information we have on Williamson to see if I can find anything that may have been missed. Want to plan on having a late dinner when you get home? Maybe you can call me when you're on your way and I can order something from DoorDash?"

"No, you go ahead and eat whenever you're ready. There's nothing worse than autopsies on drowning victims. I have a feeling that after observing this one, I probably won't be able to eat for days."

JJ's words were prophetic: not only was she unable to eat for more than 24 hours, but for the first time ever while observing an autopsy, she vomited. Twice. Her only saving grace was knowing that Marshal Astin had vomited three times. Dr. Falla had been around the block with all manner of dead bodies literally hundreds of times, but he still took a little bit of perverse pleasure in seeing the big, strong, cops brought to their knees by the disturbing sights, sounds, and smells that he dealt with daily. Luckily, he was able to hide his smile behind a surgical mask. *Those big, strong, cops often have big egos and no sense of humor.* He smiled to himself again.

18

It had taken less than three hours, thankfully, for Dr. Falla to complete his exam and confirm that Paige's death was not caused by accidental drowning. JJ was not complaining. She was glad that he had been able to make the determination quickly so that she and Astin could move out of the autopsy space and into an adjacent meeting room. Falla joined them after removing his soiled medical coverings.

"Feeling any better?" Falla asked them, still having to fight to suppress a smirk.

That suppressed smirk wasn't lost on Astin, or JJ for that matter. "Fuck you, doc. I know that you're getting a little kick out of seeing us both lose our lunch in there." Astin wasn't seeing the humor, not in the least.

"I'm guessing it won't be the first time that you've had to hose down the floor in there after an autopsy, am I right?" JJ was still a bit queasy but slowly getting back to normal.

"Certainly not. It's damn near a daily occurrence, which is why I prefer to conduct my autopsies in private, without an audience, whenever possible. Cleaning up after any autopsy is not exactly pleasant, and drowning victims are the worst of all, but adding puke on top of that just makes a bad job worse. Occupational hazard, I guess."

"So, Dr. Falla, you've made it clear that Paige's death will be ruled a homicide, but can you give us some more details about how you came to that conclusion? I know that you probably would have told us more while you were doing the procedure, but unfortunately the Marshal and I spent a bit too much time in the restroom."

"Certainly. I was able to quickly determine, based on the water in her lungs, that she had, in fact, died from drowning. However, closer examination revealed that someone had attacked her in the water, and that was evident from several marks on her body. First, I found where she'd been grabbed around the neck, and most likely forced under water."

"Are you thinking that someone was swimming in the water and took her by surprise?" This was from Marshal Astin.

"No, that's not likely. To the best I can determine, whoever grabbed her did it from above her and likely behind her. What I mean is, it appears that someone jumped down on her, with significant force, and used that inertia to push her underwater." Seeing the quizzical looks from JJ and Astin, he added, "I'm not saying *how* someone managed to jump down on top of her – I'll leave that to you guys to determine – but it's clear that that's what happened. Maybe someone snuck up on her in a passing boat, or maybe a standup paddle board. Regardless, my guess is she was taken down at least several feet, and, while I can't be certain, I'd be willing to bet that's when she got the huge volume of water in her lungs."

"You mean, like maybe she was caught by surprise and tried to scream, thereby sucking down a lot of water?" JJ could remember many times as a kid where she'd sucked-in water while playing in the pool and the resulting choking and gagging. Out in the open ocean, with someone attacking you? That would be horrifying.

"That would be my guess. I can't be 100% certain, but it's a very reasonable assumption."

"What else did you find, Dr. Falla?

"Well, Marshal, I found some bruising around her throat, even to the point of some damage to her trachea. Not enough to be fatal, but it would have added to her pain and distress. I also found some hair pulled from her scalp, and my conclusion is that happened as her assailant struggled to keep her head under water until she succumbed.

Because she had swallowed so much water, I'd estimate that she died in approximately one minute, possibly less."

JJ asked a question, though she was sure she already knew the answer. "I assume that there's no way that we'll get any fingerprints or DNA samples from the body since she was in the water so long?"

"Unfortunately, Agent Jansen, not in this instance. I can tell that she struggled mightily, but I was not able to find any kind of skin samples from under her nails or any other type of physical evidence left by the killer."

JJ thanked Dr. Falla after they'd learned everything possible. She was also glad to be walking out into the fresh air. Turning to Astin, she said, "As bad as that experience was, as least we were able to get confirmation about cause of death. I really appreciate you being here for this; I know it wasn't pleasant for either of us."

"That's an understatement, to say the least. But I'm glad I was here, regardless."

"Were you able to pave the way for me to interview the Warden and prison psychologist at Victorville?"

"All taken care of. They're expecting you tomorrow. You OK to go up there alone?"

"I'll be fine. In fact, I'm going to take Kristyn with me. She's an excellent interviewer and has incredible instincts, so she could add a lot of value. Plus, I feel better knowing that she's close by where I can make sure she's safe. Not that I don't trust the security that we have, but I guess that's just part of the control freak in me."

"Let's get you home so you can get some rest before you have that long drive tomorrow. And touch base with me to let me know what you learn when you're done at Victorville."

"Will do. And you keep me informed on anything else you learn about Williamson and his whereabouts. It bothers me that he's been on the run this long."

"You're preaching to the choir, JJ."

As they were walking to Astin's car, JJ's phone rang. The Caller ID indicated a Blocked number. Despite being too tired and emotionally spent, she knew that she should take the call anyway in case it was related to the case or the movie production. "This is Special Agent Jansen."

"Well, hello there, Special Agent Jansen. This is Brookes Williamson."

19

JJ felt her blood run cold, and all color drained from her face. Even in the dim light of the ME's office parking lot, Astin could see her terrified expression. JJ leaned on the car as her knees grew weak. For one of the few times ever, she felt real terror. *How did he get my number? What else does he know about me? About us?*

Astin looked at JJ and mimed, "Who is it?". He knew, instinctively, that something was wrong.

JJ muted her phone and quickly said, "It's Williamson." She saw Astin's stunned and questioning look. Surely the same things that were going through her mind were also going through his.

"So, I'm not going to even waste my time asking how you got my number. I guess you get an 'A' for resourcefulness. What do you want?"

"Oh, Agent Jansen....or may I just call you JJ? I just wanted to welcome you back to L.A. and ask how you enjoyed your little mini vacation to Houston with Ms. Reynolds?"

She wouldn't have thought it possible, but her blood ran even colder. No way, though, could she let him sense any weakness. "Wow. Make that an A+ for resourcefulness. You must be a lot fucking smarter than I gave you credit for. Or anybody else, for that matter. Most people I've talked to had you pegged as just a spoiled little rich kid with average intelligence, at best. Obviously damaged, even before getting yourself tied up in the Murder Game and sent to prison."

"I'm sure that you and the other incompetent investigators have spent countless hours trying to delve into my psyche to find out what makes me tic, what crazy things I did in my misspent youth, and where I might strike next. It's not really much of a mystery, JJ."

"Meaning that you're going to keep trying to shut this movie down...."

"That's certainly a given, but do you really think that's the end game?"

"No, I suppose the end game is killing me and Kristyn, but only after you've ruined this production, and everyone involved with it."

"Very good, JJ. See, you're not nearly as clueless as I first suspected. You obviously catch on quickly."

"I certainly caught onto the fact that you're just another in a long line of pathetic little incels that fancies himself a real man, a real assassin, like the Slayers, when the reality is that you're just a pissant little wannabe. You're nothing but a little shrivel-dick pretender that isn't fit to lick the sweat from their balls, much less consider yourself the heir apparent to their legacy." JJ kept trying to press his buttons, hoping to goad Williamson into a rage and, with luck, a mistake.

Shockingly, he didn't fly into a rage. He simply laughed. "That was a good one, JJ. Vey witty, I have to admit. And that mouth of yours! Do you kiss that beautiful, achingly hot lesbian lover of yours with that mouth? I mean, after you go down on her and lick, nibble, and tease her to orgasm after orgasm, do you kiss her with that cum covered mouth of yours?"

JJ was getting pissed, and she was frustrated that she was letting him push *her* buttons instead of the other way around. "I'm glad that I can contribute to your fantasies like the little, dickless asshole that I suspected. Probably fantasizing about girl-on-girl action is what you use to get yourself off, because you're not man enough to get, much less please, a woman on your own."

"Touché, JJ. Again, so quick, so witty. But let me assure you: once I've shut down this production, permanently, I will be coming for the two of you. I promise that I won't kill you right away; my plans are much better than that. You're going to watch as I fuck her in every way imaginable and *with* everything imaginable. Then she's going to watch me do the same to you. For days. Maybe weeks. You'll both be begging for death. But death is the easy way out. And after what the two of you have done, you don't deserve the easy way."

JJ was trembling, trying hard to push down the fear and not show any weakness. "Just remember, you sick little fuck, that we took down the Slayers so taking you down should be a walk in the park. Hopefully that ends with you in a body bag, but if not, we'll relish the thought of you sitting in a cell for the rest of your life and being the prison bitch for God knows how many different groups. And after we make it known the things that you've said and done – and believe me, we can embellish those statements to the point that every gang and group in that prison is going to want a piece of you – you'll be everybody's favorite boy toy."

Williamson's tone turned darker and more sinister. "Keep thinking that, you snotty bitch. You think the extra security at the studio and at your house is going to stop me? Think again. Maybe I've got eyes on your house right now, watching Kristyn walking through the kitchen. Or maybe I'm watching you and Marshal Astin right now as you head home after overseeing Paige Madison's autopsy. Maybe through the scope of my rifle...."

JJ grabbed Astin and pulled him to the ground beside her as a bullet hit the car mere inches from where she'd been standing. She heard laughter and realized that it was coming from her phone next to her on the ground. Picking it up she heard, "Good reflexes, JJ. But that was just a warning shot, a bit of fun. If I'd wanted you dead, and the Marshal for that matter, you'd both be laying on the ground with your brains splattered from here to Malibu. I just wanted you to realize that I can take you anytime I want and any place I want. You think you can take me? It's time that you realize that you're way out of your league. *I'm* way out of your league. Until we meet again...."

JJ and Astin took some time getting to their feet on trembling legs, careful not to present a large target in case Williamson was still there. Before JJ could say a word, she felt the bile coming up in her throat. After vomiting twice during the autopsy, she didn't think she had any-thing left to throw up. That may have been true, but that didn't stop her from having dry heaves that felt like it would rip her lungs out. And Marshal Astin was matching her retch for retch.

20

"Call LAPD and have them issue a BOLO for Williamson before he gets too far away, and ask them to send a CSI team down here to scour the area for evidence," JJ practically shouted. "I need you to take me home as fast as we can get there. While you call LAPD, I'm going to call Kristyn's security detail and tell them to get her into the panic room immediately."

"Let's go. You don't think that Williamson will try to get to Kristyn now, do you? Not right after taking a shot at us and knowing that we're going to call the cavalry?"

"Honestly, no, but I'm not taking any chances."

They both jumped on their phones, both struggling to hear their own conversations over the other's voice and the roar of the engine and squealing of the tires as they sped towards JJ's house. It took a few minutes for JJ to convince the security team, and for them to convince Kristyn, that this was a viable threat that needed to be taken seriously. She tempered that by reiterating that she felt chances were low that Williamson would try anything tonight. She neglected to add that she reached this conclusion because she was certain that he wanted to drag this out and terrorize them even more.

As they ended their respective calls, JJ asked the question that had been burning in her mind since Williamson had called her. "How the hell did he get my mobile phone number? It's not like it's out there on a million sites; I've only given it to a handful of close friends and my closest coworkers on the production. My primary phone number, the one that I use for my day-to-day life, would be understandable, but not this line."

Astin was lost in his thoughts for a moment before he spoke. "That could be an important point to consider. Think about it: if he'd gotten hold of your primary cell phone number, the one that is out there on countless sites and databases, from Amazon to banks to doctors' offices and everything in between, that would indicate that he'd simply hacked your shit. Not easy for most of us, but not the biggest challenge for people with strong computer skills. Not sure whether he has those skills or knows someone with them, but people get hacked all the time."

"I think I see where you're going. The fact that he managed to get this particular number probably means that he found some way to access the information associated with the production, like the studio's servers."

"Some way, or *someone*."

"Damn. That makes a lot of sense. We're going to have to dig into that angle; I'll get on that first thing tomorrow. I think my mind is too fried to take that on tonight. It's been a long day, to put it mildly, and I need a drink. Maybe several. Between rushing here from Houston, witnessing the autopsy, and then throwing up to the point that I hurt all the way down to my toes, it's been a lot."

"Don't forget the proverbial cherry on top," added Astin. "You were just shot at by a crazed serial killer wannabe. That kinda shit can ruin your whole day."

"You're right, and I have someone at home that is going to need some serious comforting when I get in. For that matter, I could use some of that, too."

Pulling up to the house, JJ called the security team to let them know that they had arrived. The last thing she needed was for a well-armed security team to be startled and start shooting as she and Astin rushed to the door. Three of the members of the security team met them as they approached the door and told JJ that they had not seen anything suspicious or out of the ordinary since she'd called. She breathed a sigh of relief. While she hadn't really expected Williamson to show up tonight, she knew better than to bet on it.

"Can you all stay posted out here and seal the perimeter while we head in. How many more guards are inside with Kristyn?" JJ was practically breathless by this point.

"Kristyn is in the panic room, as you instructed, and we have two guys in the house, one on each floor." Chris Hall was the leader of the security team and the one who had assigned the extra guards on such short notice. JJ thanked him profusely for all that he'd done.

Rushing up the stairs, she went straight to the panic room door and was about to start knocking on it and calling out Kristyn's name when she saw the latch turning and the door slowly being pushed open. "Wha...What are you doing opening the door before you know it's safe?"

"Silly, I saw you on the monitors inside. Remember? There are several cameras around this room and the rest of the house, and they all feed into the console in the panic room. I saw you as soon as you came through the door and headed up the steps." Kristyn smiled and threw her arms around JJ's neck.

They embraced for even longer than usual, both feeling totally beat down from the long day and the stress of the situation. "You had me a bit worried, but I'm glad it turned out to be a false alarm. And I must admit, even though I thought it was a silly waste of space when we first looked at this house, I'm thankful for that panic room. Not to mention all this security. You didn't have time on the phone to tell me what created the urgency." Kristyn looked to JJ and Astin, expecting to hear the full story.

For the next half hour JJ and Astin walked Kristyn through everything that had happened, including the warning shot and the disturbing sights, sounds, and smells of the autopsy. JJ felt a wave of nausea as she relived the scene, and Astin and Kristyn looked pale, too. They also explained how Dr. Falla had determined that the cause of death was murder, not a simple accidental drowning. When JJ got to the part where the ME had determined that Williamson had pounced on her while she was swimming and caused bruising to her neck, throat, and shoulders, Kristyn looked at them quizzically.

"What? Now Williamson can walk on water and sneak up on Paige? I don't get it."

"To be honest, I don't either," said Astin. "And there's no reports of any boats anywhere near the area, certainly not that close to the beach. Surely somebody would have seen that if that were the case."

"I've been giving that some thought, too. Before Dr. Falla told us about Paige being assaulted from above and behind her, I'd been thinking about someone attacking her from below, like someone SCUBA diving in the area. But that's obviously not the case."

"I think I have an idea what it could be," responded Kristyn, and it was obvious that the wheels were spinning in her head."

"We're all ears. Let's hear it," said JJ.

"A couple of years ago I did an article about a large SUP club in Dallas that held races out on Cedar Creek Reservoir on most weekends...."

"What's a SUP club? You mean like a dinner club that's held outdoors by the lake?" Astin looked totally confused.

Kristyn smiled. "No, SUP stands for Stand-Up Paddleboard. You know, they look like oversized surfboards, but instead of using them to catch waves at the beach you stand up on it and use a paddle to move through the water. Sort of like you paddle a canoe; except you're standing on the board instead of sitting in the boat."

"That makes sense, actually. If Williamson has any experience at all on a paddleboard, he can definitely paddle faster than Paige could swim. Any sound as he approached would probably be minimal, and with her head in the water she'd probably never see or hear him coming." JJ was once again impressed by Kristyn's keen mind.

"At least not so long as he kept to her blind spot, that is, the side *away* from where she lifted her head to breathe." Kristyn saw JJ smiling at her appreciatively. "I used to be on the swim team when I was a kid, and I know that I always turned to the right to breathe. Probably because I'm right-handed. I'm sure if I even tried to breathe to my left, I'd probably swallow water and end up choking."

They all talked for a while longer and made plans for Wednesday. Astin would try to track down any paddleboard rentals in the immediate area of Paige's Malibu house, and failing that, he'd try to find any witnesses that may have seen Williamson in the area. JJ planned to update Isaksen and ensure that the FBI was moving on their end, and she was also going to reach out to the FBI forensic experts to see if they could determine if Williamson had somehow hacked her phone. She had her doubts on that point.

"One final thought," said Kristyn as they were winding down. I think it's high time that JJ and I did some digging into every single person involved with the movie production. Call me crazy, but based on what we've seen, it sure feels like we might have an inside person working against us. Or at least working with Williamson, willingly or not."

"I learned long ago not to consider any of your ideas or theories crazy," JJ said with a smile. "And I'm not about to start now."

21

What a blessing to have true security professionals like Chris Hall and his team on the job. Not only had they secured the premises and ensured JJ's and Kristyn's safety, but they had also taken the initiative during the night to travel to LAX to pick up JJ's car that had been left there a few days ago. Before leaving LAX the two operatives had done a thorough check of the car to determine if there were any tracking devices hidden away, but, surprisingly, the car was clean. Still, they were insistent that another car be used for the trip to Victorville, a vehicle that Brookes Williamson was unfamiliar with. After a quick stop at the Hertz counter, one of the security team drove out of the lot with a white Chevy Malibu, likely the most ubiquitous rental car on the road. On the way back to the house, they made one last stop at an all-night convenience store and picked up several prepaid mobile phones since they felt it was a virtual certainty that Williamson had somehow compromised their current phones.

Hall had been insistent that two members of his team travel to the prison with JJ and Kristyn. At first JJ pushed back hard, arguing that she was a trained professional and fully capable of taking care of them. Finally, with Kristyn acting as mediator, JJ relented and agreed to the 'intrusion'. Kristyn was relieved, though she tried not to show it; she figured that having extra manpower and firepower couldn't hurt. Besides, as she'd told JJ, it would give them time to think, strategize, and multitask on the way to and from the prison. JJ couldn't argue with that logic.

Their appointment with the warden of Victorville prison was scheduled for 10am, and since Victorville was only about 100 miles from their Santa Monica home, the drive should be less than two hours. Or at least that would be the case almost anywhere in the US, but not in or around L.A. regardless of the time of day. JJ and Kristyn considered the possible routes, checked Google Maps and Waze, but eventually they just had to admit that it was going to be a 3-hour drive plus a 30–60-minute exercise in frustration clearing through security. The last thing they wanted was to get up early to get on the road by 6am, but if that's what they had to do, then so be it.

"If you were still with the FBI, would we have been able to requisition a helicopter for this trip? If so, would you consider going back to the Bureau?"

"No, and hell no. Trust me, in all my years with the FBI I never once rode in a helicopter, at least not outside of training at Quantico. For that matter, I never even had a decent car; since I was basically treated like *persona non grata* for most of my career, I got nothing but hand me down cars."

While the trip felt interminable, even with the security team driving, it was still more pleasant than what awaited them when they got to the prison. JJ and Kristyn went in alone, but first they had to endure multiple searches of their car, not to mention searches and X-rays of their briefcases and purses. They had to pass through three different metal detectors, even after having their mobile phones and JJ's gun taken and locked up for 'safe keeping'. After what felt like hours, they made it up to the warden's suite of offices where two guards took up a post just outside of the door. Whether that was for their protection or a sign of the warden's own paranoia, they weren't sure.

"I don't think I'll ever complain about the whole TSA thing at the airport again," Kristyn said with a barely suppressed smirk. "This whole process was somewhere between a third date and an all-out sexual assault."

"On the bright side, at least we didn't have to strip down and submit to a body cavity search. But I'm guessing that was the next step if they'd found anything suspicious or if we gave them shit about what we were already being subjected to."

The door to the warden's office opened and several people shuffled out and they were escorted in by his administrative assistant. "Warden, this is Jessica Jansen and Kristyn Reynolds, your 10 o'clock appointment that we accepted at the request of the US Marshals." With that, she turned and left.

"Ladies, please come in," Warden Tom Josupait said as he rose and came around from his desk to greet them. "Please make yourselves comfortable," he added as he led them to a surprisingly comfortable seating area with a couch and two expensive looking side chairs.

JJ and Kristyn were both taken aback by Josupait. They didn't say anything to each other, but they didn't have to. Not that the subject had even come up, but based on their experience, not to mention a thousand movies and TV shows, they were both expecting some older, hardened, and grizzled veteran of the prison system. Someone who would probably delight in cracking heads and watching the prisoners beat the shit out of each other, and someone who would turn a blind eye to, maybe even encourage, his guards to abuse the prisoners at every turn. Looks could be deceiving, but in this case looks would have to be *extremely* deceiving: the Warden could have stepped out of central casting for an English Lit or Philosophy professor. Mid- to late 30's, tall, thin, bookish, and looking like he just walked out of a Midwest corn field. If he'd been wearing a tweed blazer with leather elbow patches it would have completed the stereotype.

"I understand that you had quite a long trip this morning from Santa Monica. I took the liberty of having some coffee and other drinks and snacks brought in for us since you had such an early start. Excuse me one second while I have my assistant bring it in." He stepped away momentarily and when he came back in, he was followed by two staff members who carried in enough food and drinks for a half-dozen people.

JJ and Kristyn helped themselves to the lovely spread, thankful that Josupait had been thoughtful enough to order it. They hadn't had time for breakfast or time to stop along the way to pick anything up beyond a quick cup of coffee. "This is lovely," said Kristyn. "And you're right, it was a long trip, and it didn't afford us any time to stop and eat along the way."

"So, the US Marshals asked me to extend our cooperation and every courtesy to you with regards to Brookes Williamson and John Westbrook. I'm more than happy to cooperate in any way that I can. As you can imagine, I'm very interested in seeing Mr. Williamson apprehended and back behind bars. That, of course, would always be the case, but even more so since he's suspected of multiple murders since escaping from Victorville."

JJ asked, "What can you tell us about Williamson during his short time here? Did he ever do anything to raise your suspicions, or any instances of violence towards other prisoners, any gang affiliations, etc.?"

"There's really nothing much to say, unfortunately. Not just because of his short time here, but because he just wasn't on our radar. Hollywood notwithstanding, most of the prisoners here, or in any prison, are mostly just going through the motions and existing. Doing what they can to stay busy, stay safe, and alleviate the endless boredom. Williamson was no different; he just went about his daily routine and never caused any problems or did anything to bring himself to our attention."

"Were there instances where he was beaten up or assaulted by other prisoners that you were aware of?" asked Kristyn.

"No, not that I'm aware of. I mean, I did hear that in one or two instances early in his time here that he was hassled by a couple of our more troublesome inmates. Nothing as serious as you might expect, but just some guys trying to assert their dominance over the 'new guy', but from what the guards told me, it never escalated beyond that."

"And why do you think that is?" asked JJ. "As a new guy thrown into a world of meaner, bigger, stronger, and more violent men, he'd be an easy mark for anyone that wanted to take advantage of him. Whether that would be for money, sex, or whatever, I don't see things going well for him in those situations."

"True, but somehow or another Williamson connected with a 'guardian angel', so to speak: John Westbrook. Once Westbrook 'adopted' Williamson, the rest of the inmates took a hands-off attitude towards him. There aren't many inmates in here that would stand up to Westbrook. His reputation preceded him if you will."

"Do you think their relationship became sexual? As in, Westbrook would protect him from all the other inmates, but he expected sex-on-demand in return?" Kristyn asked the same question that was on JJ's mind.

"I can't say with any certainty, unfortunately, but my best guess is that the answer is 'no'. It's a very reasonable question and assumption but based purely on the scuttlebutt from the guards and staff here, I don't believe that to be the case."

JJ asked the question that had been haunting her. "Warden, if Williamson and Westbrook were friends, co-conspirators in their escape, and Westbrook was even, in your words, Williamson's 'guardian angel', why do you think Williamson murdered him once they escaped?"

Warden Josupait looked down at his hands and was thoughtful before he spoke. "The honest answer is that I have no idea. What scares me is to think that, even with the time spent digging into his background, practically back to birth, not to mention the time spent with our own staff of psychologists, we didn't see it coming. Not the escape, and certainly not the murder. To my untrained eye, I think we're dealing with a very sick, demented, and dangerous psychopath. And I'm afraid that the longer he's out there on the run, the more people he's going to kill."

22

WEDNESDAY, MAY 31

The meeting with Warden Josupait lasted about an hour, but in the end, JJ and Kristyn agreed that they'd learned nothing new. The warden had certainly reaffirmed some of the information and assumptions that they already had, but nothing new and earthshattering came to light that put them any closer to understanding Williamson or tracking him down. Their next meeting was with the head of the prison psychology department, and they hoped that it would prove more useful. Hopeful, but not overly optimistic, considering the overwhelming volume of prisoners under their care.

They had to wait in the administrative area for their escorts to arrive to take them to the medical wing, and while they relaxed JJ pulled out a report that she'd pulled off the internet early this morning regarding the incredible volume of men and women in American prisons and the numbers being treated for mental disorders. Even with her FBI background, she was stunned by the numbers.

"Kristyn, listen to this. It's mind-blowing: 'It's no secret that the US incarcerates more prisoners than any other country, more than 2 million people, and it's estimated that 15-20% of those prisoners suffer from psychological issues and need treatment. Those 2 million are spread among 1,566 state prisons, 102 federal prisons, 2,850 local jails, 1,510 juvenile correctional facilities, 186 immigration detention facilities, and 82 Indian country jails. Plus, there are military prisons, civil commitment centers, state psychiatric hospitals, and prisons in the U.S. territories.

108

Bottom line, the US has more facilities dedicated to incarcerating its citizens than many countries have hotels. Little wonder that there is a constant need for more clinical psychology and psychiatry practitioners. With a team of over 400 psychologists and over 650 clinical service providers, the Federal Bureau of Prisons is one of the largest employers of mental health professionals in the United States.'"

"Holy cow! I knew the number of prisoners was huge, but I didn't realize it was that many. And I had no idea there were that many being treated for mental health issues. Kinda makes you wonder if being in prison is the best thing for them versus being in a mental health facility where they can get better treatment and care."

Moments later their guards showed up, and it took nearly 20 minutes to be escorted through the maze-like prison before they reached the office of Dr. Joanne Adducci. As they were led into a conference room, they were amazed at the contrast between the stark and austere environment that they'd just passed through and the soothing and calming atmosphere of this clinical area. Rising from the conference table, Dr. Adducci greeted JJ and Kristyn warmly. Dressed stylishly in a well-cut and very expensive looking black pantsuit, cream colored silk blouse, and 4" black heels, she made quite an impression. Standing nearly 5'10" in her heels, with great hair, designer glasses that highlighted her gorgeous dark brown eyes, and a beautiful made-for-TV-smile, one could imagine that she was the subject of many inmates' sexual fantasies. On the upside, it probably didn't take much encouragement to get inmates to keep their appointments.

"Welcome, and please come in and make yourselves comfortable. May I get you anything before we get started?"

"No, thank you. Warden Josupait took great care of us when we arrived. I must say, the contrast between this area and the rest of the prison is just startling. I assume that's by design?" asked Kristyn.

"It is, yes. We do our best to present a calming environment by incorporating soothing colors, aromatherapy, and relaxing background music. Much like a spa, if you will. We want this to be a safe space, from a mental health perspective, and a place that oozes a sense of tranquility. Sorry, I know that sounds kind of new age for a clinical psychologist, but I'm sure you understand what I mean."

JJ smiled. "Yes, we do, and I think it makes total sense. Hopefully it leads to calmer sessions and better outcomes for the inmates who come to see you and your staff. By the way, do you lead the mental health practice for all of Victorville? I know that this facility is massive."

"No, I just lead this particular part, referred to as Medium 1, which is one of two Medium Security Federal Correction prisons here at Victorville. In addition, there is also a Maximum-Security Penitentiary and a minimum-security Female Satellite Camp. Each institution has their own department of Psychological Services. We work and collaborate closely, as I'm sure you can appreciate, but we work somewhat independently."

"I'm confused on one point. I thought that only psychiatrists were doctors, but it's my understanding that you're a psychologist rather than a psychiatrist. Right?" JJ asked the question to get the ball rolling.

"You're on the right track, but I think the confusion starts with the word 'doctor'. It's true that only psychiatrists are MDs – medical doctors – meaning that they completed medical school and then specialized in psychiatry, much like one might specialize in surgery or oncology. And because they're MDs, psychiatrists can prescribe medications, something that psychologists can't do. My title, if you will, is Doctor of Psychology, which denotes that I've attained credentials beyond my bachelor's and master's degrees by completing the requirements for a PhD."

"Ahhh, thank you for explaining that to me. Makes perfect sense." JJ opened her notebook and quickly browsed the list of questions that she wanted to ask. "So, Dr. Adducci, it's our understanding that you personally oversaw sessions and treatments for Brookes Williamson, from the time of his initial intake until his escape. Do you usually stay involved with patients for the duration of their stay here at Victorville?"

"Not as a rule, no. In most cases we assign one of our staff psychologists to work with the inmates after the initial intake assessment. I chose to stay with Williamson because I had openings in my schedule, and to be honest, I found him somewhat fascinating."

"Really? In what way?" Kristyn was intrigued to hear what would differentiate Williamson from the other prisoners currently housed in this facility.

"He was smart, witty, and very engaged in our sessions. Many inmates attend their sessions, shall we say, under duress. They do only the bare minimum required to keep coming to our sessions because that gives them time out of their cells. Brookes Williamson, in contrast, took our time together seriously and truly seemed to be baring his soul and confronting his demons. In my opinion, he was striving to be a better person."

"You don't think it was simply a matter of telling you what you wanted to hear? Or maybe because he enjoyed your company, maybe even had a little crush on you?" JJ saw the confused look on Dr. Adducci's face. "Sorry, I'm not questioning your expertise or medical judgement at all, it's just that you're a very attractive woman who is engaging him in conversation, paying attention and showing interest in him. Obviously, that's not something he's getting from anyone else in his life, certainly not in here."

Dr. Adducci hesitated for a moment, slowly shifting in her seat. When she looked back up at JJ the smile had returned. "I did not detect any feelings towards me, romantic or otherwise. He was unfailingly polite and cordial, but I attributed that to being well raised rather than a romantic interest or even innocent flirting."

Kristyn had to bite her lip. "How do you reconcile that image with the fact that he was an active participant in a game that wagered considerable sums on the murders of innocent, randomly picked victims? And now, after having escaped from prison, he murders his accomplice, terrorizes hundreds of people involved with a movie, and murders and mutilates two different women? I'm a layperson, admittedly, but that sounds like anything but 'well raised'". She could feel her blood pressure rising and was fighting hard not to lash out.

Dr. Adducci bristled but fought hard to hide it. Kristyn had struck a nerve, and while she may have been a well-credentialed PhD in Psychology, she was a less-than-gifted poker player. "If Williamson has suffered some sort of psychological break, there was no evidence that such a condition would manifest itself while I was treating him."

JJ didn't like the sudden change in the tone of the conversation. "Was it possible that something happened here that pushed him to a breaking point? Like maybe threats from other inmates, or a sexual assault from John Westbrook or some other prisoner?"

"Even if I knew of such events, particularly sexual assault, I would not be able to share that or any other details related to discussions that we had during his treatment sessions. Doctor/Patient confidentiality. I'm sure you understand."

The conversation went nowhere from that point on, with Dr. Adducci asserting that confidentiality and HIPAA laws restricted her ability to provide further information. With no real authority, much less a court order, to compel her to divulge more information, JJ and Kristyn decided to end the interview. As they stood to leave and thanked Dr. Adducci for her assistance, such as it was, JJ threw out one final question.

"One last thing, Doctor. Why do you think Williamson killed Westbrook? They were friends, or apparently what passes for friends in this place, and Westbrook had been his protector. They planned and executed the escape together and got away clean. Why take the risk of killing Westbrook when he was clearly a more violent and experienced killer, someone who may have been able to turn the tables and kill him in the process? Why not simply split-up and head off in different directions."

"I don't know what to tell you. To hear of his violence and terrorist threats over the past few weeks is very much out of character for him, at least from what I've witnessed during our sessions. I have no idea who or what's in his head at this point, but I will say this: you should be very concerned about your own safety and the safety of those around you. I don't think he'll stop until he's caught. Or dead."

JJ had been thinking the same thing for days, if not weeks. *I vote for dead.*

23

❧

WEDNESDAY, MAY 31

"That bitch is lying to us. I can see it in her eyes, her body language. I don't know how she's involved, but mark my word, she's part of this." Kristyn couldn't hide her distaste for Dr. Adducci.

"I'm getting the same vibe. I'd like to dig deeper into her, see how many inmates she personally treats, if there's some link or thread between them. For that matter, see if there's been any ethical complaints or even just rumors about her. First things first though: we need more to go on if we're going to convince the FBI and Marshals to get a warrant for her records and communications."

"Maybe when we meet with this inmate, we can steer the conversation in that direction and see if we can learn anything useful."

Their final interview was with Miguel Torres, an inmate housed just a few cells down from Williamson's. They'd learned that the two men had been friends, but friendships were often forgotten if there was something to be gained by betraying that trust, like a plum work assignment, someone to watch your back, or access to drugs, cell phones, and other valuable contraband. Torres had provided the authorities with some information and background after the escape, but nothing that was helpful in tracking him down. Whether he had anything more to contribute or would even talk to them in their 'unofficial' capacity remained to be seen.

JJ's first impression when she stepped into the meeting room and saw Torres: *Thank God he's shackled and cuffed to the damn table.* He was, hands down, one of the scariest men she'd ever seen, and she'd seem *many* scary individuals over the course of her career at the FBI. At 6'2" tall and 240 pounds of rock-solid muscle, even his shapeless prison jumpsuit couldn't conceal his ripped and powerful physique. Almost every visible part of his body was covered with tattoos, including his face and bald head. In short, he was not the kind of man that you'd want to come across in a dark alley. A high-ranking member of MS-13 in Los Angeles, he had been convicted of killing three rival gang members and suspected in the deaths of at least a dozen more.

JJ kicked things off. "Mr. Torres, thank you for meeting with us. I read through your files, and I have to say, I was more than a little surprised. I read about your convictions and sentence, life without parole times three, yet you're sitting here in a Medium Security facility instead of in Maximum Security. How's that work?"

That's when JJ and Kristyn got their first surprise. Torres was extremely polite, articulate, and respectful, the exact opposite of what they expected. "Please, call me Miguel. What's not reflected in those files is that I helped the police and prosecutors close at least a dozen murder investigations after my convictions. Some involved my crew, and others were committed by rival gangs. They managed to keep my name out of things, thankfully, and in return for my help they let me do my time here at Victorville Medium 1. I was able to move my family close by, and while this is still a prison, it's a lot better environment than the other alternatives. I feel truly blessed."

JJ and Kristyn were both momentarily stunned into silence. Finally, Kristyn asked, "Is that why your file shows that since you've been incarcerated, you've completed your GED and attained a college degree in English Literature? That's quite a change, Miguel, if you don't mind me saying."

"No argument there, ma'am. I needed to make some changes in my life, obviously. Unfortunately, I waited too long to make them. I ruined my life by running with the gang, doing drugs, selling drugs, manufacturing drugs, killing people, you name it. If it was bad and illegal, I was into it. I ruined my life, and because of that I'll never be a free man.

I've accepted that. The best I can hope for now is to improve myself and, with God's help, show others how they can be a better man who's ready to re-enter society when the time comes. Better educated, better trained for a trade, and better able to handle life without depending on drugs or alcohol or gangs."

When JJ was feeling cynical about people, especially criminals, she put little stock in people changing or turning their life around. If she had a dollar for every prisoner that suddenly 'found God' and was a changed man, she could retire to Costa Rica. Torres was different; she didn't doubt his sincerity even a bit, and she had to fight the tears that she could feel starting to well up in her eyes.

For the next 20 minutes Torres went on to tell them about Williamson and his time behind bars. The two men had become friends when they discovered a similar taste in books, and Torres shared many from his collection to help Williamson pass the time. He concurred with Warden Josupait's assessment that John Westbrook was not using Williamson for sex, though he admitted that he wasn't sure what brought the two of them together. "Westbrook was unquestionably his protector, but I suspect that Williamson was paying him in ways other than sex. My best guess is that Brookes convinced him to help put together their escape and promised him a substantial amount of money once they got out. Brookes never hid the fact that he came from a wealthy family and that he had access to a lot of his own money once he was back out on the street."

"Was Westbook, or Williamson, for that matter, into drugs?" A reasonable question from Kristyn.

"Not really. I mean, sometimes inmates take some drugs just to escape reality for a while, but I can say for certain that they weren't heavy users. Now, selling drugs to other inmates is a whole different matter. I know for a fact that Westbrook did a big business inside these walls."

JJ asked, "And where did these drugs come from? Any ideas? I'm not naïve; we all know that drugs are rampant in prisons everywhere, but any clue as to who was supplying them?"

"Nothing that I can prove but based on what I've observed and the rumors I've heard, my money is on the medical staff. I'm sure that some of the less-than-honorable guards are distributing, too, but I think that's small time compared to what goes on through the medical team."

"Are we talking prescription pills, like opioids?" asked Kristyn.

"Without question, but also crystal meth, fentanyl, cocaine, and heroin. It's basically like DoorDash in here: place your order and it will be delivered to your door. One more thing you should understand is that the guards know that this goes on, but even the best, most honest among them turn a blind eye. So long as someone doesn't OD or turn violent, they just ignore it. They figure that a happy and high inmate is a more mellow inmate and easier to control. For the most part, life inside a prison is all about keeping the peace and keeping things in balance."

"Makes perfect sense," said JJ. She decided to shift the conversation a bit. "So, Miguel, we know that Williamson was seeing Dr. Adducci for ongoing counseling. To your knowledge, does she personally counsel many of the inmates?"

"Not really, no. Since she's the head shrink for this facility, a lot of her work is administrative so that limits the number of actual clinic hours. I don't know the details of her schedule, but I can say that, of all the inmates that I'm aware of that are receiving treatment from the clinical psychology staff, Brookes is the only one that I know of that was treated by Dr. Adducci personally. Everyone else was seeing one of the other staff members that work under her."

"Interesting. And why do you think that is?" JJ asked as follow-up.

"Simple. Because he was fucking her practically from the time he arrived here. Pardon my French, ladies."

24

JJ and Kristyn both sat in stunned silence for several beats. They looked at each other and could read each other's minds: *we got her.*

Kristyn dove in. "Do you know this for certain Miguel, or is this just a rumor or innuendo that you heard?"

"Brookes told me, in confidence. Not like he was bragging about it, per se, but more like he was sharing something important that was happening in his life. I don't think he shared it with many other people, if any. Well, maybe with Westbrook."

"Unfortunately, we can't ask either of them. Williamson is on the run, and Westbrook is dead. If we want to get a warrant for Dr. Adducci's records, we're going to need something more than that." JJ believed it but knew that a judge would demand more before signing off on a warrant. With just this hearsay, the FBI and Marshals wouldn't even approach a judge.

"How about this video clip?" said Miguel, trying hard to suppress a smirk.

Once again JJ and Kristyn were stunned into silence and gobsmacked. This time it was JJ that spoke up. "You have a video clip. How? I mean, how did you record it, and how do you have access to it now with cell phones being off limits in here?"

Miguel just smiled. "You know that cell phones are second only to drugs when it comes to contraband in prison, right? And let's just say that some of the guards look the other way for well-behaved and trusted inmates. Like I said before, it's about keeping the peace and maintaining a balance. Anyway, I didn't record it. Brookes did. Whether or not that was for insurance or for his 'alone time', I'm not sure. He sent it to me via email and I made sure to save it to my cloud account, just in case."

"Can you show it to us now?" Kristyn looked at him pleadingly.

He could, and he did. They didn't need to see the whole thing; just a few minutes gave them all the evidence that they needed. Miguel forwarded the video clip to both of their new prepaid mobile phones.

"Miguel, I can't tell you how helpful you have been. Would you like us to let the warden or anyone else know, or is this kind of thing better kept quiet? I feel like we really owe you, but we'll follow your lead." JJ understood that spreading the word about his help make him a target for breaking the 'prison code'.

"Thank you, ma'am, but no. This is better kept between us. I'm just happy if I can help you guys capture Brookes and prevent anyone else from being killed."

"Fair enough. One more question before we go, and I realize that this may call for conjecture since you may not have direct knowledge." JJ took a moment to collect her thoughts. "Do you think it's possible that Dr. Adducci could have anything to do with the illegal flow of drugs into the prison that Brookes and Westbrook were distributing? You mentioned that the medical staff was a likely route, and I realize that medical and psychological staffs here are quite large, but could she be involved?"

Without hesitation, Miguel responded, "I think it's more than possible. I think it's a virtual certainty."

"Even though," asked Kristyn, "she's not able to write prescriptions for the opioids and other narcotics?"

"Yes. Remember, it's not just prescription drugs, there's also crystal meth, fentanyl, and other street drugs. My guess is that she's not involving anyone else here at the prison that has access to prescription drugs. I think she's getting it all on the street – some stolen, some from trailer park meth labs -- and then bringing it into the prison to distribute via her selected 'dealers'."

"Sounds possible, even plausible," said Kristyn.

"Plus, there's one other thing: every day that woman dresses like she just stepped off the runway at Fashion Week. *Every day*. She makes an OK salary here, but not enough that she could afford designer clothes and shoes, high-end jewelry, and a top-of-the-line BMW. And my understanding is that she has a sweet house a few miles outside of town that would probably be way beyond her means. Not ironclad proof, but I bet once you get that warrant and do a little digging, you're going to find that she's up to her ass in this mess. Pardon my French again, ladies."

25

WEDNESDAY, MAY 31

As they were being escorted out of the prison and to the waiting car, JJ and Kristyn barely said a word. They had no way of knowing who might be involved in the drug distribution conspiracy, so they weren't taking any chances.

"We've got a long ride back to L.A., so let's divide and conquer," said JJ. "I'll touch base with Isaksen and Astin and update them on what we've learned and ask them to try to expedite warrants for Dr. Adducci. We need to dig into her quickly, both her personal and professional life. That includes searching her office here at the prison, her home, her bank accounts, everything. I especially want to find something that definitively connects her to this drug distribution and use it for leverage."

Kristyn added, "We also need warrants for her cell phone and email accounts. How much do you want to bet that she's been in touch with Williamson since he escaped, maybe even helped him along the way? If we can connect her to the drugs and make her an accessory to his escape and the subsequent murders, that gives us a whole lot of leverage over her."

"Good point. And I was thinking back to what you said yesterday, about your feeling that someone somewhere, like maybe someone connected to the movie, was feeding information to Williamson. I still think that's a real possibility that needs to be explored. While I talk to Isaksen and Astin, why don't you track down Jackson Taylor and tell him we need names and background information on every single person connected to the production. Tell him to keep it as quiet as possible; we don't know who we can trust."

"Agreed. I still think we're going to find that Dr. Adducci has been in touch with him, but it makes sense that someone involved with the production may have provided Williamson with information like our mobile phone numbers, our trip to Houston, and more. No way that Adducci could have provided that."

JJ first connected with SAC Isaksen, and before diving too much into the details he suggested bridging Marshal Astin onto the call so they could all talk and collaborate more strategically and ensure that everyone heard the same information and details. It was decided that they would attack this on two fronts: Isaksen would seek Federal warrants for the drug distribution and tax evasion, and Astin would seek warrants for evidence that would tie Adducci to the escape and events that transpired after that, including the murders of Laura and Paige. Since it was already 3pm, they weren't optimistic at getting the warrant applications created and approved by their respective judges by the end of the day, but they committed to touching base on Thursday at 11am Pacific Time and see where they stood. When the warrants were ready, they planned to execute them immediately. They didn't want to give Adducci any time to plan her own escape or destroy any evidence. JJ felt confident that they hadn't tipped their hand while meeting with her, but she wasn't taking any chances.

For her part, Kristyn was initially met with some resistance from Jackson Taylor as he worried about everything from invasion of privacy to liability to just a general waste of time and resources. "The guy knew about our private phone numbers, our travel to Houston, and other personal information. He didn't learn this shit from a Google search."

"I understand that Kristyn, but I've got to look at the bigger picture....."

Kristyn had reached the end of her rope and was tired of the back and forth and excuses she was hearing. "Look, Jackson, let me say this as clearly as I know how: it's a virtual certainty that *someone* associated with the production is providing information to Brookes Williamson, and that information has enabled him to not only track JJ and me, it's given him what he needs to track down your phone number and private social media accounts as well as stalk and murder Laura McIntosh and Paige Madison. If we don't identify this leak and shut it down, it's going to put more people at risk. Not to mention the production and the millions of dollars already invested. Are you willing to risk all of that?"

Jackson didn't like it, but he couldn't argue with the logic. Obviously, he didn't want to see anyone else in danger, but almost as important to him was getting the production moving again on Monday. They'd already missed a week of production, and while he hadn't yet received any pushback or second-guessing from the studio, he knew that it was only a matter of time. If delays and lost money kept piling up, there was a very real chance that they'd shut the movie down for good. Millions of dollars lost for the producers and investors, hundreds of people losing their jobs, and a blemish on his reputation that might be unrecoverable.

"OK, you've made your point. I have access to electronic personnel files, so I will forward them to you by the close of business today. I trust that you and JJ will treat them with the appropriate privacy and discretion; we don't need confidential information flying around out there. What are your plans once you have the files in hand?"

"Hopefully JJ and I can dig into them and find a common link with Brookes Williamson. We're both pretty good at finding those kinds of details when sorting through a lot of data, but if we can't find it, JJ will likely enlist the help of the FBI technicians in Quantico. If they can't find it, it likely doesn't exist."

"And if a link doesn't exist, where does that leave you?"

"We're working a few different leads right now, and we're pretty confident that at least one of them will pan out and help drive this case forward. Obviously, it would be even better if we got lucky on multiple fronts since we think there is more to this story than just one guy's desire for revenge. That may be the main driver, but it's starting to look like there are other factors at play here."

"Care to share?"

"Not at this point, no. We've got like a dozen plates spinning in the air right now, and it's too soon to know which ones are going to come crashing down to the floor. But as soon as we sift through this data, we'll reach out right away to let you know if there's a snake in our midst. In the meantime, don't say anything to anyone. We don't want word reaching this person, assuming they exist. And for my money, there's little doubt."

26

THURSDAY, JUNE 1

Making movies is a complex business with a million different moving parts. Production costs for today's big-budget movies often surpass $100 million, and like any big business, it takes a lot of people to keep track of expenses, ensure that the production stays on budget, and ensure that everyone gets paid on time. Chris Zimmerman was the lead Set Accountant for *The Murder Game* production, so it was his job to monitor the project's finances. Starting his career as an entry level Production Assistant, he had leveraged his degree in accounting and on-the-job-training to become not only a top-notch accountant, but also a highly regarded specialist with encyclopedic knowledge of the movie production process.

Chris felt truly blessed to be working at a job he loved and in such a glamorous industry. To his way of thinking, it beat the hell out of crunching numbers for one of the many Fortune 500 companies back home in Minneapolis. If he never experienced another winter like he grew up with it would suit him just fine. Not that he got to hobnob with a lot of movie stars here in L.A., as many of his friends assumed, but he did often see them, and sometimes even meet them, around the studio. He made a decent living that, along with his wife's well-paying job in the tech industry, afforded their family a comfortable lifestyle in the Valley.

Like everyone associated with the production, he'd grown increasingly anxious and concerned about the events over the past few weeks.

As the person ultimately responsible for payroll and ensuring that all bills were paid on time, he was growing increasingly worried about the impact that ongoing delays and bad publicity might have on the movie. The deaths of Laura McIntosh and Paige Madison had been shocking, of course, but so were the acts of vandalism and increasing vitriol on social media. He'd read many of the disturbing Instagram and Twitter posts and was taken aback by how many times they had been forwarded or retweeted. He had his own social media accounts and understood the algorithm 'voodoo' that was employed, and it was obvious that whoever was posting these messages understood it, too. They were counting on others to jump on the bandwagon and make the postings go viral, and so far, that plan seemed to be working.

Despite his concerns, he was thankful for the break afforded by Memorial Day weekend and the production shutdown. Movie production timelines often last a year or more, and it's rare for someone in his position to get much time off, even on weekends. His role wasn't as high profile as the director, producers, or screenwriters, but it was his department that controlled the purse strings. Any delays or mistakes could effectively grind things to a halt. That's why, even during the shutdown, he planned to work at least a few hours each day to make sure nothing fell through the cracks.

His team of accountants was a tight-knit group, and most of them had worked together on multiple productions over the years. Depending on the film's budget, he might have anywhere from a handful of staff to as many as a dozen; the bigger the production, the bigger the bills and the more people and service providers that must be paid. Up until a few weeks ago things had been going well, his team working like a well-oiled machine and the production itself on schedule and, amazingly, under budget. Things started falling apart, though, when one of his team members, Dawn Steen, suffered near-fatal carbon monoxide poisoning at her home due to a corroded and broken fitting on a natural gas pipe feeding her house. It was only by a stroke of luck that her husband returned early from a business trip and found her unconscious but was able to drag her outside to the fresh air. When the

EMT's arrived, she was barely alive. When she arrived at the hospital, the doctors determined that there was apparent heart and neurological damage due to a prolonged lack of oxygen. Her chance of survival was estimated at 20%, but even if she lived it was expected that she'd have permanent brain and neurological issues. Chris was not the cynical type, but he couldn't conceive of these recent events being a coincidence. He believed in facts, not random, one-in-a-billion chances, so he wasn't surprised when the fire department's arson investigator deemed the whole thing 'suspicious' and opened an investigation.

It fell to him to notify his team about Dawn's situation, and they were devastated. Chris felt guilty in announcing that he'd have to begin the search for her replacement immediately, but they all understood. Everyone knew that they needed to get back to full strength to handle the workload, and quickly. "If you guys know anyone that might be available, let me know. We've all got a lot of contacts in the industry, so reach out to your networks."

After a few days of fruitless searching, he was almost at the point of giving up in frustration when he received a call from an old friend from high school and college. She was calling for a friend, Michael Glover, that was an accountant at an L.A.-based tech company, and, like many people, he had dreams and aspirations of working in the entertainment industry. They spent some time discussing his background, experience, and education, and Chris came away duly impressed and *very* thankful for the call.

"This might work. He sounds like exactly what I need. Is he able to start soon? I need someone ASAP."

"Since he's local and already left his previous employer, he should be available immediately. Want me to have him contact you and you can interview him yourself?"

"Yes, that would be perfect. Give him my contact phone numbers and email address. If he's half as good as you say, he should make a great addition to our team. But I know you and trust your judgement. I'd be surprised if this doesn't work out."

"Perfect! I'll have Michael reach out to you, probably by the close of business today. And thank you for giving him a shot at the career he's so passionate about."

"Anything for you, and you know it. Take care, and thanks for reaching out. What great timing!"

Chris sat back and felt a wave of relief wash over him. Assuming that this Michael Glover was as advertised, he could be the lifeline that Chris needed. How lucky for him that his old friend had taken the chance on reaching out! He was considering how best to thank her.

Calling his favorite wine store, he told the clerk, "I'd like to send a bottle of your best champagne to a friend in Victorville, CA. Her name is Dr. Joanne Adducci."

27

THURSDAY, JUNE 1

At exactly 11am PT, JJ jumped on the video conference bridge along with SAC Isaksen, his L.A.-based counterpart, Donald Alexander, and Marshal Astin, as well as assorted team members from the FBI and Marshals service. Kristyn joined JJ in her home office; she needed a break from her heads-down work of reviewing all the production team's files searching for a link to Brookes Williamson. It was critical work, but after sitting at her desk until nearly 2:30am last night and back at it this morning by 7am, she was feeling drained.

JJ was tired, too, both from the long hours and the constant stress. She wasn't in a particularly chatty mood, so as soon as everyone was on the video bridge she got right down to business. "How are we coming with those warrants for Dr. Adducci?"

SAC Isaksen spoke first. "SAC Alexander was able to get a judge to sign-off on a federal warrant this morning, and we're ready to roll. The warrant allows us to search her office at the prison, her home, her car, and all her electronic devices. And because of the probable tax evasion, we are also authorized to pull all her bank records, brokerage accounts, and access any safe deposit boxes. We might have to go back to the judge to get an amended warrant if Adducci has other properties that need to be searched, like a storage unit or other homes, but that won't hold us up too much. The judge is very accommodating."

"Excellent. That's the kind of news I need today. Thank you for the quick turnaround, SAC Alexander. Marshal Astin, how about on your end?"

"We're also good to go. I went before the judge first thing this morning and, though she balked initially because of Dr. Adducci's profession and concerns about doctor-patient confidentiality, she quickly changed her mind once I showed her the video clip of Adducci and Williamson having sex. That convinced her to issue the warrants right away, and I was in and out of there in less than half an hour. Oh, and she made it a point to say that, in California, the whole HIPAA argument doesn't hold water in the case of a state or federal prisoner. That really shouldn't come into play now, but it might when we drag their asses into court."

"I guess we couldn't have wished for anything more. Great work, guys. I don't know about you, but I think we need to execute these warrants ASAP. Let's figure out a plan and get it in motion." JJ was feeling the rush of adrenaline, and that was slowly replacing the fatigue that had her ready to crawl back into bed just a few short minutes ago.

She realized that she was falling back into 'FBI Special Agent mode' and acting like she was leading the operation, so she made a conscious effort to take a step back and let the people with the badges and the real authority take the lead. "Sorry," said JJ. "I think I'm letting myself get a bit too caught-up in this and trying to take over when I know, or *should* know, that I need to defer to you. You're the ones with the badges and the responsibility for bringing this to an end, not me. I want to help, and *will* help in any way I can, but you guys are in the driver's seat. I'm just a passenger, albeit a mouthy passenger." She smiled and hoped that they'd see that she was sincere.

"No need to apologize," responded Alexander. "We know that this case has serious implications for you and Kristyn, and without you two we wouldn't be here and this far along in the case. I'm sure I speak for everyone when I say that your input will be invaluable as we plan this operation, and in addition I'd like you to ride with us when we execute the warrants. We'd like you there to offer your trained eyes and perspective."

JJ was impressed. She'd heard of SAC Alexander during her many years at the FBI but had never crossed paths with him, but she was aware of his meteoric career rise and stellar reputation in the Bureau. Coupled with his movie star looks, a cross between Denzel Washington and Michael B. Jordan, and with a deep, sonorous voice as engaging as Morgan Freeman's, he was destined for great things.

The discussions and planning went on for more than an hour, but everyone was aligned with the plan once they were done. It was agreed that they'd arrest Adducci on her way home from the prison, then separate teams would conduct the searches of her prison office and home. Banks and investment advisors would be served copies of the warrants tomorrow as soon as they opened, and forensic accounting experts would immediately start digging into her information to see if there were offshore accounts or other properties in her name or under an alias or LLC.

With guidance and input from the FBI lawyers in the room, the decision was made to charge Adducci with multiple felony counts that carried significant prison time, likely running into hundreds of years. JJ lobbied to charge her as an accomplice to capital murder, which made sense since she had facilitated Williamson's escape from prison which led to the subsequent killing of John Westbrook and others. Any leverage they could use to get her to flip on Williamson was worth a try.

There was also a discussion about how to keep Adducci *incommunicado* for as long as possible. They knew that this was a very fine line that they couldn't cross without risking the dismissal of all charges for violating her civil rights. JJ was the one who argued for coloring just inside the lines. "We don't want to do anything to compromise our prosecution in this case, but we need to do anything and everything to keep her from contacting Williamson, whether directly or through a third-party like an attorney. We can't risk him fleeing, or destroying evidence, or maybe even escalating his craziness in retaliation."

"Do you think Adducci would use her one phone call to try to warn Williamson rather than reach her attorney? I would think that getting herself out of jail is priority one."

"True, Kristyn, but it's not quite like that," said Isaksen. "The whole 'one phone call' thing is really just Hollywood BS. In California, as in many states, the penal code allows for up to three phone calls."

"But her right to make those phone calls doesn't begin until she's gone in front of a judge or magistrate," added Astin. "So, she can kick and scream about calling someone all she wants when we first pick her up, but until she's been processed, she can't reach out and touch anyone."

"Which is kind of where I was going with this," said JJ. "I remember a case a few years back where the police and FBI got a bit creative and did a little bit of 'hide and seek' with the suspect to delay their appearance before a judge or magistrate and to keep the suspect's lawyer from screwing up the works. As you can imagine, the defense screamed bloody murder at the trial, but the judge declared that the police had bent the rules but not broken them and let the conviction stand. The decision was even upheld on appeals in both state and federal courts."

"So, are you suggesting what I think you're suggesting? That we grab her in Victorville and then hopscotch her ass around the state instead of going straight back to L.A.?" Isaksen asked the question but could barely suppress the smirk on his face. "You know we're playing with fire, to put it mildly."

"That's exactly what I'm suggesting. We arrest her in Victorville, then instead of processing her there, we carry her to the jail in Barstow. Then later tonight we make a midnight run down to San Bernadino, and maybe tomorrow mid-morning we make another move to Anaheim or Irvine or wherever the hell makes the most sense for keeping her 'hidden' and unable to contact Williamson."

"And all the while, we can ramp up the pressure by adding charges as we uncover more evidence of her involvement. Not to mention additional prison stretches. I like it," said Astin.

"With a little luck, we may end up with a delayed arraignment since, tomorrow being Friday, it might be harder to find a magistrate or judge after 5pm. It would be a shame to have to hold her all weekend, wouldn't it?" Now JJ couldn't suppress her own smirk.

28

SACs Isaksen and Alexander, along with Marshal Astin, took the lead in assembling the various federal, state, and local law enforcement teams and briefing them on the plan. Between the FBI, US Marshals, California Highway Patrol (CHP), and the Victorville police and sheriff's office, they had a team of nearly 40 people set to participate in the arrest, evidence gathering, interrogation, and forensic accounting on this operation. Everyone involved rendezvoused for a last-minute briefing at the CHP location on Amargosa Road in Victorville, only about 6 miles from the prison and minutes from the planned spot where they'd intercept Adducci.

During the briefing, many still expressed concerns about Adducci being able to contact Williamson before they could take her into custody. Shades of the OJ Simpson 'chase' came to people's minds, and a lot of ideas were considered but ultimately rejected for legal and/or logistical reasons. The favored idea, to use a short-range cell phone jammer, had to be rejected since they are illegal in California and most other states. Existing case law was not clear if using the technology would get her case thrown out of court, but it would undoubtedly give the defense teams grounds for a possible appeal if they lost. It could also lead to charges against the prosecution and members of the task force. As one of the FBI lawyers in attendance reminded everyone, if it was legal to use cell phone jammers then every prison in America would line up to buy and deploy them. It's no secret that cell phones are constantly smuggled into jails and prisons by visitors and guards; next to drugs, they're the contraband of choice. It's little wonder that the most violent and well-connected prisoners continue running their criminal enterprises even while behind bars.

The assembled team settled on a plan: a CHP helicopter would track Adducci as she left the prison grounds, and two officers in a single CHP Police Interceptor Utility SUV would pull her over about a mile from the prison, ostensibly for a minor equipment infraction. One of the CHP officers would offer to show her the problem, and once out of the car she would immediately be cuffed and placed face down on the ground. More than a dozen CHP and local Victorville officers would quickly converge on their position in an overwhelming show of force to secure her car and belongings, especially her cell phone. Everyone agreed that the plan was simple, well-conceived, low risk, and could be executed in three minutes or less.

Shortly after 5pm the CHP car parked near the exit gate for Victorville prison sent a radio message to the team. "I've got eyes on Adducci. She's exiting the prison and turning east towards your location now."

"10-4," responded SAC Isaksen. "Hold your position. Chopper 1, keep her in sight and let us know as soon as she approaches the intercept point. CHP Leader, Officers McMillan and Gaston, she should be proceeding past you in about 30 seconds, so be ready to pull in behind her."

Marshal Astin added, "Prison team, as soon as we have Adducci in custody, you'll have the green light to enter the prison and start the search. We'll reach out to the Warden and administrative staff to announce your arrival and make sure they know that we have warrants in hand. Watch your back in there; we don't know who can be trusted. That goes for the guards as well as the prisoners."

"This is Chopper 1. Adducci is just approaching the intersection of Air Expressway and preparing to turn right onto National Trails Highway. She should pass the intersection with Powerline Road in approximately 10 seconds and then CHP can fall in behind her."

"Roger that. Officers McMillan and Gaston, you're up." The tension, coupled with too much coffee, not enough food or water, and enough adrenaline to drop a water buffalo, had his stomach in knots.

McMillan and Gaston spotted Adducci's car as it passed, and they pulled out onto National Trails Highway a few seconds later. The plan was to pull her over about a mile before the ramp for I-15, so that gave them about a half-mile area to execute the stop. The rest of the task force vehicles were staged at various businesses along the Highway in front of them as well as several cars that were staged behind them on Powerline Road. Should Adducci try to make a run for it, she would be blocked-in from all directions. The whole take-down operation was probably overkill, but everyone involved understood what was at stake.

JJ and Kristyn were in the Mobile Command Center with Isaksen, Astin, and Alexander, and the tension was palpable. JJ turned to Kristyn and said quietly, "I know it's crazy, but it's harder and more stressful for me to be sitting here away from the action than it is to be out there on the street."

"I understand, but I'm glad that for once you – *actually, both of us* – are at a safe distance and not in the thick of things. I'm scared enough sitting here. I can't imagine being out there." Kristyn squeezed JJ's hand and forced a smile.

"This is CHP Leader, we're in position and ready to light her up. Everyone on your mark and ready to converge in two minutes and counting." Officer Gaston reached over from the passenger seat and hit the lights.

Not sensing anything suspicious, fortunately, Adducci turned on her emergency flashers and pulled over onto the right shoulder of the road. McMillan pulled the CHP Explorer behind her, leaving a good 25 feet between the vehicles. Unfolding his 6'3" frame from the vehicle, somewhat encumbered by his vest and the sheer amount of equipment strapped to his belt, he strolled casually towards the BMW SUV. Officer Gaston exited from the passenger side and took a position by the rear of her car. Both officers double-checked that their body cams were turned on and ready to capture every second of the encounter.

Adducci lowered her window as McMillan approached. "Good after-noon, Officer. Was I doing something wrong?" She knew that she hadn't been speeding, or at least not going faster than the flow of traffic.

"No, ma'am, not at all, and sorry for the inconvenience. I pulled you over just as a courtesy because we noticed your brake lights flashing on and off continuously, even as you braked to pull onto the shoulder. That could be dangerous if the cars behind you can't tell that you're braking; I'd hate to see you get rear-ended. It might be a short in the wiring, or possibly something in the back that's touching the wiring harness. If you pop the back hatch, we can take a quick look to see if it's something that we can correct and get you on your way."

"Thank you, Officer." Adducci pressed the button to pop the hatch, and then stepped from the car. As she walked towards the rear of the car with McMillan, she asked, "If it's not something that we can fix here, I guess I'll need to call a tow truck?"

"Yes, ma'am, that would be best. Even though it's not dark out yet, the fact that the brake lights are inoperable is a major safety hazard."

As they rounded the back of the car, McMillan took her by the arm and quickly spun her around while putting one cuff on her left wrist and saying, "Dr. Joanne Adducci, you're under arrest for......"

Before he could say another word or secure the other cuff, she spun quickly around and threw a lightning-fast punch to his throat, practically crushing his windpipe. As he was sinking to the ground, she threw a quick knee to his face that shattered his nose and knocked him unconscious. Gaston reacted quickly and drew his gun from his holster, but before he could raise the weapon, Adducci jumped forward and threw a perfectly executed roundhouse kick that knocked the gun from his hand. Before he could make a move, she landed a spinning back kick that hit him square in the face. He dropped like the proverbial sack of potatoes. It had taken her mere seconds to take them both down, even with a handcuff dangling from her left wrist. Quickly grabbing the gun from McMillan's belt, she calmly walked over to the unconscious Gaston and put two quick shots into the back of his head. She followed that by doing the same to McMillan. As she walked back to the driver's side of her car, she turned and shot five rounds at the oncoming traffic; she didn't care about injuring or killing anyone, she just wanted to cause panic on the highway and an accident that would jam-up traffic and help her make a clean getaway.

Mission accomplished.

29

⬯

THURSDAY, JUNE 1

Cries and screams erupted inside the mobile command center as everyone saw what was happening in real-time thanks to the camera feed coming directly from Chopper 1. Before the chopper pilot even recognized what was happening, Isaksen was practically shrieking into the radio. "All units, all units, two officers down. Converge on Adducci immediately. Swarm!" His voice was trembling with rage and shock.

"Jesus Christ," the Chopper pilot practically shouted. "She took down McMillan and Gaston and shot them both in the back of the head! We're going to need multiple EMT units on the scene ASAP. She fired several shots at oncoming cars and caused a multi-vehicle accident. I can't tell the extent of injuries but there are four cars involved in the accident."

"I'll radio for the rescue and EMT's," announced JJ, tears already starting to roll down her face and on the verge of hyperventilating.

Inside the large mobile command center many were close to panic and the volume level was escalating with everyone shouting into their radios, at each other, at God. Sirens from a dozen or more local police and CHP cars flying past added to the cacophony and confusion.

"This is Chopper 1. The suspect is back in her car and pulling out heading east. All units coming from the east prepare to intercept in less than a quarter mile. All units coming from the west, you need to get around the four-car accident by staying to the left shoulder and block her in. She's about 30 seconds in front of you."

"Do not let her get past you and up onto the freeway," cried Astin, barely able to keep himself under control. He'd seen people killed before, even some of his fellow US Marshals, but he'd never witnessed the cold-blooded execution of two men, *two cops*, like he'd just seen.

"We need her alive," JJ said to everyone assembled in the command center. "She's our only link to Williamson."

SAC Alexander turned to JJ and said, loud enough for all to hear, "We want her alive, but that's up to her. If she engages our people, we'll use whatever means necessary to either apprehend her or take her out."

JJ wanted to speak up and argue the point, but she couldn't. Alexander was right; Adducci had just executed two cops and was attempting to flee, not to mention the fact that she had one of the fallen officers' guns in her possession. While JJ hoped and silently prayed that this would end quickly and without further bloodshed, she couldn't fault the cops for defending themselves if they came under gunfire. Even if that meant Adducci was killed and they lost their only link to Brookes Williamson.

Kristyn was fighting a losing battle in trying to hold it together, but she still had enough of her wits about her to ask, "I know that we can't jam her mobile signal, but are our tech teams still monitoring her calls in and out? I know that the warrants we secured allow for that."

Isaksen responded. "Yes, we're still up on her cell phone, or at least we're monitoring the one that we have a record of. Hopefully that's her only one." Turning to one of the techs, he asked, "McLean, any traffic to or from Adducci's mobile?"

"No sir. We've been up on her number from the time we moved into position for this operation, and there hasn't been a single call in or out."

"Thank God for small favors," said JJ. "McLean, let us know if she tries to call Williamson. Hopefully she won't have time for that before we have her."

The video feed from Chopper 1 showed Adducci accelerating as fast as the BMW SUV was capable of, but she had nowhere to go. Several

CHP and Victorville patrol cars had already crossed the median and were coming at her head-on, and several others had made it past the carnage that she'd left behind and were closing quickly from the rear.

Sensing that she was trapped and seeing no way around the patrol cars that were blocking all lanes and both shoulders, she slowed and considered her options as the car gradually lost speed. Picking up the gun she'd taken from the fallen McMillan, she prepared to make her final stand. A quick check revealed only eight bullets left in the magazine: seven shots, plus one for her final *fuck you* to the world. No way would she allow herself to be being taken alive, interrogated, and used against Williamson. She had even less intention of spending the rest of her life in prison.

As her speed dropped below 20mph and the gauntlet tightened, she lowered her window. Surely the cops were hoping that she was going to stop and surrender peacefully, but they weren't taking any chances. As they closed in, Adducci raised the pistol and squeezed off all seven rounds before they had a chance to react. A few of the cars sustained some damage, including one with a shattered windshield, but no one was injured. Almost immediately one of the CHP Explorers, equipped with a front bumper 'bully bar' accelerated and smashed into the BMW hard enough to knock it sideways and partly off the road. The impact was severe enough to set off the airbags in the Explorer, leaving the CHP officer momentarily dazed.

Adducci had a large gash on her forehead where her head had hit the steering wheel that was bleeding heavily, and her left shoulder had been dislocated in the impact. She was barely conscious, and it was only the excruciating pain that kept her from passing out. While her plan had been to swallow the last bullet, she now turned her attention to the cop that had just rammed her. She could see him strapped into the Explorer as the airbag slowly deflated, barely 10 feet away from her. *What's one more dead cop?* She felt around for the gun, having dropped it in the collision. Finally locating it on the passenger seat, she slowly, painfully, raised her arm and tried turning to take aim at the cop that had rammed her.

Before she could get a shot off, she heard several shouts of, "CHP! Drop your weapon!".

She just smirked and screamed, "Fuck you!" and was about to fire when a fusillade of semi-automatic weapons tore into her SUV. Dozens of bullets shattered the windshield, the side windows, flattened the tires, and made Swiss cheese of the car's body. She was only hit two times, surprisingly. As she sank into unconsciousness, her last thought was *'I'm sorry Brookes. I failed you'*.

In the mobile command unit, Isaksen and the others had observed the entire thing via the video feed. Isaksen raised his microphone. "CHP units, report. What's the status of our officers? And what's the status of the suspect?" The tension in the room was palpable, as everyone had witnessed the wreckage and shooting but were not able to tell from the Chopper video feed if anyone was injured or killed.

"This is Sergeant Adams, CHP, sir. All of our officers are OK, a couple of them shaken but no serious injuries. Damage to a few CHP and local PD cars. The suspect sustained multiple gunshot wounds, the most serious being one to her left shoulder. She needs immediate medical attention, but my guess is that her injuries are survivable."

JJ and Kristyn looked at each other and breathed a sigh of relief. Adducci was injured but would be taken into custody, and most importantly, she had not been able to get a warning call or text to Williamson.

SAC Alexander spoke to Adams. "Great takedown Sergeant. You and the team did a helluva job keeping her contained. And under such conditions, great shooting, too. We really needed her alive."

"Thank you, sir." Adams knew that wasn't exactly true. The stress and adrenaline had impacted his marksmanship; he was going for a head shot and had every intention of killing her. In his mind it was more than deserved after she had executed two of his fellow officers, two of his *friends*. No matter how much the FBI and Marshals wanted and needed her alive, she deserved to die. Violently. He wanted retribution. He *needed* retribution. *Fuck!*

30

THURSDAY, JUNE 1

"The EMT's are taking Adducci to Desert Valley Hospital, and I want at least a dozen people guarding her and ensuring that she has zero communications with anyone, for any reason. Got it?" Isaksen was beyond pissed but trying to maintain.

"And since she has not yet been charged with any crime, under no circumstances do we let her push for an attorney. Make sure everyone understands that. No phone calls, no texts or emails, nothing." SAC Alexander was every bit as pissed as Isaksen but was having an even harder time keeping it under control.

"The second she's patched up we want her the fuck out of there. I know she's injured, but we stick as close as possible to the original plan and get her away from here the second she can be released." Astin was less worried about Adducci being able to contact Williamson directly than he was about someone identifying her as the person involved in the shootout and spilling it all over the news.

JJ added, "I guess it's at least somewhat in our favor that her wounds aren't too serious, according to the EMT's. The shoulder wound was a through and through, so likely no major damage. The other wounds are less worrisome. Fingers crossed that she won't need surgery so we can push for her discharge tonight."

"I think we need to take a couple more precautions before we rush out of here," said Kristyn. Everyone turned to look at her, their impatience evident. "Every reporter within 100 miles is going to be swarming here to report on this, so if we want to keep her name out of this and not have it broadcast across the whole state, if not the whole country, we better do everything we can to keep her from being identified. That means getting the tags off her car before they can be photographed, covering up her car and hauling it away to somewhere where it can't be found, and making sure that the hospital has her listed as a 'Jane Doe'. And we better pray that no one at the scene was able to whip out their cell phone and video tape or photograph her or the car; if they were, everything we're doing to try to keep Williamson in the dark may be for nothing."

Isaksen spoke first. "Damn, you're right. Great call, Kristyn." Turning to the officers in the mobile command unit he told them, "Get the word out to everyone still on the scene as well as those who are on their way to the hospital. They're to do everything that Kristyn said, and more if they come up with other ideas, to keep Adducci's name out of this. And obviously it goes without saying, absolutely no statements to the press or the public. *None.* Is that understood?"

They all arrived at the hospital barely 10 minutes behind the ambulance, and when they went inside, they were led to the area where Adducci was being treated. They were happy to see that her right hand was cuffed to the bed as well as shackles on both legs. The doctors were none too happy about it, but the cops made it very clear that they were not giving her any freedom of movement except for the left arm the doctors were working on.

"You're not making this any easier for us," said Dr. Raymond Jarvis, the lead doctor for the ER. "Her movements are too restricted by these cuffs, and that's keeping us from being able to position her where we need to take care of her wounds."

"You're going to have to deal with it; we're not about to take off or even loosen any of her restraints. And trust me: you don't want us to. She's already killed two men, two *cops,* and would have zero compunction about killing you and your whole staff to get away from here." Alexander wasn't about to sugarcoat it. He wanted Dr. Jarvis and the whole staff to be on the verge of pissing themselves. Maybe that would help expedite getting her treated and released.

"And Dr. Jarvis, make sure that you and your team treat this just like you would if you were in surgery: count every single instrument, every single syringe, *everything*, to make sure that every piece is accounted for and she hasn't taken anything that can be used as a weapon." JJ didn't feel that she was being overly dramatic. After seeing how Adducci had overpowered and executed two highly trained CHP officers, there was no way of knowing what she's capable of.

Dr. Jarvis looked at her nervously, visibly shaken, and nodded his understanding. Being an ER doctor always carried more risks than anywhere else in the hospital, but in his 20+ years of ER experience he had never seen such measures or such heavy police presence. That was surprising since they were one of the closest hospitals to the Victorville Federal Prison, but he assumed the police had their reasons for having this strong of a presence. He just wanted to get her stitched-up and out of here as quickly as possible and get his team back to their normal shitshow routine.

"How long do you think this will take, Doctor?" asked JJ.

"We'll want to do some X-rays just to make sure that there's not more damage; I don't believe there is, but we need to make sure. If we find anything medically suspicious then we'll want to do a CT scan, but I doubt that will be needed. I'm thinking just a few hours to do that, clean the wounds and stitch her up. Then we'd like to keep her overnight for observation, just in case. Mainly to make sure that we don't see any signs of infection."

"Sorry, doc, but that's not possible. Keeping her here overnight puts you, the staff, and your patients in serious danger. We have reason to believe that her crew is already on their way here from L.A. to rescue her and keep her from being interrogated and jailed. We don't want to put this entire place and hundreds of innocent people at risk." SAC Alexander was laying it on thick and going well beyond a 'little white lie', but it seemed to be having the needed effect.

Dr. Jarvis and the nurses assisting him were shaken. "I'll do what we can. If all goes well, and I think it will, we should have her patched up and ready for transport in maybe two hours. And I'll have the staff prepare a bag that has everything you may need to take care of her for the next day or two, like extra bandages, antibiotics, something for the pain, and a sling for her arm. You'll need someone with at least basic medical or EMT training to make sure that she doesn't get worse once she leaves here."

"That works, Doctor. Thank you. And we'll make sure to have an EMT travel with us at all times and when we reach our final destination, we'll have a doctor check her out again." Alexander was feeling cautiously optimistic that things were mostly under control.

JJ was hopeful but not convinced that the plan would still work. Yes, so far they had managed to prevent Adducci from contacting Williamson, and they'd managed to take her alive – *barely* – but they weren't out of the woods yet. *Two cops dead, dozens of witnesses, a multi-car crash, bullets flying in the middle of rush hour on a heavily traveled road.......Sure, this should be easy to keep under the radar.* JJ could feel the tension headache cranking up to a '10'.

31

✎

Brookes Williamson was growing impatient. He'd been sitting in the darkened apartment that reeked of stale food, dirty cat litter, and pot for nearly four hours. He had originally planned to be here for no more than 30 minutes, but the software program being created by the apartment owner, Max Perry, was not quite complete. *Maybe if this asshole would lay off the weed for even five minutes, we could get this shit finished.* Max was every stereotype one would expect of a total tech-nerd: tall, gangly, tatted, with filthy hair, a scraggly beard, and body odor that was off the scale since he didn't have a very close relationship with soap and water.

Brookes had heard about Max Perry during his short time in Victorville, and the scuttlebutt among the more tech-savvy inmates was that Max was one of the most skilled hackers and developers anywhere. More importantly, he had a non-existent moral compass, a barely-under-control drug habit, and would do literally anything, regardless of how illegal or destructive, for the right amount of money. He was basically a mercenary, but his weapon of choice was the internet instead of a gun. Despite his incredible talent he'd been fired from every IT and tech firm imaginable and was considered *persona non grata* in Silicon Valley and beyond. It didn't help that he burned bridges and created chaos, including 'missing documents', misappropriated funds, and strong suspicions of ransomware attacks at a dozen or more companies.

"How much longer, Max? You said that this would be ready today by 1pm, and now you're dragging your ass and keeping me stuck here in this shithole."

"Greatness and perfection cannot be rushed. It will be done when it's done."

"You've had several days to complete a job that you swore shouldn't take more than two. I gave you those video and audio files, as well as the script that I wanted you to develop, with plenty of lead time to have this completed by now. Maybe if you'd get your head out of that fucking bong long enough to actually get some work done, I could get on with my life."

"Hey, if you've got a problem with the timeline or accommodations, feel free to get the fuck out and take your chances finding someone else with the talent and skills to create this for you. I'm more than happy to hit the delete button and scrap this shit altogether."

Brookes held his tongue, at least for the moment. He needed this job finished, and quickly. He didn't care so much about the $10,000 he'd already advanced to Max, but he needed the product. As soon as it was done and he was satisfied that it would work as planned, he'd gladly put an icepick into Max's brain. *Even the Slayers never used an icepick for their murders. They could learn a lot from me!*

"Just give me an ETA for Christ sakes. Are we talking a few minutes, a few hours, or what? I need it tonight, bottom line. So, are you almost done, or do I need to order dinner to be delivered?" The thought of eating anything in this nasty smelling apartment almost made him gag.

"Putting the last few lines of code in now, then we're ready to view the whole thing. Give me five minutes." Max hated it when clients rushed him. He considered himself an artist, not some kind of hourly factory worker.

True to his word, Max announced that he was done in less than five minutes and invited Brookes to pull up a chair beside him to view the final product. Brookes declined, knowing that he couldn't stand to be that close to Max for even a few seconds, and instead insisted that he display it on the large monitor so they could view it together.

Brookes was in awe. Even though he knew what to expect, had even provided the script and the video and audio samples, he was floored by the quality and realism. He'd seen deep fakes before, but this was like the Michelangelo of deep fakes. As he saw a virtual image of his hated nemesis on the screen and heard 'her' speak with perfectly synched movements of her mouth and facial muscles, he was amazed. "My God, this is incredible. Her own mother couldn't tell that this was a fake. And you think this will work even if I use this over FaceTime?"

"I think FaceTime will actually make it even easier to fool the person on the other end. Not that it's bad quality video but it won't be as crisp and clear as people have come to expect with video conferencing via Webex or Zoom on a 70" video conference system. I think that plays into your favor."

"Makes sense. And you were able to create a way for me to go off-script and talk to her in real time if needed?"

"I was. For starters, I was able to leverage AI and Machine Learning to enable insertion of some alternate script questions and responses for you. You simply hit the Pause button on the video and click on the question-and-answer choices from the drop-down menu." Max demonstrated, and again, Brookes was stunned by the quality of the audio and video, as well as the simplicity of the application.

Max continued. "And just in case you have to go totally off-script and think on the fly, the program will capture your words and communicate them in Jessica Jansen's voice and synced with her video image. No way will anyone be able to tell that it's not her, at least so long as you don't say the wrong thing that raises a red flag for the person on the other end."

"Incredible. Just incredible. I gotta tell you, Max, I had my doubts that this would work based on examples I've seen in the past, but now I'm a believer. You're right: you are an artist."

"Well, in fairness, technology is advancing at a logarithmic rate, so anything you may have seen even six months ago is behind the times. And if it's a year or more old, it may as well be from biblical times. Plus, this is the first time you've ever seen one of my creations; not to brag, but it would be false modesty for me to say that there's anyone else out there that can do what I do."

"I can't disagree with you on that point. You've absolutely proven your worth."

"If you're satisfied with what you've seen then I assume you're prepared to pay the balance of my fee?"

"Definitely. Final payment of $10,000 in mixed denominations, as agreed." Brookes reached into his bag and removed the stack of bills that he had banded together.

Brookes walked around the desk and handed the stack of bills to Max. "Feel free to count it."

"Oh, trust me, I will." Max unbundled the bills and started counting them out. He was barely up to $200 when he stopped, trying to understand what he was feeling. At first it felt like a bee sting, then less than a second later he felt a sharp pain and loss of motor control and vision. Before he could fully process what was happening, his head fell face first onto his desk, the ice pick still sticking out at an upward angle from the base of his neck.

Brookes took his time collecting the money and helping himself to some of Max's technology and toys. Mostly he was using the time to think about how to make a real statement and visual impact, something that would show the cops exactly what he thought of Max and his disgusting existence. It only took a few minutes to come up with the perfect staging concept: Max's dead body covered in garbage from around his nasty apartment, and his mouth stuffed with the dirty kitty litter that he'd been too lazy to clean for what appeared to be days, if not weeks. He smiled at the thought; surely not a crime scene that the cops had seen before. *Who's the real brains, the real artiste now, Max?*

32

SATURDAY, JUNE 3

Members of the task force had barely slept all night, constantly moving between locations to keep Adducci's whereabouts unknown. They tried taking turns and sleeping in one- to two-hour shifts, but that was hard to do in the cramped confines of their cars and SUV's. Adducci probably got more rest than all of them combined, since she was drowsy from the drugs administered for the pain and handcuffed to a stretcher inside the ambulance. Isaksen and Alexander refused to take any chances: two well-armed officers were in the back of the ambulance along with one of the EMTs.

They'd finally rolled into Orange County around 7am and went directly to the Irvine Police Department building on Civic Center Plaza. SAC Alexander had called ahead to Chief Robert Mauro to request their cooperation, and despite waking the Chief out of a dead sleep at 4:30 on a Saturday morning, he quickly agreed to the request and had his officers waiting on the task force's arrival. Adducci was moved to a holding cell and the EMTs that had been traveling with the group since the arrest in Victorville checked on her and changed her bandages one last time.

"So far, so good," said EMT Haskins. "The bleeding has stopped, and no outward signs of infection, at least not yet. If you keep getting those antibiotics into her, I think we'll likely head off any infection that she would otherwise be susceptible to. And I'd suggest that you keep giving her those Vicodin for the pain. It's always better to stay ahead of the pain than trying to catch up to it."

"That's a valid point," responded Isaksen, "but we don't want her to take so much that she's too comfortable and disinclined to talk. I'm thinking that we hold back a bit between doses. I think the prescription says every four hours. If that's the case, then I'll probably plan on six to eight hours per dose unless she's being *very* cooperative."

"I got it," Haskins said with a smile. "Kinda like giving a dog a treat as a reward for peeing outside instead of on your expensive carpet or furniture. It's all in your hands, sir. Good luck."

"Thank you for your assistance, and my apologies for dragging you halfway across the state and keeping you away from home all night. There's a hotel room at the Embassy Suites just a few miles from here where you and your partner can get some rest and freshen up before you head back up to Victorville. The rest of us will be heading there shortly to do the same thing, even if it's only a couple of hours of sleep."

Isaksen, Alexander, and Astin gathered everyone in a conference room, including the Irvine officers that Chief Mauro had assigned, for a quick meeting. It was obvious that JJ, Kristyn, and every member of the task force was dragging at this point. That was partly due to lack of sleep, partly due to the long hours on the road, but mostly the inevitable crash after the adrenaline rush they'd had hours ago when apprehending Adducci.

"First things first, especially for those of you that are just joining our merry little group" Isaksen said, trying to lighten the mood. "The suspect is not, under any circumstances, to have communication with anyone outside of this room. I don't care if it's someone claiming to be her doctor, her lawyer, or her goddamn preacher, nobody talks to her. And further, under no circumstances is her name to be released to any-one outside of the room, especially the press or your media relations people. Is that understood?" Seeing nods all around, he continued.

"Good. Second point: The suspect has not yet been formally charged. We hope to get to that later today, but as of this moment she has not been charged and has not been in front of a judge or magistrate.

Bottom line, she does not yet have a 'right' to demand a phone call. If she starts up with that shit again, and I'm pretty certain that she will, ignore her. Tape her mouth shut if you have to, but she does not get access to a phone."

"Third point: all of us on the task force are exhausted, and we need some rest, a shower, and some decent food. Personally, I'd like to sleep until tomorrow morning, but we don't have time for that. It's nearly 8am now; I say we head over to our hotel and get a few hours of sleep and plan to be back here at 1pm sharp. Agreed?" Once again, nods and agreement all around.

Astin spoke up. "Maybe we should give the suspect her next Vicodin before we leave. It's been nearly four hours since her last dose, and I'm sure the folks tasked with babysitting her for the next few hours would appreciate it if she were mellowed out instead of her usual mouthy self."

"Good call," said Alexander. "And what's the worst that could happen? Would it really break our hearts if the bitch OD'd." He was smiling as he said this, but everyone in the room knew that he was only half-joking, at best.

33

⚬⚬⚬

SATURDAY, JUNE 3

After checking into the hotel, JJ suggested that Kristyn head up to the room to shower while she grabbed breakfast for the two of them from the buffet. They were both so tired they had trouble deciding whether they wanted to prioritize sleep over showering and eating or the other way around.

"That's too much for me to wrap my head around at this point," said JJ. "I feel like my mind is trapped in quicksand."

"I think the shower will at least make me feel a bit more human. I feel disgusting after traveling all night in such close quarters. And I could use something decent to eat, too. Living all night on coffee and donuts and crappy junk food isn't cutting it."

JJ got up to the room about 15 minutes after Kristyn and was glad to see that she was already out of the shower. "Ready to eat? I'm going to inhale this and then jump in the shower before taking a nap. I think we had better set every alarm we can get our hands on to make sure we wake up in time. I feel like I could sleep until tomorrow morning."

Kristyn nodded in agreement. Even with the shower, she still felt like a zombie. *Maybe a few hours of sleep will help. And maybe some pizza when we get back to the Irvine station.....*

Both of their iPhone alarms went off right at noon, and that was followed less than a minute later by the in-room alarm clock. JJ fell right back asleep, but soon Kristyn snuggled up to her and started lightly stroking her shoulders, her neck, and her breasts. JJ wanted so badly to sleep, but she couldn't fight the growing arousal. As Kristyn started lightly caressing her stomach and planting butterfly kisses on her neck, JJ couldn't hold out any longer. Arousal was, not surprisingly, winning out over her need for sleep.

"What are you doing to me? You know I'm exhausted, plus we've got to be out of here in like 30 minutes." JJ was saying this softly, already breathless with desire.

"Then you better make the best use of your time," Kristyn said as she drew JJ to her and started passionately kissing her. Their hands started roaming and touching each other as their passion and fire grew, their legs intertwined as they practically wrestled for dominance and control.

JJ could feel the wetness growing between her legs, and as she reached down to touch Kristyn it was evident that she was just as turned on. The stress of the last few days had put a damper on their usually voracious sex life, and having this time to connect – even when they were under the proverbial gun – was just what the doctor ordered. JJ wasted no time in kissing, nuzzling, nibbling, and licking her way down Kristyn's always intoxicating body, and in minutes she was bringing her to a raging climax. Luckily Kristyn buried her face in a pillow to keep the entire fourth floor of the hotel from hearing her lustful screams.

Never wanting to leave the love of her life hanging, Kristyn eagerly reciprocated. The pillow was once again put to good use.

***

"So, we're all agreed then," said Isaksen. "Marshal Astin will take the lead in the interrogation since we're focusing on the capture of Brookes Williamson. We're not going to put too much emphasis at this point on charges related to her support of Williamson and his escape. She's smart enough to realize that we have enough other charges to throw at her, including the murders of two CHP officers, that her involvement with that asshole is secondary."

"JJ, I'd like for you to observe the interrogation via video and let me know if you pick up on anything, any details that she may provide that might not register with me. You know what's going on with Williamson probably better than anyone. In fact, depending on how the conversation progresses, I might ask JJ to join me in the interrogation room at some point." Astin looked at JJ and then to Isaksen and Alexander for their agreement. No one raised any objections.

"JJ has done hundreds of interrogations during her time with the FBI, so I have no doubt that she can handle this." Isaksen looked at Astin. "You let us know if and when you need her, or any of us, for that matter, in the room."

Astin headed to the interrogation room, along with two officers who were going to be posted outside the door. Four others, two from the FBI and two from the local Irvine PD, went to escort Adducci from her cell after putting her in full transport restraints.

Kristyn walked with JJ towards the observation room and whispered, "While you're observing the questioning, I'm going to focus on Adducci's background and financials, see if there's anything there that jumps out. I'm also going to keep checking into the backgrounds of the entire movie production crew. Maybe I'll find some link between someone on the crew and Williamson."

"Good idea, and we need something to go our way quickly. We're not going to be able to hold her much longer. We're already pushing our luck."

34

Marshal Astin had been questioning Adducci for nearly an hour but had made little headway. Most of his questions elicited little more than silence, smirks, or smart-ass responses. Any mention of Brookes Williamson was met with venom and bile as she constantly ranted about how brilliant he was compared to the *'idiot civil servants tasked with his capture.'* Astin was having problems maintaining his cool and it pissed him off to know that she was getting under his skin, as she no doubt had planned. It pissed him off even more to know that they were wasting time; every minute that passed put them one minute closer to being tracked down by the media, her attorneys, and God knows who else.

The media coverage of last night's events in Victorville was non-stop statewide and on every major 24-hour news network. That was to be expected with the death of the two CHP officers and the broad daylight car chase and shootout. Astin knew that they were fortunate that Adducci's identity hadn't been uncovered and revealed until mid-morning, but now that her name and ties to the prison were made public, the story wasn't going to fade away anytime soon. The fact that the media had few facts to go on didn't matter; they, and their audience, were more than happy to continue with baseless speculation.

Astin had reached his limit. He needed coffee, he needed a bathroom break, and he needed some time to calm himself down. He also realized that it was time to tap out and let someone else continue the questioning. "I'm going to step out for a few moments to get some coffee and hit the head. Can I bring you anything, Dr. Adducci? Coffee, soda, water?" He'd been trying hard to remain professional and civil, but every minute it got harder.

"Oh, aren't you just a dear, Marshal Astin. Fuck you!" She gave him the finger despite being cuffed to the table. Most people in her position would have been worried about the growing intensity of the interrogation, the discomfort of being shackled in this windowless and airless room, and the likelihood of a long prison sentence, if not the death penalty. Not Adducci: whether it was narcissism, the fact that she was probably a sociopath, or just someone that was resigned to her fate, she didn't seem to have a care in the world. At least, not beyond ensuring that they didn't find Brookes Williamson before he'd accomplished his mission.

Astin walked into the observation room. "I think we need to change the game a bit. I've been with her an hour and basically don't have squat to show for it."

"Not your fault, Marshal. You've done and said all the right things, you're just faced with a suspect that is willing to hold out and play the long game, figuring it's just a matter of time before her attorneys come riding in here like white knights to save the day. And she's not wrong; time is not on our side." Isaksen patted Astin on the back to show his support and understanding.

Isaksen looked at JJ. "I think you should take a shot at her, JJ. Since you and Kristyn are the ultimate targets, and obviously the ones that Williamson has a serious hardon for, I think you should take the lead. Remind her how you guys took down the Slayers and he's just a little pissant wannabe, how you're going to take him down and cut his balls off, whatever it is that you have to say to make her lose her cool and start blabbing."

"So basically, what you're telling me is that I should go in there and be my usual smartass and annoying self, right?" JJ smiled and barely suppressed a giggle.

"I have no doubt that you can annoy her to the point that she'll start talking just to make you stop," he responded with his own smirk. "I've had years of experience with your world class annoyances."

JJ gathered her notes and PC and headed for the door, then stopped to speak to Kristyn. "When I go in there, listen carefully to everything that's said. We need to verify everything that comes out of her mouth and take nothing at face value. I assume most of what she says will be bullshit or outright lies, but maybe something will be said that can be validated and cross-referenced and help in our search. Text me if you get anything."

As JJ entered the interrogation room, Adducci burst out in laughter. "Oh my God, talk about sending in the 'B' team! You're not even a cop anymore! You're so worthless that the FBI fired you, so why the hell should I talk to you? Not to mention that you'll be dead in a matter of hours, or a couple of days if you're lucky. Don't you have someone else that you'd rather spend those last precious hours with?" She was trying hard to get a rise out of JJ right off the bat, but it didn't seem to faze her at all.

"Nowhere that I'd rather be than right here, right now. I can't wait to hear the words that are going to send you straight to death row. And I can't wait to be there in the gallery to watch them put the needle in your arm. Too bad that your boy Brookes Williamson won't be there to see it for himself, but by the time you even stand for your first arraignment, he'll already be in custody."

"Hah, don't kid yourself. One, he's much too smart for you and the other incompetent fools on this so-called 'task force'. And even if you should be so lucky as to find him and try to arrest him, he'll never let you take him alive."

"Wow, you really seem to have a soft spot for that deranged psychopath. All along I just assumed that he was someone that you were fucking, like all the other inmates, but it actually sounds like you're in love with him. How rich! What do you think this is, some sort of star-crossed lover story, or a 21st century remake of *Bonnie and Clyde*?"

Adducci tried to jump up from her seat in anger, but the restraints stopped her. "Fuck you!" she screamed. "Don't you dare speak of our relationship! You know nothing of real love or having a real man as your soul mate. You're nothing but a hideous dyke."

If she thought that would get under JJ's skin, she was dead wrong. JJ loved that she was finally seeing Adducci rattled. "It seems like you were having a veritable smorgasbord of lovers in there, from what I hear. Were you fucking John Westbrook in addition to some of your other dealers?"

"Fuck you. You have no idea what you're talking about."

"Wow, so defensive. Help me understand one thing, though: did Brookes enjoy fucking you more than he enjoyed getting fucked by John Westbrook? And was he anyone else's little bitch besides Westbrook? I don't understand why he even needed to be with you if he was enjoying so much cock from all the other inmates. Was he doing you just so he could keep the drugs flowing and sucker you in to helping him escape?"

Adducci screamed and tried her best to leap across the table and grab JJ by the throat. She barely made it halfway across the table before the shackles stopped her, but she grew even more outraged when JJ didn't even flinch. "I'm going to kill you, you bitch! I swear to God, I will kill you with my bare fucking hands." She fought against the restraints, to no avail.

JJ just laughed, knowing that this would egg her on even further. "Let's talk about that for a second. You'll 'kill me with your bare hands'. That's interesting. I have to say, you surprised us last night in Victorville. That was no small feat overpowering two large CHP officers. Shooting them was a bit of overkill, if you'll excuse the pun, but disarming them and knocking them out the way you did was impressive."

Adducci was still seething and practically spitting fire. "Do you think I'm stupid, that I'd spend every day locked up with those animals and not be able to defend myself? I can't rely on the guards to protect me every minute, so I have to rely on myself. I've taken years of Krav Maga and Muay Thai training since I was in college. I can defend my-self against any man, and I think I proved that last night." That last statement brought a satisfied smirk to her face.

"And was it in college that you started down this path of falling in love with the ultimate 'bad boys' or did that start once you started working in Victorville? Because I gotta tell you, I've seen lots of women that had bad boy issues, or daddy issues, or 'I need a man to be fulfilled' issues, but you take the cake."

"Not that it's any of your fucking business, but I don't have *any* issues and I come from a loving, stable, and well-respected family in Minneapolis. I attended Providence Academy, a private Catholic school, and St. Olaf's College, a private Lutheran school. I excelled academically, which was expected of me, because my family spent a small fortune sending me to the best schools around. That's about as mainstream and white bread as you can get, so don't even begin to think that you can psychoanalyze me or criticize my family."

"So maybe mommy and daddy put too much pressure on you, and you couldn't handle it? I can imagine that you're just one big disappointment to them. They spend all that money on your education, only to see you wasting that degree as a prison psychologist. I bet they'll really disown you when they find out about your little drug empire and how you get passed around like a $2 whore by all the inmates. Real classy, doctor."

"Hah, fuck you! What about you, Miss Former FBI agent, who can't even hold onto a pathetic government job! Who gets fired and pushed out in disgrace! My impression of you is that you grew up in some inbred, white trash town in Appalachia where you spent time fucking your farm animals for entertainment and marrying your first cousins. Or in your case, your female first cousins."

JJ didn't take the bait. "I should be so lucky. My first cousins are *hot*."

That enraged Adducci even more. Nothing she said seemed to be getting the rise out of JJ that she expected or knocking her off her game.

JJ heard a ding on her computer and looked at the screen. There was a short text from Kristyn. "911!! Get in here, now!"

35

✦

SATURDAY, JUNE 3

Kristyn could hardly contain herself. "I knew that you'd get her talking and she'd eventually say something to give us a lead."

Everyone in the observation room gathered around. "Did you find Williamson?" asked JJ.

"No, but I think I know how we're going to find him."

"Let's hear it," said Isaksen excitedly.

Kristyn continued. "I've spent hours digging into every member of the production crew trying to find a link between one of them and Williamson, but I kept coming up empty. But when you got her talking about her childhood and education, something clicked. I don't think it's Williamson that has a connection with a production team member, it's Adducci."

"I'm not sure I follow," Astin added. "Say more."

"When she said that she'd grown up in Minneapolis and attended Providence Academy and St. Olaf's College the bells went off in my head. I knew that I'd seen those schools before as I was reviewing backgrounds, and I was right. The main Set Accountant, a guy named Chris Zimmerman, also grew up there and attended the same high school and college. And before you ask, I did a quick check and verified that they attended both at the same time. That can't be a coincidence."

SAC Alexander asked, "Are you suggesting that this Chris Zimmerman is really Williamson and he's using that name as an alias?"

"No, definitely not. Chris Zimmerman is legit; he's been with this production since the beginning, and he's been in the industry for quite a few years and done a lot of movies, many of them with some of the same crew members."

"So then, what's his connection to Williamson?" asked Isaksen.

"We'll need to verify this, but I think I know the connection: a few weeks ago, a member of the accounting team almost died from carbon monoxide poisoning that investigators are calling suspicious. Chris Zimmerman hired a replacement, a guy named Michael Glover. I've reviewed his file, and everything seems clean and aboveboard, but it's possible that someone just has a talent for creating a well backstopped cover story."

"You're thinking that this Michael Glover is really Brookes Williamson? And somehow Adducci was able to leverage her relationship with Chris Zimmerman to get him hired?" Reasonable questions from Alexander, as he anxiously tried to hurry things along.

"Yes, that's exactly what I'm thinking. I believe the next step is to reach out to Chris Zimmerman right away and see if he's had contact with Adducci, see if she maybe recommended Glover for the position, etc."

"You think we should risk talking to Zimmerman in case he might tipoff Williamson, or at the very least try to reach out to Adducci and her people?" Isaksen trusted Kristyn's instincts, but he wasn't completely sold.

"I think that's highly unlikely, sir. Regardless, I think it's a chance worth taking. Look at it this way: we know that Zimmerman is legit and has years in the industry working with many of the people on this film. No way is he some kind of sleeper agent or deep cover kind of guy. He's just someone who was duped by an old friend and hired someone that looks good on paper but happens to be a psychopath."

"I agree with Kristyn," added JJ, "and I think we should reach out to Zimmerman right away to see what information he can provide about Williamson's whereabouts, the information he has access to, and any information he has about his movements during the time of the murders and vandalism."

"I see your point. I think it's on us to warn Mr. Zimmerman about Williamson, too, so he can take steps to ensure his own safety and that of others on his team." Isaksen was ready to get things moving right away.

"Kristyn, you've got Zimmerman's file and all his contact information. Let's reach out to him right away and see what kind of information he can provide. I especially want to focus on getting confirmation of the dates and times he communicated with Adducci on this." JJ was anxious to get moving, too.

Isaksen added, "And since the warrant we have for her phone and other electronics has already let us access her data, we should review it to confirm the calls or texts to Zimmerman, too. That should help tighten the noose a bit."

"I love that imagery of a noose tightening around her neck, sir. Or my hands. Either works for me." JJ couldn't hide her smirk. For the first time in hours, she was feeling like they were finally making progress.

36

SATURDAY, JUNE 3

The level of activity and progress grew quickly. They were able to reach Chris Zimmerman on his mobile phone and, after explaining the situation, confirm their suspicions about Adducci's involvement in the hiring of Michael Glover, née Brookes Williamson. To say that Zimmerman was shocked, and frightened, was understating things.

"Chris, we have a lot more to talk about, but we need to wrap things up here first and get Adducci in front of a judge or magistrate. We're leaving Irvine to head back to L.A. shortly, and normally I'd want to meet with you in person, but we can't afford to waste the next couple of hours. Are you OK if I call you back and we continue this conversation once Kristyn and I are on the road?"

"Yes, that's fine. I'm heading back to my house now and should be there in about 15 minutes. Call me as soon as you can."

As JJ terminated the call, she addressed the whole room and filled them in on the details of her call with Chris Zimmerman. "Kristyn and I are going to dig deeper with Zimmerman while we're driving back to L.A., and I'll reach back out to the team to fill you in on the details when I'm done. Sound like a plan?" Once again, she was trying to be sensitive to the situation and not overstep her bounds.

"Later today I'm going to head up to L.A., too, along with my handful of Dallas-based agents, at least for the next few days. SAC Alexander will continue to take the lead, of course, and I'll be there to support him and the local teams." Isaksen was dead set on seeing this through to the end.

Astin spoke up. "Since we need to divide and conquer, I'm going to escort Adducci back to Victorville for her arraignment along with a contingent from my team and the CHP. I wish I could be in two places at once so I could continue the search for Williamson, but right now we don't know where to start. Hopefully you guys will get some information from Zimmerman that gets us moving in the right direction. Keep me in the loop; I'll be back in L.A. by morning."

"One last important point, especially for those transporting Adducci back home: not a word about our conversation with Zimmerman or our suspicions about Michael Glover being Brookes Williamson's alias. If she learns that we've uncovered this link, she's going to get word to Williamson through her attorneys and that would put Zimmerman's life in immediate danger." JJ didn't have to add the obvious fact that Williamson would likely disappear again, and they couldn't afford to be back at square one.

As the meeting broke up, Isaksen pulled JJ and Kristyn aside. "Great work in there, JJ. And you, too, Kristyn for uncovering that connection. I finally feel like we've caught a break. Hopefully Zimmerman can provide more information that will help us close-in on Williamson before he can kill anyone else."

"Since his ultimate goal is to kill Kristyn and me, I kinda hope you're right. Maybe I'm just being selfish and self-centered." JJ smiled as she said this, but there's was no denying that there was more than a hint of truth to her statement.

Walking out of the building, Kristyn offered to drive so that JJ could focus on her conversation with Zimmerman and take notes. As they jumped on the I-405 North for the drive back to Santa Monica, JJ phoned Zimmerman. "Hi Chris, it's Jessica Jansen and Kristyn Reynolds. I have you on speaker, but it's just the two of us in the car so you can speak freely."

"Sure, I don't know what more I can add, but I'm happy to answer any questions that I can if it will help you catch this guy. I feel really stupid and embarrassed that I was conned into offering this monster a job, and then he used his position to kill people involved with the production." He was obviously upset and, even over the phone, it was evident that he was on the verge of tears and racked with guilt. "I feel responsible for letting this happen."

"You can't blame yourself, Chris. You had no way of knowing his true identity or what he was capable of." JJ muted the call for a second and whispered to Kristyn, "We need to ease into it with this guy. He's scared, understandably."

JJ unmuted. "Tell me more about your relationship with Joanne Adducci and why you put that much trust in her and her recommendation of Michael Glover."

"I've known Joanne since we were in high school together, and we've always been close. We ran with the same crowd, had a lot of classes together, went to all the same parties. I've always considered her one of my closest friends."

"Did you two ever date? Not to be nosey, just trying to understand the background a bit."

"No, we never did. I think it was a combination of consistently bad timing – if I wasn't dating someone, she was, and vice versa – and that old trope about good friends not wanting to jeopardize their friendship for a quick romp in the hay. But we were the best of friends; I was literally the shoulder she would cry on, and over the years I helped set her up with countless guys and she hooked me up with lots of her friends."

"And then you ended up at the same college together. Was that unusual?"

"No, not really. A lot of kids around that part of Minnesota went to St. Olaf because it's a good school and a lot of the Minneapolis-based Fortune 500 corporations look to them for internships and new hires. I went there partly because I needed to stay close to home due to some family issues, plus I really didn't know what I wanted to study or where I wanted to take my career. Luckily St. Olaf helped me focus on economics and accounting, which admittedly isn't very sexy, but it helped me get to where I am today. And I love the movie business. Hope-fully this whole mess won't have me blackballed by every production company in Hollywood."

"Once Adducci recommended Michael Glover to you, I assume that you still interviewed him before offering him the job?"

"I did, though I had every confidence that he would be the perfect hire based on his resume and what Joanne had told me. Of course, now we know that his resume was completely fabricated and his references fake, but I have to admit he fits in very well with our team and is doing a good job. I guess that's why I continued to be fooled."

They talked for another 30 minutes about Glover/Williamson, in-cluding any differences between his official description and pictures versus how he presented himself at work, who he hung out with in the office, if there were any known places where he liked to eat or drink after work, any mentions of outside friends or girlfriends, and dozens of other questions that JJ and Kristyn could come up with. Zimmerman was open and talkative, but he didn't have a lot of information that would help them zero-in on his location. Kristyn had already checked the address that had been used on his application, but according to Google Earth, it was a vacant lot about 20 miles from the studio.

JJ had one last idea. "What about his paychecks? Were they being direct deposited or mailed to him?"

"We only offer direct deposit, and his checks were being deposited at Bank of America. I can send you the information if you need it."

"Definitely. I don't know if it will help, or if he's even bothered to access it since he apparently has a lot of money at his disposal. But if nothing else, hopefully we can nail down when and where he opened the account and use that as one more data point for building a case against him."

Zimmerman had his own question. "Do you think my family and I could be in danger? Like, should we get out of town for a bit until this is all over?"

JJ and Kristyn exchanged a look and practically read each other's mind, then JJ responded. "Honestly, I don't think you're in any danger.

We made sure not to discuss the fact that we uncovered the connection between you and Adducci with anyone except the task force leaders, so that should keep things under wraps. Still, I'd be lying if I said that we can guarantee your safety with 100% certainty. We've seen Williamson pick and choose random people to kill just to further his goal of stopping this production. We don't know who he might choose to target next, and while there's no reason to assume it's you, there's no way to rule it out, either."

Kristyn jumped in and added, "Bottom line, Chris, we don't think it would hurt for you to take off for a few days, maybe take the family and head out of town for a little vacation. Hopefully this will all be over in a few days, but until then I don't think there's anything wrong with playing it safe and disappearing for a bit." She looked at JJ, who nodded in agreement.

"I'm going to take your advice. Worst case, I can always work remotely while the family enjoys the vacation. One favor though: will you keep me posted about any developments with tracking and capturing this guy? And if there's any change to Joanne's status?"

"I'm happy to do that. I expect she'll be arraigned tonight or Monday morning at the latest. And it's a virtual certainty that she'll be remanded to jail without bail. I don't think she'll ever see the light of day again."

"As much as I hate to say this about a friend, or at least someone that I used to consider a friend, she deserves whatever she gets. Probably more."

"Very true." JJ couldn't help thinking, *and the same goes for Williamson. And then some.*

37

⚜

SATURDAY, JUNE 3

No industry spent as much time giving itself awards, accolades, and overpriced plastic statues as the entertainment world. Whether it was movies, television, theater, or music, rarely did a month pass without some segment of the industry being feted. That was true throughout the year, but even more so in late winter and spring, the proverbial 'awards season'. Some of the bigger, more prestigious awards, like the Oscars, Emmys, Golden Globes, and Grammys, even garnered a coveted prime time slot on the major television networks. The fact that ratings were decreasing every year did not diminish Hollywood's appetite for celebrating their successes and giving themselves another pat on the back.

Tonight was another in the long line of awards celebrations, though one with less cache and visibility than the major events. There was no live TV and only a small press contingent compared to, say, the Oscars. The Beverly Hills Hilton was the setting for the Directors Guild of America (DGA) awards, and there was the expected mix of Hollywood blockbuster directors, next generation 'artistes', and serious filmmakers that spent their lives toiling in the documentary and short-subject world. It seemed that the directors of blockbuster films secretly longed for the anonymity and freedom of the documentary filmmakers or the *avant garde* flair of the younger indie players. Then again, the documentary and next generation directors all longed to trade places with the blockbuster players, assuming that life would be much easier with bazillion dollar budgets, the latest technology, fawning actors begging to work with them, and the love and admiration of the adoring public.

As the director of *The Murder Game*, a big-budget Hollywood production that was generating a lot of early buzz even though its release was at least 9 months out, Steven Carter was invited to attend. Even without the current project he would have been invited to attend based on his past accomplishments and resume, to say nothing of his three DGA awards and multiple Emmys and Oscars. While not exactly royalty on the level of Steven Spielberg or James Cameron, he was certainly well-known, highly respected, and had a coveted seat at one of the tables closest to the stage. Many others would have traded places with him in a heartbeat: not just for his table at tonight's show, but for his entire career.

Carter enjoyed attending the DGA show each year, and not just because it was a chance to catch-up with old friends and bask in the glory of Hollywood's achievements, but because this show didn't start in the late afternoon like most of the others. Most of the big awards shows start at 5pm Pacific Time in deference to the all-powerful TV networks and their large east coast audiences. The networks that broadcast these awards shows want it broadcast squarely in prime time, and in their perfect world scenario they would hand out the last award promptly at 11pm ET/8pm PT to ensure they kept their viewing audiences around until the last award, and the last high dollar commercial, had been shown. A 5pm start time generally meant an arrival around 4pm – especially if you wanted to see and be seen – and that necessitated leaving the house by 2:30. In other words, the whole day was shot, which isn't too bad if you're up for a big award, but otherwise it seemed like a bit much. Since the DGAs weren't televised, they didn't start until 7pm. Much more civilized, in his opinion.

The red carpet wasn't a big draw at the DGAs. In fact, if not for the handful of Hollywood stars and starlets that were there to present awards, the crowd would be practically non-existent. Even the handful of professional photographers paid little attention to the parade of attendees, and it seemed that half the pictures taken were requested by excited attendees who wanted a souvenir of their big night.

Carter was luckier than most; he was always recognized by the press and asked to stop for a quick picture and interview. He didn't take that for granted and always made it a point to dress in a stylish but conservative tuxedo and to graciously answer every question asked of him by the press. Now that he was in his early 40's – *gag!* – he liked to be perceived as one of the industry's most distinguished professionals. To help drive and maintain that aura, he always made sure that his slightly-younger-but-not-young-enough-to-be-a-trophy-wife spouse, Kathleen, was dressed in a beautiful but *very* classy designer gown with perfect hair, makeup, and jewelry. No see-thru gowns that looked like they leapt off the pages of a Victoria's Secret catalog, no skirts with a side slit *up to there*, and no dresses that made it likely that her more than ample breasts would spill out at any given minute. The perfect Hollywood couple: not quite 'A' list', but definitely very high up on the 'B' list. Almost everyone at the show would have traded places with them in a second.

As the Carters made their way into the auditorium, they stopped and chatted with dozens of industry friends and acquaintances. Finally, just a few minutes before the ceremony was about to start, they made it to their table and took their seats. Steven was happy to see that he knew every person at the table, making it more like a reunion of friends. Turning to Kathleen he whispered, "What great seats! Perfect view, people we know, and some serous industry power players."

"I always like it when that happens, but what I like best about this show is that we're seated at tables where we can set our drinks and purses. I really get annoyed at those shows where I feel like we're seated in a movie theater."

He couldn't help but smile, but she was right. "Speaking of drinks, I think I could use a glass of wine. How about you?"

"Yes, definitely. I think I'll have champagne. I'm sure you're going with your usual red wine?"

"Sorry to be so predictable, but yes. I'll go with a glass of Cabernet."

He flagged down a waiter and placed the order, and a few others at the table did the same.

The waiter was back in less than five minutes and placed the drinks in front of each person that ordered. After collecting a few empty glasses from those that had already had one or more rounds of drinks, he headed towards the kitchen. After setting down the dirty glasses he made his way towards the rear kitchen exit and took off his red uniform jacket and dropped it in the hamper reserved for soiled linens. As he reached the door, he looked directly at the security camera above the door. Brookes Williamson just gave a big smile and flipped the middle finger.

The awards show had been barely underway for five minutes when Steven Carter collapsed on the floor, his body seemingly paralyzed and unable to breathe. Panicked screams went up, and the awards host yelled for someone to call 911. Despite the valiant efforts of several of the attendees, and the EMT's arriving within five minutes, he was pronounced dead at the scene.

When talking to the police, a devastated Kathleen said that she had no idea what could have happened. Steven had been acting and feeling fine, and he had been looking forward to this evening after having production on *The Murder Game* shut down all week due to recent events. Most of all, he was looking forward to resuming work on the movie on Monday and getting things back on track.

That's when a scary realization hit her: was this something other than a heart attack or stroke? Could this be another targeted killing of someone involved with the movie? She started to shake, almost uncontrollably, and the tears that she'd been shedding turned to pained sobs. "I think Steven was murdered."

The cops looked at one another. They hadn't said anything, but they'd already concluded the same thing based on what people had told them and on their own observations. Almost certainly poison, some sort of paralytic, but it would be up to the ME to determine what kind.

Welcome to Hollywood, where even award shows have their own drama.

38

SATURDAY, JUNE 3

It had been an incredibly long and stressful couple of days, and all JJ and Kristyn wanted was to get back to their house, have a quick dinner, and get to bed early. Not exactly the glamorous Hollywood lifestyle, but they were way too tired to care.

"I don't know about you, but I'm too tired to cook. Feel like just ordering something for delivery, and maybe a glass of wine while we're waiting for it to get here?" JJ was in the mood for some good Italian food.

"Yeah, that works. How about Sal's? I'll just have my usual." Apparently Italian was good for Kristyn, too.

As JJ was fumbling through the DoorDash app, her phone rang. She was about to ignore it but then saw that the call was coming from Jackson Taylor. Her pulse immediately quickened. *What now, God?*

"What's up, Jackson? Although I'm scared to ask."

He hesitated a moment before speaking. "Sorry to hit you with this, JJ, but I wanted to let you know right away: I just got word from the police in Beverly Hills that Steven Carter died a little after 7pm while attending the DGA awards at the Hilton."

"Oh my God! Do we know what happened?" JJ was hoping that it was just natural causes. Hell, she'd settle for an overdose of illegal drugs at this point. She just couldn't handle the thought of another murder tied to the movie.

Kristyn knew JJ well enough to know that something bad had happened; she could see it in her face and hear it in her voice. She caught JJ's attention and motioned for her to put the call on speaker so she could hear firsthand, which she did.

"There's nothing in writing yet, but by all accounts, it sounds like he was poisoned. He and Kathleen had just sat down at their table and ordered some drinks, and within minutes he was on the ground and unable to breathe. According to witnesses, they said he looked like he was completely paralyzed and his body just totally shutdown."

That definitely sounds like poison. "Any leads from the police yet?" She knew that it was probably too soon for that, but she had to ask.

"No, but they did find a red jacket from a waiter's uniform in the laundry hamper by the back door in the kitchen, so they suspect that someone was posing as a waiter in order to get close to Steven and slip something into his drink."

Williamson! "Any video of the incident or of this supposed waiter?"

"The police told me that there's a camera by the back door that should have captured something and they're starting to review it now."

JJ requested and got the Beverly Hills PD contact that Jackson had spoken to. While her gut told her that this *poseur* was Brookes Williamson – *how the fuck?* – she wanted to see that video for herself. She could positively ID him, even if he was wearing a disguise. It was unlikely that the cops were familiar enough with him to do that.

It took only minutes for the Beverly Hills PD to forward the video clip to JJ's phone, and as soon as she and Kristyn started viewing it they saw Williamson in plain view, first casually taking off his waiter's jacket and throwing it in the hamper and then turning to face the camera.

"He knew that the camera was there. Hell, he's practically fucking posing for us," Kristyn screamed. "He wants to make sure that everybody knows that he did this."

"And look," said JJ. He's looking right up at the camera, smiling, and notice his right hand down by his waist? He's giving us – *maybe the whole world* – the finger."

JJ immediately reached out to all three leaders of the task force to let them know what had transpired, and to say that they were all stunned and pissed would be sugarcoating things. Astin was still a few hours away from L.A. but promised to high tail it back there, and Isaksen and Alexander promised to update the task force team right away. So far, the word hadn't spread to the FBI or even local PDs beyond Beverly Hills because they had no idea that they'd just become part of something much bigger than the murder of one man.

"I'm going to call back to the on-scene leader with the Beverly Hills PD to read them in on this and ask them to initiate an APB and have all hands on deck for this. Maybe we'll get lucky, and someone will have spotted Williamson as he slipped away." JJ had her fingers crossed. God knows they needed the break.

His luck can't hold out forever. Can it?

39

While all thoughts of dinner flew out the window, the same couldn't be said for the wine. The last few days had been exhausting and mentally draining. While they needed to stay alert, neither of them could stomach the thought of drinking another cup of coffee, and they weren't sure that their stomach linings would survive if they did. Hopefully wine would do the trick, if only for a few hours.

It was shortly after 9pm when Captain Moriarty of the Beverly Hills PD called JJ and reported that his team had caught a break. A store located across the street from the back entrance to the Hilton had security cameras and, in a real stroke of good luck, the owner was onsite and cooperating with the police and sharing his video.

"We got your guy, Williamson, slipping out the back and getting into a black Dodge Charger parked right near the alley. We even managed to get a full license plate and traced it to an Enterprise rental car location at LAX."

"Have you already issued an APB?"

"We have, and I'm forwarding the video to the FBI and task force teams now. I guess that task force also includes the US Marshal service. It seems that everybody is hot for this guy."

JJ said, "And with good reason. He's already left a lot of dead bodies in his wake, and he's doing everything possible to set himself up for his grand finale."

"And what's that?" asked Moriarty.

"Killing me and my partner, Kristyn Reynolds."

"Damn. This Williamson guy doesn't sound like someone you'd want as an enemy."

"Too late. He's already in a snit because we took down his heroes last year and, through that whole clusterfuck, he ended up in prison, too. Now he's out to prove that he's every bit as vicious and capable of a killer as the creeps that he worshiped."

"I guess everyone has their dreams and aspirations, especially here in LaLa Land. You guys be safe and watch your six."

"We will, Captain, but one more quick thing before you go: do you already have your team, and hopefully the entire LA metro area cops, checking traffic cameras and every other possible video source for signs of Williamson's car? This may be our shot at tracking him and ending this thing. This is the first time where we can say with certainty that he was at a specific place, at a specific time, and traveling in a specific vehicle. We need to leverage this to the hilt."

"We're on it, and we've looped-in our counterparts in the surrounding cities and areas and are working together to locate him and track him. As soon as we have anything I'll call you ASAP."

"Thanks, Captain, and if it's not too much trouble, can we plan to check in, say, every 30 minutes? Regardless of the time? If we locate him then I want to make sure that we don't lose our shot at taking him down."

"You got it. I'll be in touch."

After ending the call, JJ and Kristyn tried hard to relax, sip their wine, and let their minds focus on more pleasant topics. Food. Wine. Travel. Love. It didn't take long before they both concluded that they were just going through the motions and nothing short of a nice long anesthesia-induced nap – or Williamson's demise – was going to set their minds free.

JJ perked up when her phone rang again just 20 minutes later and seeing that it was Captain Moriarty she practically dove across the table to pick it up. She once again put it on speaker. "You have something, Captain?"

"We do." He sounded almost as excited as JJ. "We spotted him on a few cameras as he was heading out of Beverly Hills and back towards Santa Monica, and then he was tracked on the 405 and finally back towards LAX."

"Did he go into the airport, like maybe he's dropping off the car and catching a flight?" Kristyn asked.

"That's what we assumed was going to happen, but he didn't stop at the airport or even the rental car return. He drove over to the La Playa area and parked his car in a lot close to the beach."

"Do we know where he went from there? He doesn't seem to be the long-walks-on-the-beach kind of guy." JJ's adrenaline was starting to pump again, and she was surprised that she had any left in reserve after the past few days.

"We couldn't see exactly, but we're almost certain he went into one of the restaurants along the block there. We lost him for a few seconds in the crowds, but our best guess is that he went into a restaurant called Playa Provisions."

"We know that place well," said Kristyn. "I'm guessing that it's pretty packed at this hour, being as it's Saturday night."

"Captain let's get everyone moving that way, ASAP. I know that it's well outside of your jurisdiction, but since the crime happened in your backyard, plus you were instrumental in tracking him down, I don't think anyone will begrudge you for being there. Obviously, that's just my unofficial, civilian contractor opinion."

"I'm heading that way, but of course I'll let LAPD and the rest of the task force take the lead. It's their show."

"I'll reach out directly to our FBI leads and US Marshal Astin. Since Williamson is an escapee, I guess technically the Marshals have the lead, but since Astin is still making his way back here from Victorville, I guess the brass will have to make that call. Hopefully they do it quickly; we don't have time for all the usual pissing matches and dick measuring."

"Are you guys heading down there, too?" Moriarty asked the question, but he was pretty sure he already knew the answer.

JJ and Kristyn looked at each other and smiled nervously. "We wouldn't miss it for the world."

40

After a fantastic dinner, Brookes Williamson headed to the bar for one last drink before driving back to the beach house he was renting this week. He'd had two glasses of wine with dinner, but he decided that after his exciting evening, a nice bourbon on the rocks was in order. Looking over the restaurant's extensive list of spirits he settled on Blanton's Silver Edition Single Barrell Bourbon; fortunately for him, money was not an issue, which was good since this bourbon retails for about $5,000 per bottle. The restaurant, of course, adds their own markup. Brookes just smiled to himself and then told the bartender, "Make it a double."

"Wow, you must be celebrating something big to order Blanton's!" said the comely blonde sitting a couple of seats down the bar.

Brookes eyed her appreciatively. She was the quintessential California girl: tall, blonde, blue eyes, and toned arms and legs showing a healthy tan. Surfer girl? Beach volleyball player? Actress wannabe? She could have been any of those. Or all of them. She was certainly attractive, but no doubt she knew it. And no doubt she used it to her advantage to get what she wants. Did she think he was an easy mark because of the drink he ordered?

"I am celebrating a big day, actually a big week. Unfortunately, I have to celebrate alone, but that's no reason not to go big, right? Would you care to join me and help make my celebration a little less sad?"

That's all she needed to hear. *Free drinks for the rest of the night. And he's kinda cute. If he's not a total creep, I might even have to go home with him.* She rose from her barstool and approached him. Sticking out her hand, she said, "Hi, I'm Mandy."

"Michael," he answered as he shook her hand and held it for just a heartbeat too long. He was already thinking about how he wanted to take her back to his place and ravage her for hours. Whether or not he'd kill her after was another matter, but not something to concern himself with now. "May I order you a drink? Maybe you'd like to try the Blanton's?"

"I'd love a drink, and bourbon is my drink of choice, but I could never ask someone to buy me something as expensive as that. Just a regular Jack Daniels or Makers Mark is good enough for me."

"Nonsense." Brookes signaled the bartender. "Can I get one more Blanton's for the lady, please. And make it a double." He smiled at her and, growing even more appreciative of her stunning good looks, made up his mind that he'd definitely take her back to his place. He was not without considerable charm when it suited his purposes, and his track record with women was evidence of that. He only needed to be charming for a short while since the restaurant closed at 11pm. If she seemed reluctant to go home with him, he had no qualms about slipping Rohypnol into her drink. It certainly wouldn't be the first time he'd gone that route.

***

Outside the restaurant, the surrounding streets were crowded with so many cops and federal agents that the onsite commanders were worried about the civilians in the area noticing and blowing the whole operation. Marked cars were kept at least two blocks away, and other than a small handful of uniformed officers spread around the area, everyone else was in street clothes. JJ and Kristyn had managed to snag a parking space in the same lot where Williamson's car was parked, and they stayed in the car and kept an eye on the restaurant entrance.

"I wish we could go in and arrest him right now, but one of our plain clothes guys walked in there and he said that there are still at least 50 people in the restaurant. We're going to have to wait until he's out on the street." JJ was anxious.

"I've got an idea. I'll be right back." Before JJ could object, Kristyn slipped out of the car.

JJ wanted to go after her and stop her from doing something crazy, but she didn't want to cause a scene that might expose them. She watched as Kristyn casually made her way towards Williamson's rental car, and then saw her duck quickly out of sight. *What the hell?*

In less than a minute Kristyn was back in the car. "That should slow him down."

"Are you crazy getting out of the car and exposing yourself like that? Potentially exposing the whole operation and ruining our chances of catching him?" JJ was not mad, just shocked that Kristyn would do something that risky and without deciding on it together. "What did you do?"

Kristyn held up the pocketknife that JJ had given her months ago for protection, since she wasn't big on guns and didn't have the necessary California permits to carry one. "I cut off the valve stems on two of his tires, so he's not going anywhere with them flat. I thought you'd be impressed."

JJ couldn't help but smile. "Pretty smart. But you scared the shit out of me! My heart is about to beat out of my chest." JJ reached out and held her hand. "Good thinking. Like I've said a million times, you would have made a great cop."

Moments later, they spotted Williamson and a woman exiting the restaurant and heading towards the parking lot. JJ keyed her radio. "All units, I have eyes on Williamson. He has a woman exiting with him, and there are still a large number of civilians on the street in the immediate area."

The LAPD commander onsite responded. "Teams 1 and 2, converge on the parking lot but wait for my command. Let's wait until he reaches the parking lot before we approach."

Moments later Williamson had almost reached his car when he saw the flat tires and, knowing something was wrong, reached for the gun tucked into his back waistband. As he was turning back towards the street, he heard shouts of 'LAPD, get on the ground' coming from multiple people and directions. Thinking quickly, he grabbed Mandy to use her as a human shield, and he started firing at the cops heading his way. Two officers went down almost immediately while the others took cover. Gunfire rang out from seemingly all directions.

"Where's your car?" Brookes screamed into Mandy's ear.

"Right there," she cried as she pointed at a blue Explorer.

"Get in! You're driving!" As he dragged her towards the car, he felt a searing pain in his left leg as a bullet grazed his thigh. As he spun around, he saw JJ aiming another shot from about 125 feet away. He fired off two quick rounds in her direction that sent her scrambling for cover behind a car.

"Go! And don't you stop for anything!" Brookes screamed at Mandy. In her terror, she did exactly what he said and drove like a bat out of hell. After inserting a new magazine, he unleashed at least a dozen shots at the cops, at cars, and at the people on the street to create chaos and confusion. When LAPD cars tried to cut them off, he fired directly at them and caused two of them to crash into parked cars.

Minutes later they cleared the immediate area and Brookes was trying to stop the bleeding from his leg. It wasn't a bad wound, as gunshots go, but it still hurt like a bitch. "Pull over right here," he practically screamed at Mandy. She did as he asked. As the car came to a stop, he turned and shot her twice in the head, sending blood, tissue, and brain matter all over her designer clothes and the car's interior. He climbed out of the car, every step causing intense pain that he had to push down in order to focus on finding a way out of the area.

Seconds later, a car approached from the other direction. He stepped in front of the oncoming Mustang and raised his gun and pointed directly at the driver. It worked. As the car stopped, he dragged the man from the car, pushed him to the ground, and then put a bullet in the back of his head. Not the cleanest getaway, but a getaway, nonetheless.

41

SUNDAY, JUNE 4

Last night's attempted capture of Brookes Williamson was a disaster. Actually, it went beyond *disaster* and all the way to *clusterfuck*. Three officers shot, though thankfully all with survivable wounds. Four other officers were injured in car wrecks or from flying glass when shots hit their car windshields. Two civilians dead, including a possible witness, Mandy Adams, who had been with him in the restaurant. Two vehicles were carjacked, including Mandy's, and no sighting of the Mustang that he made his final escape in. Bottom line, Williamson had gotten away, and they were no closer to apprehending him. If anything, they may be falling further behind and the body count left in his wake was growing.

"I was just contacted by a homicide detective with LAPD, and they found a dead body early this morning and they think it could be related to our case," said Marshal Astin. He looked incredibly tired and haggard, which was understandable after yesterday's events, to say nothing of his long trip transporting Joanne Adducci back to Victorville.

"What's the connection?" JJ almost shuddered at the thought of another death at the hands of Brooks Williamson. *He's losing control. Or maybe already lost it.*

"Apparently it was some world-class hacker and computer geek named Max Perry. He has the reputation, at least in Dark Web circles, of being one of the preeminent experts in creating deep fakes. Apparently, his stuff has been seen all over the Web, and he's suspected in any number of blackmail and extortion plots in multiple countries."

"What makes them think it was Brookes Williamson?" A reasonable question from Kristyn.

"They spotted him on several different CCTV feeds around Perry's apartment complex, plus a couple of witnesses were questioned and identified him from a 6-pack spread of photos."

"Cause of death and estimated time of death?" JJ couldn't stop herself from reverting back to her FBI mentality in stressful situations, and this situation qualified.

"According to LAPD, he was killed by an icepick to the base of the skull and right up into the brain. Too early to know for certain, but the preliminary information estimates TOD to be around mid-afternoon yesterday."

"Christ. He kills this Max Perry dude in the mid-afternoon and then just casually makes his way to the DGA awards ceremony and poisons Steven Carter. And then, just as casually, he bebops down to La Playa for what was apparently a celebratory dinner and drinks, based on his ginormous tab at the restaurant." JJ was seeing this whole case spiraling out of control.

An hour later everyone from the task force, which seemed to be growing by the day, met in the conference room of the L.A. FBI office. SACs Alexander and Isaksen were still leading the group, along with Marshal Astin, and so far, the teams were still working well together and no egos or turf wars had reared-up. That's often the case, but thankfully not here. At least not yet.

Marshal Astin kicked things off and spent the first 15 minutes informing everyone about the killing of Max Perry and how that factored into yesterday's timeline. One of the LAPD team members asked if they should send someone down to Perry's apartment to see if they could find any evidence, especially computer evidence, to further tie this to Williamson and whatever he had planned next.

Astin responded, "I think we should, though I don't expect we're going to find much in the way of computer evidence, based on what the LAPD Homicide detectives told me. It appears that a lot of things were missing, and what was left seems to have been trashed. Still, we might get lucky; maybe this Perry asshole went old school and wrote a few things down on paper or kept some files or backups hidden somewhere in that hovel he called an apartment. Let's see if we can get a team down there to go through the place with a fine-tooth comb, and let's make sure that at least one member of that team is a computer or technical expert."

SAC Isaksen spoke next. He looked like he'd aged at least five years in the past five days; the case and the pace were wearing on him. "I don't need to tell you that this case is now the lead story in every paper and every news broadcast in California, and it's trending on all the cable news shows and social media sites, as well. This couldn't get much higher profile unless he shot the damn president. I don't need to remind you that there are millions of eyes on this now, and half of them are going to be criticizing you for not catching him sooner and the other half are hoping to get their 15 minutes of fame by starting a podcast talking about how much we screwed up and focused on the wrong man."

"In other words," continued SAC Alexander, "be careful out there on the street in everything you do and everything you say. If anyone approaches you for information, regardless of who they are or which paper or news organization they claim to represent, your only response is 'no comment'. If they want more than that, then they'll need to go through the usual FBI PR channels. Everyone got that?"

Seeing nods all around, Isaksen asked JJ and Kristyn if they had anything to add. Kristyn stood up and spoke first. "Let me add one more thing to what SAC Alexander said: every person out there on the street has a mobile phone with a video camera and can't wait to record you and share it on social media. We've all seen that happen, and it's only getting worse. But let me add one more wrinkle: every person out there wants to claim to be a 'journalist' and have their 'first amendment rights' to film you, record you, question you, interfere with you and your job. While I don't suggest that you take physical action, if it can be avoided, I would suggest that you try to disengage from the interaction and keep the 'no comment' advice in mind."

JJ was the last to speak. "I know that for everyone in this room, the interruption to the movie production is the least of your worries. Even though Kristyn and I have direct involvement as producers and writers, we absolutely agree. Still, production has been halted for a week already as we were dealing with the two earlier deaths, and we were supposed to resume work tomorrow. Obviously, with the death of Steven Carter, that's out the window." She paused and looked around the room; she still had everyone's attention.

"The reason that I mention this is that shutting down this movie was one of Brookes Williamson's two main goals. I'm sure there are a lot of people associated with this movie – investors, studio executives, and probably even some of the crew – that prefer to cut their losses at this point and walk away. Maybe they're scared, or maybe they just want to move on. Regardless, unless someone in this room can give me a better idea, I plan to reach out directly to the studio honchos and tell them that we want to put out an announcement in the press that the movie is still moving forward. Yes, we'll have to hire a new director, but we are not stopping production."

A lieutenant with the LAPD raised his hand to ask a question. "Just curious, ma'am, why you're so adamant that the production should keep moving forward? Couldn't that put even more people at risk?"

"It might, but I'm hoping that it might push Williamson a bit over the edge, maybe drive him to make a mistake in his anger and frustration. Or, at least, have his anger drive him to accelerate the move on the final goal: killing me and Kristyn."

Sure, let's try to piss off the maniac even more and have him focused on killing us. Am I crazy?

42

It was early afternoon when Isaksen asked everyone to join him in the conference room. Nearly half of the people that had been there earlier in the morning were now out in the field working on the case, but he still wanted to update everyone that was available, particularly his key players.

"I just received word from LAPD that one of their patrols just located the Mustang that Williamson carjacked last night, and they think it might have been abandoned in the general area of where he's holed-up."

"Why do they assume that sir? I don't necessarily disagree, but what's to have stopped him from stealing another car, or calling an Uber, and traveling miles from there?" Detective Morgan was the lead investigator from the LAPD, and his years of experience and intuition had so far proven to be very valuable to the investigation. That it hadn't brought the task force to the point of capturing Williamson was a sore point for everyone.

"It's certainly not a slam-dunk, but they've checked traffic cameras and other CCTV video from the area, and they've seen him walking for more than a half-mile from where he abandoned the car. It seems that he was making his way closer to the oceanfront area, and that seems consistent with what we've suspected: he moves between homes every few days, and almost always at the beach or up in the Malibu Canyon area." Isaksen was having that tingly feeling that told him that this could be a good lead.

Detective Morgan responded. "That sounds reasonable, sir, and I assume that we've checked for any ride share or taxi pickups in that area last night?"

"Exactly, Detective. Per the LAPD team, they couldn't find any record of passenger pickups or drop-offs in that vicinity within several hours of the times that he was caught on camera."

JJ spoke up. "This sounds like a really solid lead. What's our next step?"

Kristyn rose from her seat and addressed Isaksen directly. "Sir, I think I can use a few portals and databases from back in my reporter days to track him since we now have a known, relatively small area to search." Seeing the skeptical looks on a few people's faces, she quickly added, "Not that the area is super small, but at least we're not searching through the entire L.A. metro area and Valley."

"Go on," said Isaksen. "Tell us how you'd accomplish this search."

"As you said earlier, we strongly suspect that he's been changing locations every few days, and usually at the beach or up in the Canyon area. While we know he's not using any credit cards in his name, we haven't run any searches about transactions in the name he's used as an alias, Michael Glover."

"Good point," added Morgan.

Kristyn continued. "And even if we don't get hits on Michael Glover, I can search for anyone that has had multiple rentals of 1-3 days over the past few weeks in the target areas. We may find that he's used the same portals, like VRBO or Airbnb, or the same realtor, to find and book these properties; obviously tons of people rent homes in these areas for vacations, but I'm betting there's very few that have done multiple short-term rentals in the past few weeks."

JJ smiled. "I think she's onto something, sir. Her logic seems spot-on to me."

Isaksen asked for other opinions or questions. No one objected or challenged Kristyn's idea, and they all seemed energized by seeing a plan of action coming together. Isaksen asked for agreement from Alexander and Astin, and they agreed without hesitation. Turning to Kristyn, he simply said, "Let's do it."

After everyone filtered out of the conference room, JJ slid up behind Kristyn and put her arms around her in an embrace, nuzzling her neck and kissing her lightly on the ear. "I am so proud of you! That's absolutely freakin' brilliant! And the way that you felt confident and self-assured enough to stand right up there in this room full of testosterone and take the lead was so awesome. And you convinced everyone to follow your instincts; that's what's really amazing, that a room full of cops and federal agents would concede that this very blonde, very beautiful reporter....."

"Ex-reporter...."

"Yes, ex-reporter, had come up with a plan that they hadn't thought of first. I think you earned a lot of respect and brownie points here today!"

"Gee, that's what I live for," Kristyn said with a smirk.

"Well, you also impressed the hell out of me, though that's nothing new. And when this day finally ends, I promise to give you a little sample, maybe a very big sample, of what you *do* live for." JJ's lecherous smile pretty much said it all.

43

It was approaching 4pm when Kristyn jumped up from her desk and excitedly announced that she'd found him. Immediately everyone gathered around her desk to learn firsthand what she had uncovered.

"This has to be him. I found five different addresses over the past few weeks, and all the rentals were for the entire home and not just a room or guest house. Plus, every one of them was within a block of the beach in Santa Monica, Venice, or Malibu."

"Were all of them under the same name?" asked JJ. She wasn't hopeful, but it would make their work easier.

"No, but luckily for us it wasn't a different name for each rental. He only used two different names – neither of which was Michael Glover – but he screwed up by using the same couple of credit cards for each rental. Oh, and all of them were booked on VRBO."

"I'll reach out to my tech team here at LAPD and have them pull every traffic cam and video feed they can get their hands on and try to place Williamson in and around those places on the corresponding dates." Morgan was feeling re-energized, as were other members of the team. Kristyn's breakthrough was just what the team needed.

Isaksen spoke up, excited for the breakthrough but hesitant about one detail he hadn't yet heard. "Kristyn, you said you found all these rental locations. Please tell me one of them is his current location."

"Sorry, sir, I should have led with that! Yes, I have his current address and, as we suspected, it's within about a quarter mile of where he abandoned that car last night."

Finally, Isaksen let out the breath he'd been holding and allowed himself a smile. "Thank God for small favors. Alright, listen up: get all members of the task force in here ASAP and let's put together a plan to take this asshole down. I want us ready to roll, in force, within the hour."

Everyone scrambled to round up the task force members, some of whom had headed home earlier for some much-needed rest. Others had stepped out for a bite to eat or just to clear their head, the intensity of the past couple of days weighing on everyone. Still, within 15 minutes almost every member of the task force was assembled in the conference room, and those that weren't there in person were attending via video conference.

Once again, it was SACs Isaksen and Alexander, along with US Marshal Astin, that took the lead in crafting the plan for going after Williamson. Detective Morgan offered his ideas and committed to getting as many LAPD and LA Sherriff's office personnel as needed to box him in and secure the area. That included a commitment for the SWAT team, as well. Much of the task force discussion focused on when to attempt the takedown. Most of the team wanted to move now and not take the chance that he might move again, while a very vocal minority pushed hard to wait until later in the evening when they would have the cover of darkness and fewer people on the street, especially on a Sunday night. The discussions were getting progressively louder, more intense, and aggressive.

Finally, it was SAC Alexander that put a stop to all the back and forth. Standing up at the head of the table, all eyes turned to him, and the room quieted. "Alright, time to dial this down a bit and get this plan locked and loaded. This is one of those times when it's not a matter of one side being right and the other side being wrong, it's making a choice between two less-than-perfect options."

Looking at Isaksen and Astin for their support, he continued. "In a perfect world, I'd want to do this later tonight, but unfortunately, we don't live in a perfect world. After last night's events, with the carjackings, the killings, the shootout, I'm not 100% certain that Williamson is even still here. If I were him, I'd have been the hell out of here last night, or this morning at the latest. The bottom line, though, is that we can't wait any longer. We go now." Isaksen and Astin nodded in agreement.

Decision made, now it was just a matter of setting up the big chessboard and getting people moving. By 5pm, the entire task force, including the additional LAPD and LA Sheriff personnel, were ready to head out.

Before they all stood to leave, JJ rose from her chair and added one more important point. "I think we have a solid, well-thought-out plan in place and an incredibly talented group of cops ready to make this happen. But one word of warning: I've been working on this for a few weeks now and studying this guy's moves and thinking. Or at least what passes for thinking in his case. Anyway, he's got zero conscience and doesn't shy away from killing, even when it's not necessary. I think last night's killing of the two carjacking victims proves that."

"What's your point?" asked one of the local FBI agents. He wasn't trying to be rude, just impatient to get things moving.

"My point is this: If he's still here, I don't expect him to go quietly. He'd rather die in a hail of bullets than be taken alive. But if he's already bolted, then my gut says that he's still going to do everything possible to take out as many of us as he can."

"Are you suggesting that he'd booby-trap the house?" This from Alexander.

"Yes sir. That's exactly what I'm suggesting. His brutality has been increasing, while the gap of time between killings has decreased. That's a dangerous shift. I think it's an absolute certainty that he will try to kill or injure as many people as possible to show the world that he's smarter and more capable than the law enforcement teams aligned against him."

The room was silent for a few moments. Nobody argued the point that JJ raised. Finally, SAC Alexander spoke. "Detective Morgan, please arrange for members of your bomb squad to roll with the task force and accompany our teams on this mission. I'll do the same with my FBI team. Better to be prepared in case all hell breaks loose."

***

The raid on Williamson's rental home was the proverbial good news/bad news story. The bad news is that he wasn't there, and it was evident that he'd left in a hurry. There was blood and bloody bandages and towels still on the floor; not that they needed confirmation, but they'd still go through the motions and test the DNA. The best estimate they had, based on neighbors' statements and videos from a few private residences, is that he had left just a few hours earlier, on foot. They didn't expect him to be on foot long, whether he had another car stashed, planned to rent one, or heaven forbid, carjack and kill another person that's in the wrong place at the wrong time.

The good news? JJ had been right about the house being booby-trapped, but the assembled experts from the bomb squads were able to locate and disable all of them. It did slow down the search, but that was a small price to pay for having every member of the task force able to go home safely at the end of the day.

JJ thought of one other small measure of good news, and it made her smile: Williamson will totally lose his shit when he learns that his plans for taking out every cop that came in or near his house was a total failure. Too bad she didn't have a way to let him know that she was the one that foiled his little plan. Seeing him throwing a tantrum like a spoiled toddler would absolutely make her day.

44

JJ may not have been prescient, but she was right on the money when she predicted that Brookes Williamson would throw a major shit-fit when he learned that his booby-traps had been disabled. He was surprised – shocked, actually – that the police had found his rental house so quickly and raided the place barely two hours after he'd left. Still, he'd left his little surprises spread around hoping to create more death, mayhem, and destruction, whether for the cops or the home-owner and their cleaning service team. He didn't care. All he wanted was more carnage and to be regarded by the press and the masses as the most prolific Slayer of them all.

He was now settled into a decidedly mid-market hotel chain that catered to traveling businessman and trades people that needed rooms for weeks, if not months. His ocean views were now replaced with views of the 405. The sweet smell of the salt air was replaced by pervasive car exhaust smells, and the sound of the crashing waves had been replaced by the ever-present sound of cars and trucks passing by just yards from his window. As if he wasn't already pissed enough, the thought of being trapped here in this plebian environment that was, in his narcissistic view, well beneath his station in life, was the final straw. He pledged to strike again, and soon, and he swore to himself that his pursuers, his enemies, would rue the day that they involved themselves in his business.

He took some satisfaction in knowing that he'd thrown a monkey-

"

wrench in the movie production, if not shut it down for good. With the director now dead, which in his opinion was one of his finest, most cunning assassinations yet, there would at least be significant delays. He was cautiously optimistic that the studio would throw in the towel completely after all the death and destruction he had unleashed, not to mention the tons of lost money and lost investors.

Only two things kept him going and helped him maintain focus: the pain in his leg where he'd been grazed by JJ's bullet, and killing her and Kristyn. He was so pissed-off that he considered just heading out into the street and killing dozens of random people, but he realized that a mass shooting barely registered with the public anymore. Hardly a day goes by in the US without a mass shooting, followed by the same political fighting and the worthless 'thoughts and prayers'. No, he had to take a breath, put the focus back where it belonged: tormenting and torturing Jessica Jansen and Kristyn Reynolds until they begged him to take their lives and end their pain and misery. Tomorrow was the day to put that plan in motion.

45

MONDAY, JUNE 5

It took some convincing, but JJ and Kristyn managed to reason with the studio executives who were considering the fate of the movie production. To say that the execs were torn would be downplaying the acrimony in the room. Some wanted to cut their losses, some wanted to shut it down 'out of respect' for the lives lost, some wanted to shut it down for fears that more tragedy might befall the production and create a huge legal and financial liability. There were a few executives who supported moving forward with the project, and they aligned themselves with JJ and Kristyn. After a couple of hours of sometimes heated discussion it was agreed that production would move forward on Wednesday, the day after Steven Turner's funeral. They would announce this to the production crew and the Hollywood press, and the official press release would state *we're continuing the production out of love and respect for our recently departed colleagues so their sacrifices will not be in vain*.

"Well, I'm glad that's over," said JJ. "In the end I guess we got exactly what we wanted, but the fact that they couldn't even be honest with themselves in a closed-door meeting was irritating as hell. No matter what side or argument they supported, it all came down to the financial risk versus reward."

"No kidding. That was obvious, especially with the finance guys. You could almost see them calculating in their heads how much each additional death would cost them in delayed production costs. It reminded

197

me of the stories about the Ford Pinto from back in the late '70s when they were catching fire in rear end collisions, and supposedly Ford's actuarial people calculated the cost per death to see if it was worth issuing a recall and paying for the repairs."

"Great analogy. Sad story, but great analogy."

Kristyn took a sip of her drink and then continued. "I don't know about you, but I really don't care for most of these studio jerks. I understand that they're running a business, but damn, they are some cold, calculating, and heartless bastards."

"Speaking of which, wouldn't you love to be a fly on the wall to see Brookes Williamson's reaction when word gets out about the movie production starting up again? I'm guessing that's going to cause a major snit. Again. I love it."

Kristyn nodded, and then added, "Yeah, but I just hope that the studio honchos follow through with their promise to dramatically increase security on and around the set. This guy seems to be getting more unhinged by the moment, so God only knows what he may try to do next."

"Maybe I'm being an optimist – hmmm, or maybe in this case it's a pessimist? – but I'm thinking that he may be feeling the walls starting to close in on him a bit and he might decide to accelerate his plan to the end game...."

"You mean us?"

"Right, I mean us. While there's still a ton of people associated with the movie that he could target if he just wants to run up the body count, the fact that he was almost captured the other night in La Playa....."

"Plus you managed to wound him....."

"Right, and then we managed to track his rental house and miss him by only a couple of hours, so he's got to feeling the pressure."

"Good point." Kristyn thought for a minute and then added, "Do you think he'll come after us directly? He strikes me as the kind of psycho who's going to try to be a bit craftier and creative. His end game is the same, but I think he wants to make us suffer more first. Probably from both a psychological and physical perspective."

"I tend to agree with you. He knows that we're expecting him to attack us at some point, so we're being vigilant. And he knows that we've increased security here at home, and once he hears about the production starting back up, I'm sure he'll assume that the studio will add even more layers of security. That doesn't mean he won't try a frontal attack, but I think you're right: he's going to come at us from anywhere except the front. I just hope we see it coming."

It's hard to see it coming when you don't even know what 'it' is.

46

MONDAY, JUNE 5

It was a pleasant day in Houston, with blue skies, temps in the low-80's, and a humidity level that resembled New England more than southern Texas. No one was complaining; any day that you can't literally wring the perspiration out of your clothes is considered 'comfortable' this time of year. Stacey was relaxing by the pool after a morning of running errands, cleaning the house, paying bills, and other mundane tasks. She knew that there was more work waiting for her in her home office, but the weather was too nice to be trapped inside all day.

She swam a few laps, then dozed off while floating on a large pool toy that was as tricked-out as the high-end recliner in her media room. Multiple cup holders, detachable pillows, and even a flip-up tray to use for dining. After a couple of hours, she could tell by the pink splotches on her stomach and legs that it was time to reapply her sunscreen so she hopped out of the pool and dried off. She sprayed sunscreen all over and finished the last of her margarita, which she practically spit out since the once frozen drink was now about the same temperature as the pool water. Stacey headed inside to make herself another drink before stretching out on one of the lounge chairs.

As soon as she was sitting back down beside the pool, her phone rang with a FaceTime call coming in. She smiled as she saw JJ on the video; she'd been worried since she hadn't heard from her and Kristyn since they flew back to L.A. last week. She'd been following the story on the news – it was unavoidable – and even though nothing directly concerning them had been reported, she was still concerned about their safety.

"Hi, JJ. I'm so glad to hear from you. How is....."

Before she could even finish her thought, JJ burst in, loudly. "Stacey, listen to me. You need to get to L.A. right away. Williamson ambushed us this morning and he shot Kristyn. The police and EMT's just got us to the hospital, and she's being prepped for surgery."

"Oh my God! No!" Stacey screamed and burst into tears. 'Is she going to be OK? Tell me everything."

"It's bad, Stacey. She was shot three times, and she's lost a lot of blood. One of the bullets hit her in the chest, and they're going to oper- ate immediately to stop the bleeding and look for any internal damage. Please get here as fast as you can. I've already gone online and booked you a flight from Houston to LAX that leaves in about 90 minutes. Can you make it?"

Stacey could barely talk through the tears. "Yes, I'll make it. What should I do, where should I go when I land? I'm coming straight to you."

"We're at Cedars-Sinai. I've already arranged for one of the local FBI agents to meet you at LAX and bring you straight here. His name is Agent Michaels, and he'll have a sign with your name on it, and he'll have his FBI credentials. You can trust him."

"I'll call you the second I land."

"You'll have to call me on this number. Kristyn and I both had to throw away our old SIM cards and get new temporary burner phones. We found out that Williamson was tracking us via our old phones, that's how he knew where we were pretty much all the time."

"I can't believe this is happening. My God, I didn't even stop to ask you if you're OK. Were you hurt?" Stacey was still fighting back the tears, but it was a losing battle.

"I'm fine. Not a scratch. He didn't even try taking a shot at me. I think it was more important to him to have me watch her getting shot and lying there covered in blood and fighting for her life." JJ's voice started breaking and tears were rolling down her cheek.

"That bastard. If I get the chance, I swear to God, I'll kill him myself." Stacey was fighting to stay strong.

"I'll see you in a few hours, Stacey. Try to keep it together, and if anything changes, I'll text you immediately. Hopefully the Wi-Fi on your plane is reliable."

After they disconnected, Stacey ran back into the house and threw a few quick things into an overnight bag and sprinted for her car. On the way to the airport, she called her ex-husband, John, and tearfully recounted what had happened to Kristyn. John loved Kristyn – the divorce hadn't changed that one bit -- and he was taking it pretty hard, but he was doing his best to comfort Stacey.

"I'll reach out to Austin and Amy and pick them up from school and take them home. I'll try to convince them to pack a bag and come to my house, but if they balk at that I'll just plan to stay with them at your house. Don't worry about anything here, I have it covered." They may not be married anymore, but they were still family and there was still a lot of love and history. Best of all, there was no one better in a crisis than John.

"Thanks, John, and don't forget to take care of the dogs. I'm sorry. What am I saying? Of course, you won't forget the dogs. I'll contact you and the kids this evening when I land in L.A. and let you know what's going on."

"Anything else I can do on this end to help while you're gone?"

"I know it's not really your thing, but maybe you can pray and beg God to watch over Kristyn and keep her alive."

"I can do that. You take care of yourself, and Kristyn, and don't worry about anything here. Stay as long as she needs you, and if you need me and the kids to fly out there, just say the word."

Stacey knew that she was lucky to have such a solid co-parenting partner as John. While the romance and passion may be long gone, the deep love, respect, and friendship was still strong, and for that she felt truly blessed. Especially now.

She was only about 15 minutes from Bush International Airport, but still she quite literally flew down the road and broke countless traffic laws. That was the least of her worries.

***

'JJ' smiled as the call ended. *Well that certainly couldn't have gone any better. That sick fucker Max Perry really outdid himself with this deep fake.* Williamson was so excited, so happy, that he was almost beside himself. He had watched as it was created, participated in the scripting and recordings, and knew that he was 'playing' the central character, but he had still been a bit nervous. What if a question was thrown his way that the real JJ would know but he couldn't answer? What if the software glitched in the middle of the call? What if a million different things that had to go perfectly, didn't?

But they did. All was perfect. And now for the next step in his Grand Finale: using Stacey as leverage to torture his adversaries and, eventually, leave them all so desecrated that DNA tests would be needed to identify the bodies. *Who's the greatest Slayer of them all?*

47

MONDAY, JUNE 5

Stacey was restless and anxious and bouncing off the walls during the seemingly interminable flight. Fortunately, the flight landed about 10 minutes ahead of schedule at 7pm, and she was grateful for even that small break. LAX was its usual madhouse self, even on a Monday evening. It seemed to take forever to get off the plane, and the maddening crowds were blocking her way and slowing her down at every turn. She tried calling JJ at least five times while making her way out to the main concourse, but every time the call went unanswered. No matter how she tried to make sense of that in her mind, she couldn't think of any possible scenario where that was a good thing. The tears started flowing again.

When she finally made it out to the main concourse and out of the secure area, she saw a well-dressed man holding a sign with her name on it. Approaching him, she asked, "Agent Michaels? I'm Stacey Reinsmith."

"Yes, I'm Special Agent Brent Michaels." He quickly flashed his badge for her. "Glad you made it Ms. Reinsmith, and sorry that you had to rush here under these circumstances. Let me take your bag and we can head straight down to the car and Cedars-Sinai."

"Have you heard anything more about my sister? I tried calling JJ, her partner, but didn't get any answer."

"I'm sorry, ma'am, I don't. I came straight here from our L.A. area HQ and the last I heard was that your sister was still in surgery. That was almost 90 minutes ago, but I don't have any further updates. Fortunately, once we're in the car it's a short ride to the hospital, at least by Los Angeles standards, but I'll call my team stationed there to try to get us an update."

"Thank you, that helps a lot. I'm anxious to get there, as I'm sure you can imagine, but at the same time I'm scared as hell at what I may find when I get there." She dabbed at her eyes with a tissue, but the tears didn't stop.

"Let's hurry then." Special Agent Michaels wheeled her bag and politely, but firmly, made his way through the crowds.

Once outside they had to cross the multiple lanes of traffic on the Arrivals level to reach the parking garage. The scene was pure chaos, even with traffic lights and the airport cops directing traffic. It reminded her of the old arcade video game called 'Frogger' where the frog tries to cross the road without getting crushed while zigzagging and moving forward and backward in a constant struggle to reach the other side safely. In several instances Agent Michaels simply kept moving and turned to face the driver and stared them down until they stopped in their tracks. Seeing the holstered gun on his hip probably helped the drivers make up their minds to give him the right of way.

Reaching the safety of the sidewalk, Michaels proceeded to walk into the parking garage with Stacey struggling a bit to keep up. She didn't want to say anything to slow him down. He was only doing what she had asked: get to Cedars-Sinai as fast as possible.

"Is it much further?" Stacey realized that the multi-level garage they were in had thousands of cars parked there, and even just on the ground level where they were now there were at least several hundred.

"Just a bit further. I'm parked near the back corner on this level. Apologies, but by the time I got here the parking lot was practically full. I was lucky to get a spot at all."

Another 100 yards and they finally made it to Michael's black SUV. "Let me put your suitcase in the back and then I'll help you in."

"Thank you."

Hitting the bottom on the key fob to lift the gate, Michaels quickly stowed the bag and then came around to open the door for Stacey. "Ma'am, while I'd welcome you to ride in the front, for operational safety I'd like you to sit in the back on the passenger side. Not that I expect anything to happen, but should that one-in-a-million situation arise, I'd like you to be able to take cover in the back."

"Whatever you think is best, Agent Michaels. And I hate to say it, but that one-in-a-million situation already happened today to my sister. No need to tempt fate further."

Michaels helped her step into the SUV, and as she turned to secure her seatbelt, she felt a sharp pin prick on her neck. Almost instantly her eyes were unable to focus, and she felt weakness in her arms and legs. She was aware that Michaels was forcing her down flat on the seat and felt her arms being pulled behind her back. Something tightened around her wrists, and soon she felt the same tightening sensation around her ankles. She had the instinct to scream for help, but try as she might, not a sound emerged as heavy tape was being placed over her mouth and a dark hood pulled over her head. Blessedly, before debilitating panic could take control, the darkness was complete as she slipped into unconsciousness.

Agent Michaels, née Brookes Williamson, simply smiled at the perfect execution of his brilliant plan. *And now the real fun begins!*

48

❧

TUESDAY, JUNE 6

Brookes was in no hurry. In fact, he wanted to take his time. He wanted to slowly ramp up the terror for Stacey, even though she was just a minor player in the scene he'd created in his twisted mind. Sure, he still planned to kill her in the end, but she was really just a means to that end. Getting to JJ and Kristyn was the goal.

He'd driven to his latest rental home, a long-term lease under another alias, in the Santa Monica Mountains. It was an elegant, 5,000 square foot home with views all the way to the ocean. It was multi-level and one of those oh-so-typical California homes that was built on stilts and cantilevered out over the canyon. It was in a spread-out neighborhood of similarly situated homes, with the closest house being well over 100 yards away. Secluded, but not remote. Hell, he could even get DoorDash or Uber Eats deliveries. That made it downright civilized in his mind. He especially liked the fact that the home had a large garage, so he was able to pull the SUV straight in last night before getting Stacey out of the car, so zero chance of her being seen.

He was very pleased with how well his plan was progressing since no one even knew that Stacey was missing. It was already more than 14 hours since he'd drugged her and brought her to the house, so he knew it was just a matter of time before her family in Houston started trying to contact her to get an update on Kristyn's supposed medical status. No matter. He planned to be the first one to reach out to JJ and Kristyn, and he was ready to set that part of the plan in motion.

As he finished breakfast, he went to check on Stacey. He'd locked her in one of the bedrooms after having done a few 'modifications' in advance, like covering all the windows with plywood and lag-bolting it into the surrounding wall studs, removing anything that had even the slightest chance of being made into a weapon – *lessons well learned in prison* – and putting a heavy-duty latch and padlock on the door. Being extra cautious, he handcuffed one arm to the bed frame.

Unlocking the door, he stepped into the room. "Good morning, sunshine. I trust that you had a good night's sleep." He smiled, but there was not a bit of warmth underlying it.

Stacey looked like hell. That was probably an understatement. Her eyes were puffy and red from crying, her hair and makeup a mess, and terror was still written all over her face. When she'd finally regained consciousness last night, about the time they were pulling into the garage, she thought sure she was going to die from suffocation after having her mouth taped and the hood over her head. She was so relieved when Williamson took the hood off her head that she started crying all over again and actually uttered the words 'thank you' to the monster that had put her in this situation. That had made him smile.

Last night when they'd come in, after leading her upstairs to the main level, he started acting somewhat....*human*. After securing her to a chair in the kitchen, he offered her something to eat and drink. She at first refused, but finally asked for a glass of water; there was no hiding how dry her lips were from the tape, or how parched her throat was from the hood and her labored breathing. She still couldn't even think about eating. Her stomach was in knots, and she was fighting hard not to throw up just from the panic and terror.

"Here's the deal, Stacey," he said to her, talking in between bites of the sandwich he was eating. "You're going to be here for a while. I'm not sure how long, hopefully not more than a couple of days. During that time, I'm going to try to make you as comfortable as possible, within reason. You're not being held in some grungy, rat-infested warehouse or abandoned factory; this is actually a pretty nice place. You will have your own bedroom, your own TV, and even your own bathroom. If you want something to eat or drink, all you have to do is ask. With me so far?"

Trying to be brave, she nodded her head. "Yes."

"During all times your hands will either be bound together or hand-cuffed to the bed, a chair, or whatever is handy."

"I understand."

"Good. Now let me make one thing perfectly clear: if you try to escape, or even scream for help, which is futile, by the way, I will hurt you. *Badly*. If you try to attack me, or even raise your voice to me or in any way be uncooperative, I will hurt you. *Very badly*. Do I make myself clear?"

The tears started flowing again as his threats made her blood run cold. "Yes."

Stacey fought hard to suppress her sobs, but it was minutes before she could begin to compose herself. Lifting her head and looking directly at him, she said, "I don't understand why you're doing this. What do you want from me? I've done nothing to you or anyone else to deserve this."

"Oh, Stacey, don't play dumb or naïve. We both know that you're much too smart for that. You know who I am, and you know what I want. You're basically just the bait. Nothing more, nothing less. It's that bitch sister of yours, and her bush-bumping bitch of a lover, that I have unfinished business with. And I intend to finish that business very soon."

"Meaning that you intend to kill them both."

"Of course."

Getting pissed at his smugness and his intention to use her to lure Kristyn and JJ to their deaths, she kept pressing. "So, the fact that you haven't tried to hide your face from me means that you intend to kill me, too, right, after I've served my purpose? And you want them to know it's you, which is why you didn't even bother to try hiding from the cameras at the airport and along the roads."

"Whether you live or die is entirely up to you. I don't have strong feelings about it either way. Admittedly, you will be around to see your sister and Miss Jansen killed – and I plan to drag that process out for at least a day or two, to be honest – but then you are free to walk away. If you behave. It won't really matter if you are left alive. The police will already know that I'm the one that lured them in and tortured and killed them, not to mention the others I've already dispatched over the past weeks. And I assure you, I have absolutely no intention – *zero* – of being taken alive."

"You sick bastard. Just another dickless male that can't face the fact that a couple of women took down the psychopaths that you hero worship. You're pathetic." Stacey spit in his face.

Suddenly she felt the most intense pain she'd ever experienced as 50,000 volts surged through her body where Williamson had pushed the stun gun directly into her breasts. She screamed as her muscles contracted and she fell to the floor writhing in pain, the handcuffed chair on top of her.

Brookes stood over her, glaring and fighting the temptation to kick the shit out of her, then slowly bent down, rubbing the stun gun over her exposed arms, legs, and neck menacingly but not hitting her with another shock. "I told you that I would have to hurt you if you got out of line, so let this little sample be enough to remind you not to let that mouth of yours get you in trouble again, shall we?"

"Oh, and if I hear one more rude comment come out of your mouth like 'dickless'? I'm going to show you, in every orifice you've got and for days on end, just how wrong you are. And when I'm done, I'll wash your mouth out with battery acid to ensure you never make such comments again while your sister looks on helplessly." He was trembling with rage and the venom in his voice was obvious. Ultimately his rage took over and he reached down and zapped her long and hard as she writhed on the floor in excruciating pain. Only unconsciousness stilled her.

49

⊙∞⊙

TUESDAY, JUNE 6

"Now that you're up, take a shower. You smell like a feral animal. Your suitcase is over by the table so you can put on clean clothes."

"Are you going to uncuff me?"

"Yes, but I'll be sitting right here watching the whole time. I'm sure you noticed that I took the bathroom door off so I can enjoy the view while you're using the bathroom and showering."

"It also looks to me like you've been rifling through my suitcase."

"I have. Not that I expected you to have any kind of weapons in there since you had to carry it through airport security, but one can never be too careful."

As Stacey turned to look at him, she noticed that he had both a semi-automatic pistol in his hand and that nasty stun gun. She was about to say something about him being scared of her but thought better of it; she never wanted to feel that stun gun again.

She felt his eyes on her the whole time she was in the bathroom and when she got out and dressed. He was enjoying the power, the control, and the discomfort and humiliation he was causing her. She did her best to remain stoic. As bad as this was, she knew it could get much worse. Last night was proof of that.

"Very good. You look and smell much better. Step over here and turn around so I can cuff you again." As she meekly walked over to him,

211

he suppressed a smirk. He loved seeing the fear in her eyes. *Control is sometimes so easy to assert.*

"Can I make you something to eat this morning? You haven't had anything but water since we got in last night, and I'm guessing that you probably haven't eaten since before going to the airport yesterday."

Why's he being nice today? "I could eat some toast or cereal, whatever you have around. And coffee would be great. I smelled that earlier before getting in the shower."

After bringing her to the kitchen area and cuffing her to a chair, he made her cereal and coffee, as requested, and waited while she ate it. She was growing uncomfortable with the silence.

Brookes noticed her discomfort. "Finish eating. It's time to get down to business."

He walked her to another room that he had set up as a home office, and he sat her down in a chair facing one of his monitors. He took the chair beside her. "Before we start, let me assure you that if you say one wrong word, you're going to get another taste, a much worse taste, of the pain that you experienced last night. Do you understand?"

She swallowed hard. "Yes, I understand."

"Good. So, for this call you're going to be off-camera to start, and I apologize in advance that I'm going to have to once again tape your mouth shut and put the hood over your head."

Terror flooded through her, the fear and claustrophobia and inability to breathe immediately flashing back. "Please, no, I swear I won't say a word or do anything until you tell me. Please," she begged, practically blubbering.

"While I do believe you, I'm afraid I can't do that. This is not really for you, it's for the impact it will have on them. I promise, though, I'll try to have you gagged and hooded for only a few minutes. Nothing like last night's ride getting here."

He loved that the tears were flowing and the terror was evident on her face. *The theatrics are perfect,* he told himself. To continue setting the scene, he zip-tied both arms and legs to the chair, then placed the duct tape over her mouth and the black hood over her head. "Here we go."

50

TUESDAY, JUNE 6

Monday had been a frustrating day for JJ and Kristyn. It had started off well, with the studio executives agreeing to keep moving forward with the movie, but other than that they hadn't made any headway in tracking down Brookes Williamson. Nor, for that matter, had anyone on the task force. They were desperately hoping that today would be more productive.

"Maybe when the Hollywood press makes the announcement this morning about the movie starting up production again tomorrow, that will drive some sort of response from Williamson. Not that his responses are always good things." Kristyn realized that, actually, his responses were always very bad things, including people dying.

"In the meantime, I feel like we're getting nowhere fast. It pisses me off that we lost his trail when he only had a couple of hours head start on us." JJ couldn't hide her disappointment that he continued to elude a task force made up of dozens of highly trained police, FBI, and US Marshals.

JJ's phone rang with a FaceTime call, but there was no video of the person on the other end. *Another idiot who doesn't know the first thing about technology,* she thought to herself. "This is Jessica Jansen. Who is this, please?"

No sooner were those words out of her mouth than the video image came on, and she stood there shocked. She was looking at herself, as surely as she was looking in a mirror. "What...."

214

"Hi, JJ. It's me, JJ" So good to see you again. Or is it see *me* again?"

Kristyn heard the words but was confused, and as she moved closer to JJ to see the video, she was so shocked that she spilled her coffee. "Oh my God, what the…."

"Oh, and bonus! My beautiful lover Kristyn Reynolds, too!" Brookes was laying it on thick and relishing the looks of confusion and fear on both of their faces. "How do I look, Kristyn? Good enough that you want to take me back to bed and spend the day ravishing me?"

Neither of them understood exactly what was going on, but whatever it was, they had no doubt who was behind it. They were both smart enough and tech-savvy enough to have heard about deep fakes, and they were sure that this is what they were seeing, but they had no idea that it could be this perfect, this advanced. The voice, the movements, everything, were spot-on.

JJ wanted to rebound and take control, or at least not be controlled. "I always expected you to be into cross-dressing after your time in prison. I'm impressed that you clean up so well. Quite an improvement if I do say so myself."

"Very clever, JJ. So maybe we should be interviewed on the red carpet together and let the viewers vote on 'who wore it better'. Personally, I think I'm pulling it off brilliantly."

"I'll grant you that. And the voice, the technology, kudos. Of course, we know that you aren't capable of creating something this advanced. That's why you had to contract it out to Max Perry. Wish you hadn't killed him though; would have loved to draft him to work for the good guys. A guy like that can be a game changer."

"True, but Max was far too much of a reprobate and drug user to ever consider going straight. Or even holding down a regular job."

"So, what can we do for you today, Brookesy?" She hoped that teasing him with a baby-sounding name might knock him off his game. "We're a little busy here working with the task force to close the walls in on you."

"Admittedly, you got a bit too close for comfort on Sunday, but you know as well as I that you've totally lost the scent at this point. And while I'm sure Kristyn, who has stepped out of the picture, is frantically calling your friends at the FBI to try to trace this call, there's no need to waste your time. This call is going through so many hops, courtesy once again of Max Perry, that the connection would have to be nailed up for days, if not weeks."

Fuck, once again he's at least one step ahead of us. "As interesting as this is, we've got work to do, so why don't you cut to the chase and tell us why you called."

"Gladly. Today I have a special guest that I'd like to introduce. Brookes, still in 'JJ mode', got up from his seat and moved across the room and turned the video camera to show a woman wearing a black hood and tied to a chair. "Do I have your attention now? Both of you?"

Kristyn and JJ both were back in front of the camera, terrified at what they might see. *Who the hell is he terrorizing now and probably getting ready to kill?*

Brookes slipped behind the chair, really trying to raise the drama and fear factor. He loved every minute of this. *Best. Day. Ever.* Slowly he removed the hood and removed the tape from his captive's mouth.

He heard screams from the FaceTime connection and saw Kristyn fall to her knees. Screams turned to sobs, and sobs turned to curses against him, against God, against everyone and everything. He couldn't have asked for anything more.

"Stacey, maybe you'd like to say a few words?" He turned to face Stacey and gave her a very scary and stern look as if to reinforce his threats of severe pain if she got out of line.

Stacey could barely speak through the tears. "I'm sorry. To both of you. He's using me for bait."

Brookes interjected. "Oh, Stacey. That's hardly news to them. Of course they know you're the bait. But that won't stop them from trying to come to your rescue. They'll risk everything to try to save you, especially JJ. That's who she is; it's in her FBI DNA."

Even with her years of training and hardened persona, JJ was still totally devastated. She was terrified at what might happen to Stacey and how it would affect Kristyn, both short-term and long-term. It was all she could do to stand back up, face the camera, and respond to his taunts.

"Let her go. You know she's got nothing to do with this. I'm the one who led the case against the Slayers. It's me you want. I'll trade places with Stacey right now. You can do anything you want to me. I won't resist. Just let her go and let her get back to her family."

"How noble of you, but no thanks. This is not an either/or situation. It's more of a 'one for all and all for one' situation. I'll get to you, and Kristyn, in due time. And by due time, I mean very soon. In the meantime, though, I'm going to enjoy getting to know Stacey a little better."

"Don't you dare touch her, you motherfucker," Kristyn screamed. "I swear to God, I will kill you!"

"I've already touched her, at least in some ways. Let me demonstrate." With that, he walked back over to Stacey and zapped her with the stun gun again, as she bucked and fought against the restraints before going still.

"Stop goddamn you!" shouted Kristyn.

"You know, I'm thinking that Stacey may be good for one other little bit of fun, too. I've always wanted a child, preferably a son, but just never connected with the right woman. I'm getting older, thinking that I'm finally ready to settle down and be a dad. What do you think? I think Stacey might be a suitable mate, or at least a suitable cum receptacle. She's a bit older than I prefer, but still attractive. Probably still has a few eggs left. I think it's worth taking the chance. Don't you? I think we'd have some cute kids together."

"Don't you dare touch her, you son of a bitch!" JJ screamed as tears clouded her vision.

Brookes disconnected the call, fearing that he'd break out in laughter at the terrified screams and words coming from JJ and Kristyn. *God, I was fucking brilliant, if I do say so myself!*

51

TUESDAY, JUNE 6

JJ and Kristyn were devastated, especially Kristyn who was inconsolable and sobbing to the point of hyperventilating. Try as she might, it took JJ seemingly forever to calm her down enough to talk about the immediate actions they needed to take.

"We need to get moving on this, sweety. Do you think you can get up and start making calls to find out how Williamson managed to kidnap Stacey?" JJ's mind was running a mile a minute with all the details that they needed to tend to before any more time was wasted.

It took a minute, but Kristyn started slowly pulling herself together. Having a task to focus on that could hopefully help save her sister was the push she needed. "I'll start with a call to John to see what he knows. Hopefully I won't have to call the kids, but if John doesn't have anything of value to give us then I'll reach out to them."

"Perfect. I'm going to start with calls to the task force leaders; hopefully I can catch them all at once. Why don't you take a minute to splash some water on your face and catch your breath, then call John. You need to stay as calm and matter of fact as possible, try to keep him from freaking out, especially if he's with the kids. Make sure he understands that we have half the cops in California working on this so we're doing everything possible to get her back safely."

As Kristyn headed off to the bathroom to clean up a bit, JJ called Isaksen and had him round up SAC Alexander and Marshal Astin. It only took a few minutes to get everyone on the call together. The three of them were stunned into silence, not sure if they even believed that technology was advanced enough to pull this off. They put that aside, though, when they understood the implications of Stacey being kidnapped by this madman.

"Any idea where the call came from or where he's holding her?" Isaksen launched the first probing question.

"No. I think it's a virtual certainty that it's here in the L.A. area, but there was no way to trace the call. We tried, but we would have needed the connection to be nailed up for hours, maybe days, to trace it. For what it's worth, the video appeared to be shot inside of a house, not some kind of factory or abandoned structure. I caught a quick glimpse out one of the windows when he panned the camera, and it looked like it was in the hills facing west towards the ocean."

"That's something, at least," added Astin. "I assume that Williamson made a number of threats?"

"He did, and exactly what you'd expect. He'll hurt Stacey if she gives him any problems, he intends to torture and kill all three of us, blah blah blah. And, of course, the expected threats to sexually assault Stacey just for his own fun and games."

"Thoughts about next steps?" This from SAC Alexander.

"Several, sir. First, let's assume that Stacey flew into LAX last night; we should have that confirmed by her ex-husband any minute now, but let's check with the airlines. Since she lives in Houston, let's start with United Airlines into LAX. We should check all available video feeds in the airport. I think it's a certainty that he was waiting for her when she landed, maybe posing as a cop or whatever story he told her while communicating as 'me' via his deep fake application. Let's try to track them out of the building, see if we can identify their car and where it goes when they leave the airport. Every little bit of information helps narrow the search."

"Agreed," said Isaksen. "And you'll get back to us with whatever details the ex- and her family can provide?"

"Of course, sir. Hopefully within the hour. One last thing, and this goes for the entire task force, so if you can please spread the word immediately: if you get a phone call or video call from me, *do not* trust that it's really me, under any circumstances, unless I start the call with a code word. That code word will be 'cabernet', like the wine. Don't prompt me for it; if it's really Williamson trying to fool you with his deep fake, letting him know that there's a code word will just have him shut down communications with us."

"I think that's wise. If you're agreeable, I'd like to take it one step further, like our version of two-factor authentication." Alexander took a minute to form his thought so he could express it clearly. "If there's ever a situation when any member of the task force is unconvinced that they're really speaking to you, even after hearing the code word, we can use a challenge/response prompt. If that makes sense to you, I'll work with the team here to craft one and share it with you later today."

"I think it's a great idea, sir. While the task force gets moving on this, I'm going to check-in with Kristyn to see what information she's been able to develop. I'll touch base with you soon."

***

Kristyn looked drained and exhausted, but there was no hiding the fire and determination in her eyes. She'd just hung up from a 20-minute call with Stacey's ex-husband, John, and it was Kristyn who had to stay strong and supportive of him. John was devastated not just for Stacey but at the thought of what this would do to their kids.

As JJ entered the room, she asked, "Was John able to shed any light on this?"

"He was. He said that Stacey reached out to him in a panic be-cause she'd gotten a call from you saying that we'd been ambushed by Williamson, and I'd been seriously wounded and was on the way to Cedars-Sinai."

"Did he indicate if Stacey had any hint that she wasn't really talking to me?"

"He said no, she didn't appear to have any suspicions whatsoever."

"Can't blame her; I was on the call earlier and I would have sworn that I was talking to myself, too."

"As we expected, she caught a flight out of Bush International that you supposedly arranged, and she was to meet an FBI agent when she got off the plane who would take her directly to the hospital. John couldn't remember the name of the FBI agent, if Stacey even mentioned it."

"That tracks with what we suspected. I have the task force checking all video feeds from the airport, the parking lots, and the surrounding area to see if we can zero-in on them. I'll let them know that you were able to confirm her United flight, so they don't waste time on that detail."

"What do we do now? I can't just sit around here doing nothing, but I don't know where go from here." Kristyn was anxious to do something, anything, to help in the search for Stacey but she didn't have any idea what to do.

"It's frustrating, but right now the only thing we can do, the only thing that any of us can do, is focus on basic police work. Follow the leads, dig up every bit of information we can, and keep pushing forward."

"Maybe one thing I can do to stay busy and productive is go back to my searches of rental houses on VRBO and Airbnb, as well as local realtors that specialize in short-term rentals, to see if we can identify some possible locations where Williamson might be holding her."

"Good idea. And concentrate on homes up in the hills instead of near the ocean." Seeing Kristyn's inquisitive look, she added, "When Williamson panned the camera around to Stacey, I caught a quick glimpse out the window behind her. It was definitely in the hills. I'm certain of it." *I just wish there was a lot more I'm certain of at this point.*

52

It was late afternoon and both JJ and Kristyn were tired, frustrated, and going stir crazy. JJ, especially, felt like she needed to be back out on the streets investigating Stacey's kidnapping like she would have in her FBI days, but what could she really do? Other than some vague idea of Williamson being in a house 'up in the hills', they didn't know where to start. At least the task force had been successful in digging up video from LAX that showed Williamson meeting Stacey in the main concourse, walking with her through the crowded airport and out to the parking garage, and even a grainy shot of him jabbing her in the neck with a hypodermic needle before throwing her into the SUV. They managed to ID the black SUV and its license number, which, as expected, turned out to be plates stolen from another vehicle a few days before. Still, they were able to track them using traffic cameras leaving the airport before eventually losing them in traffic on the 101.

"Are you surprised that Williamson hasn't reached back out to us yet, just to torture us if nothing else?"

JJ thought for a moment. "Yeah, now that you mention it. I'm sure he wants to torment us and twist that knife as much as he can. I've been trying to figure out his endgame: obviously, we know he wants to kill us both, but does he want to take us out at the same time, or does he want to make one of us watch while the other is killed?"

"I think he wants some kind of grand finale, like some big showdown in the old West. He wants to prove that he's better and smarter than both of us, but my money is on him doing something to incapacitate us first rather than kill us right away. Maybe lure us in close and then take us down with some kind of chemical or gas to knock us out."

"Makes sense, actually. He made threats before about torturing us and making us watch as he beat and raped and eventually killed the other. My guess is that he's still thinking along those lines, but now he's expanded the plan to include Stacey, too."

"Not exactly a comforting thought."

"Sorry, you're right. But I'm glad we're talking this out and generating some ideas. Your thoughts about using some kind of gas or nerve agent to take us down, I think that makes sense. Or I could see him luring us into a location and using something like flash-bangs to incapacitate us without any lasting effects. He wants us alive and fully aware of the tortuous plans and pain he has in store for us."

"Again, not exactly a comforting thought," Kristyn said, trying to force a bit of a smile.

"No, but this is good. You've got my creative juices flowing. I'm going to reach out to Isaksen and the rest of the task force to share our thoughts, get them thinking and planning along those lines. You're welcome to join the call, too, if you want. The more we can consider and plan for these contingencies, the better off we'll be."

"But you know that Williamson is going to insist that we come alone whenever he's ready to take this to the next step. I'm sure he'll threaten to kill Stacey, and not hesitate to do it, if he even suspects that cops are anywhere around."

"True. And one advantage of being up in the hills is that you can look down and see people approaching for miles, especially if there are enough SUVs and police cruisers to look like we're invading a small country."

Kristyn looked at the information she'd developed in trying to pinpoint a possible rental house in the hills, having looked at dozens of potential locations from the Hollywood Hills all the way to Calabasas. "One thing I've noticed, with every possible location I've identified so far, is that no matter how remote the location, there are always at least two ways out. That is, while the house may be facing west and is usually approached from that direction – and that would be the direction where any police raid would be expected to come from – there is a road that comes up from the other side of the mountain. I'd be willing to bet that this is something that Williamson considered when looking for a place to hide out."

JJ looked at the properties and then pulled up a map of the L.A. area and pinned the location for all the possible properties that Kristyn had identified. She was right. "Let's talk this over with the task force and have them factor this into their planning. For now, we'll tell them that we're still looking for his exact location, but we want them to plan for a rear approach to stay out of sight. Anything we can do to increase the chances of letting Williamson think we're being 100% compliant."

JJ's phone alerted her to an incoming FaceTime call. Her blood immediately ran cold, and she felt the tension dial up to a '10'. Even though she was totally expecting it, seeing 'herself' on screen was still disconcerting. "You seem to be getting pretty comfortable showing yourself as a woman there, Brookes. Something we should know?"

"Yes. You should know that one more smartass comment like that and I will make sure that Stacey gets a nice little zap, and I'll let her know that you're to blame for her pain and suffering. Want to try me?"

JJ bit her tongue. So much that she wanted to say, and if she were one-on-one with Williamson, she would say it and take whatever he could dish out, but she couldn't do that to Stacey. "What do you want? Just calling to torture us some more, maybe twist the knife a bit more?"

"Yes, exactly. I wanted you to know that Stacey and I have had a lovely day together. We had a nice lunch, sat out on the deck enjoying the sunshine, and watched a few movies on Netflix. Simply wonderful."

"Can we see her?" JJ didn't really think that he'd kill her yet since she still had use as bait, but better to verify, then trust.

"I don't see why not." The video showed that he was standing up and moving to the other side of the room, and then Stacey slowly came into view.

JJ had to quickly mute the phone to cover the scream coming from

Kristyn. JJ was barely able to suppress her own. Williamson pulled the black hood off Stacey's head and roughly ripped the tape from her mouth. *Why would he still be using the tape and hood when neither were necessary in the house?* Stacey screamed in pain, and probably not just from the bloody, raw lips. Her face was covered with bruises and welts, obviously from being slapped and punched, maybe even kicked. Blood was caked over her right eye and her forehead, and there was a gash on her left cheek.

After the phone was taken off mute, Kristyn screamed with as much venom as JJ had ever heard from her, "You sadistic motherfucker! Why are you doing that to her? She's no threat to you!"

That just made him smile into the camera. "Well, I could say that it's because I enjoy it, because that's certainly true enough. But in her case, she disrespected me, and I won't stand for that. I offered her dinner and something to drink, and she turned it down. After all my hard work. Then I offered to let her fuck me, in the most gentlemanly way, and she not only declined, but she spit on me. That earned her a bit of punishment, not to mention several extremely strong, extremely long zaps from my trusty stun gun. I don't think she'll turn me down again, should I make her the same offer."

They both threw hysterical screams and curses at him, finally with JJ concluding it with, "I swear to God, I am going to kill you. You'll want us to arrest you, but I promise you, you won't be given that chance."

Brookes just chuckled, and before cutting the connection added, "Come and get me, bitch."

53

TUESDAY, JUNE 6

Kristyn was sobbing, and JJ couldn't hide her own tears, but she was already working and formulating plans. She knew that she should stop and try to comfort Kristyn, but at this point she had a bias towards action. Her mind was going a mile a minute and she was cautiously optimistic that the steps she'd taken prior to the call from Brookes were going to pay off.

It took a while, but finally Kristyn came over to join her. "We've got to stop him, JJ. We can't let him hurt Stacey any more than he already has." She wiped her tears and blew her nose, still far from calm. "What are you so focused on? Have you found something?"

"I may have, or at least it's something that the task force can use as one more piece of the puzzle."

"What is it?"

"I recorded the entire FaceTime call on my iPhone, so I'm going to send the video clip to Isaksen and the team and let them analyze it. Once again, I noticed that he panned the camera past the window in the kitchen or living room, so maybe they can use it to help focus us in on the right area."

"I didn't know you could record a FaceTime call on your iPhone."

"I didn't either, but it's amazing what you can learn when you spend some time researching things on Google. Turns out to be a feature already built into the IOS software. Who knew?"

They spent a few minutes going over the video clip several times, taking note of everything from the architectural style to the furniture, art on the walls, anything that might be able to connect back to a realty listing for rental homes in the area.

"I guess there's no way to grab geolocation data from this, is there?" Kristyn's mind was starting to click on all cylinders.

"It doesn't appear to be. I don't know if that's because this is just a video capture or because Williamson disabled geolocation from his end. I'll have to leave that to someone more tech savvy than us."

"Let's get that over to the task force right away and let them get started on it. Every second counts at this point." Kristyn was hoping and praying for a breakthrough, if not a miracle.

***

"Really clever move, JJ. This could be the breakthrough that we've needed. I'll get it into the hands of the local teams right away and have them bring in anybody and everybody that may be able to help identify the location." Isaksen had been feeling the weight of this case for days, but this was just what he needed to get re-energized. This new information hit him like a triple-shot espresso, and he was ready to roll.

"So, JJ, how's everything else going? Kristyn hanging in there?"

"It's been really tough for her, sir, especially when Williamson moves the camera to show Stacey's beaten and battered body, not to mention his constant threats to hurt and even rape her. I'd say Kristyn is doing as well as we could hope, but that's not saying much. I'm not sure that anybody could stand up to the situation any better. I'm just trying to help her see that we're making some progress, slow though it may be."

"I guess that's all any of us can do at this point. By the way, I just got word from one of the tech guys that the Hollywood Reporter just broke the news that your movie production is starting back up tomorrow. Do you expect that will garner a reaction from Williamson?"

"Yeah, almost certainly. I'm not sure when he'll see it – sometime today or early tomorrow, I'd imagine – but I expect he'll have a very strong, visceral reaction. What scares me is that he'll take it out on Stacey before we can find her."

"Agreed. By the way, I sent a handful of cops and FBI agents from the task force to attend the funeral and interment for Steven Turner earlier this afternoon. I didn't really expect Williamson to show up there, but we didn't want to take any chance."

"I think that was a smart move, sir. One last question for you: it's been 24 hours since Stacey was abducted, and we've managed to keep a lid on it. How much longer do you think our luck can last?"

"Even with our direct orders to every member of the task force to keep this quiet and not even share it with other members of our respective agencies, I'd be surprised if we're able to keep it quiet for even another 12 hours. Plus, I wouldn't be the least bit surprised if Williamson makes his own announcement, especially since he's likely to go ballistic when he finds out that the movie is still moving forward. He's likely to see that as one more instance of you ruining his grand plans. Unfortunately, that may not be a good thing for Stacey."

And the last thing we need is for him to take his frustrations out on Stacey.

WEDNESDAY, JUNE 7

Brookes had the TV in the family room on and tuned to the *Today* show while making breakfast, really just for the noise and occasional distraction. He heard Savannah Guthrie speak to Carson Daly about something going on in Hollywood and it piqued his interest. When he heard Carson announce that production was resuming today on *The Murder Game*, only one day after the funeral for director Steven Turner, he totally lost his shit. He screamed. He cursed. He threatened to kill every living person and creature on Earth. *I will make them all pay.*

He flew into a rage the likes of which he'd never experienced before. Not just his normal pissed-at-the-world, psychotic raging, but totally out of control raging. He broke nearly every piece of furniture in the kitchen, dining, and family room, including slashing the sofa cushions with a large chef's knife. He'd thrown heavy pots and pans into every mirror and picture hanging on the walls and ripped the 75" Samsung TV off the wall with his bare hands.

Stacey was petrified but thankful to be locked in her bedroom and away from the worst of it. She just prayed that he would get it all out of his system now before coming after her. She curled up into a ball on the bed and pulled the cover and pillows over her head, trying to shut out the screams and the violent destruction of seemingly every item in the house. She'd seen him mad and out of control, but this seemed to be at a whole different level.

His head felt like it would explode, and, for that matter, so did his chest. His hands were bloody with cuts from broken glass as well as instances where his grip on the knife slipped while stabbing and shredding the furniture, the walls, and anything else he could reach. He grabbed the bottle of vodka from the freezer and poured nearly a quarter of the bottle into a tall glass, and then went into one of few kitchen drawers that hadn't yet been broken and pulled out the bottle of hydrocodone that he had been taken for the leg wound. He was tempted to take the entire bottle of pills and wash it down with the bottle of Tito's, but that would be letting them win. *And I'll never let them win.* Three pills washed down with the large glass of vodka had the desired effect, finally dulling the pain until he passed out on the mostly destroyed couch.

Stacey said a prayer of thanks when the violent outbursts stopped and, while she didn't know how or why it stopped, she didn't really care. She just needed her own pain and anguish and suffering to end. If that meant he was dead, so much the better.

55

❦

WEDNESDAY, JUNE 7

"Damn. The word is out there now. All the networks and online sources are reporting that production is starting back up today. I wonder how long before he hears about it?" JJ had hoped that the news coverage about the movie production resuming would be minimal, but apparently the fact that the story could be sensationalized because of the murders and vandalism made it juicier and more appealing to the masses.

"Let's hope that he doesn't hear about it. Maybe he's not someone who follows the news that closely." Even as she said this Kristyn realized that she was probably mistaken; even if he wasn't watching the news to find out about the movie production, it's pretty much a given that he'd be paying attention to what's being reported about him, Stacey's kidnapping, and the other killings that he'd been tied to.

Neither of them wanted to broach the painful subject of Stacey still being held by this psychopath and the one most likely to feel his wrath. It was always there, sometime bubbling just beneath the surface and threatening to explode once again, but they fought hard to keep it pushed down. It didn't do them, or Stacey, any good, and if anything, it kept them from giving 100% to finding the solution.

JJ and Kristyn both received a notification on their mobile phones that the task force leadership wanted everyone on a video call asap. Moving to the large monitor in JJ's office, they logged in and waited while everyone gathered either virtually or in the conference room at the L.A. FBI office.

Isaksen got right down to business, as was his style. "Two things to share with you all, and then we'll let you get back to it. First, if you're not already aware, the news broke a little while ago that the production on *The Murder Game* is resuming today. I don't need to remind you that shutting this down has been one of Williamson's key objectives or demands, so we have to assume that he's not going to take this lightly." He looked around the room and waited to see if there were any comments, but there were none.

"Second point: thanks to the efforts of JJ and Kristyn, we've had access to the FaceTime video that Williamson initiated with them yesterday. After considerable effort by our tech teams, they are pretty confident – they rate it as 85% level of confidence at this point – that Williamson's hideout is in the Topanga Canyon area."

"That's great news, sir. That helps focus the search area considerably. How were they able to narrow it to that general area?" JJ asked what everyone on the call was thinking.

"I don't pretend to understand all the information provided to us by the tech teams and their contacts in the fields of botany and biology, but in simple terms, the trees that were seen in the video outside of the house are more closely associated with Topanga versus other locations we considered like the Hollywood Hills. They said it was the clusters of willow trees and large oak trees in such close proximity, at least as I understand it. Regardless, let's double-down on possible locations in Topanga."

Kristyn interjected, "Sir, I've already identified about 10 potential target homes in the Topanga area. My next step is to search for everything I can find online about those homes – descriptions, pictures of the interior, etc. – to see if I can narrow it down to the right one when comparing it to JJ's video."

"Excellent." He looked to Alexander and Astin to see if they had anything to add.

Astin stood up to address everyone. "As I'm sure all of you can appreciate, that Topanga Canyon area is rugged and potentially treacherous. When we identify Williamson's place, we're going to have to do everything possible to contain him. By that I mean, we can't afford for him to make it out of the house and into the woods and rough terrain. There are plenty of places our cars, and even our SUV's, can't go. It will all be on foot and trying to track down an armed madman with nothing to lose, who's vowed to never be taken alive, is less than ideal. Containment is the name of the game."

"Marshal Astin, if I may," said Kristyn. It was her habit to always ask permission politely, sometimes feeling that she was 'less than' because she wasn't law enforcement, even though every member of the task force respected her, her abilities, and especially the fact that it was her sister being held captive. "JJ and I have plotted all the probable locations on a map and noted that each one has access from both the west and the east. Since the homes are all facing west, usually cantilevered out over the hill and facing towards the PCH and the ocean, that's where we think he'll be focused. If we approach from the east, via the 101, we can come over the far side of the mountain and down on his location."

"Makes sense," said Alexander. We're less likely to be seen, and we can also setup a roadblock in case he makes it to a vehicle and tries to evade capture by heading out to the 101."

"Great idea," said Isaksen. "Let's start putting together plans now for how we'll conduct this operation, what resources we'll need. We may not know the exact location for the raid, but we understand the general idea and topography. Let's try and have something ready for review by end of day."

The task force was feeling pumped thinking that things were slowly turning their way. If only.....

***

It was just after lunchtime when Kristyn's phone rang. She was happy to see that it was her nephew, Austin. She felt guilty that she hadn't made time to reach out to him or his father and sister since this all started. They were all extremely close, and she'd always been the 'cool aunt' to the kids. "Austin, how are you? And Amy? I've been so worried about you guys."

"We're scared, Aunt Kristyn. We haven't heard a word from anyone or even seen anything about Mom online. Tell us what's going on." It was obvious that he was struggling to hold back the tears.

"Of course, sweety, and I'm sorry that I haven't called since this all started. I'm working closely with the people trying to find your mom. Are your dad and Amy close by? Let's get everyone together so everyone can hear the same things and ask questions."

Moments later Austin was back with Amy and John, and they switched the call from voice only to FaceTime so they could see each other's reactions and emotions, and just feel closer to each other. "What can you tell us, Aunt Kristyn?"

"I can and will tell you everything I know at this point, but before I do there's something you have to understand and promise me: you cannot, under any circumstances, talk about this to anyone else. No one. Not the cops, not any reporters, not even your closest friends. Got it?"

"Yes, we understand. That makes it even more scary." Amy appeared to shudder a bit.

"Sorry, that's not my intention, but right now we're doing everything we can to keep this out of the press. We've been lucky so far, but it won't last forever. Right now, the only people that know that your mother has been kidnapped are us, JJ, and the task force leading the effort to rescue your mother and capture this maniac." She didn't bother to add that many on the task force, including her and JJ, had zero intention of letting him be captured alive.

"Did I just understand you to say that even your parents and Daniel don't know about this?" John asked, referring to her and Stacey's brother in Denver. "Don't you think they have a right to know."

"They absolutely do, John, but for right now, and probably for the next 24-48 hours, we're trying to limit the number of people that know about this. There's nothing that mom and dad can do to help, and Daniel is liable to go ballistic and head to L.A. with guns blazing. The task force is trying to keep this quiet because as soon as it gets out, they'll have to waste time and cycles following-up on dozens, maybe hundreds, of false sightings, fake confessions, and dead-end leads."

"How much longer do you think you can keep this quiet? You said that the task force had grown pretty big." Austin wasn't wrong. The more people involved, the greater the chances that something eventually leaks.

"I'm not sure. I'm surprised that word hasn't already leaked, but thankful. It also wouldn't surprise me one bit if Williamson leaked this himself, just to make our job harder."

"Why did he take our mom?" asked Amy through her tears. "What could this guy possibly want with her? She's nobody to him."

Kristyn chose her words carefully. "He doesn't want your mom. He took her to get to me and JJ. He's using her as leverage to try to get to us."

"Why is he after you and JJ?" Amy was not so young that she was unaware of all that Kristyn and JJ had been through when investigating and shutting down the Slayers and the Murder Game, but she didn't have a full appreciation for the magnitude of the crime and conspiracy.

"He was one of the thousands of people around the world that were involved in gambling on the Murder Game, and like many others, he was arrested and sent to prison. We'd never even heard of him; he wasn't one of the main conspirators or one of the biggest gamblers, no one special. Just another twisted individual that took pleasure in betting on violence against innocent people. Anyway, the bottom line is that he worships the Slayers, even though they're all now deceased, and wants to both avenge their deaths and prove that he has what it takes to ascend to their level."

John spoke up. "Is he as twisted and evil as the Slayers?"

Again, Kristyn thought through her words carefully. "In some ways yes, in other ways no. The Slayers were very disciplined; they never killed anyone that wasn't a target of their sick game. That is, no collateral damage. They never killed anyone randomly, and they only used the killing methods specified for each game. For this guy, he's not disciplined at all. He's killed a lot of people using all kinds of weapons, and he seems to delight in killing even if it has nothing to do with getting him closer to his goal."

"Meaning, closer to you and JJ," said John.

"Unfortunately, yes. JJ and I are well protected, so I'm not concerned about us," she said, knowing that was a little white lie, at best.

"Have you talked to my mom?" asked Austin. "Do we even know for sure that she's still alive?" He was trying to be brave, but this is just way too much for a young teenage boy to handle. The tears were evident in his eyes, too.

"I have talked to her, twice in fact. Both times were via video, so it wasn't just hearing her voice. I got to see her." She didn't want to even begin to broach the topic of the beatings and pain she'd endured.

"And she's OK?" Austin was hoping against hope that she was.

It tore Kristyn up to lie to them, but she couldn't tell them the truth on this point. It didn't serve any purpose for them to know the details of what their mother had endured and would just cause them more pain and worry. "Yes, she's OK. She's scared, obviously, but when we've seen her on video, she's been secured to a chair with zip ties but other- wise OK. Here's the bottom line: he doesn't want to hurt her, because she's the bait for me and JJ. If something happens to your mom, he'll never have a chance of getting to us."

John asked the next question. "Do the police have any clue where she's being held?"

"We don't know exactly where yet, but we think we have it narrowed down to one area in particular. I know that isn't the exact answer you guys want but consider that we've managed to narrow it down from more than 4,000 square miles to an area of less than 20 square miles in just the last 24 hours, and we're still working it."

They talked for a while longer, and before ending the call John asked, "What more can we do from this end Kristyn? Anything we can do to help and support you and JJ, and the police, for that matter?"

"Honestly, nothing that I can think of. I do want you guys to be careful, though. In fact, from this point forward, if you get any calls from me or, especially, JJ, do not say anything until you are given the code word to confirm that it's us."

"That applies to you, too? Dad told us that this guy had used a deep fake that looked like JJ to fool Mom, but does he have one of you, too?" Austin was aware of deep fakes but had never experienced one, other than what he'd seen demonstrated on TV and online.

"We don't think he has a deep fake version of me or anyone other than JJ, but we can't be 100% certain. I've seen the deep fake version of JJ on a video call, and no way would I have known that it wasn't her. So bottom line, if JJ calls for whatever reason, she must give you the code word 'cabernet' before you say anything to her. Everybody got that?"

"Anything else, Aunt Kristyn? We're scared for our mom, but we're just as scared for you and JJ, too." Amy was a sweet and sensitive kid, and Kristyn hoped this experience wouldn't scar her for life. At the very least, there were likely to be years of therapy in her future.

"Not unless you have some kind of crystal ball that can help us locate your mom faster," she answered, trying to show a bit of a smile to end the call on a slightly lighter note.

"Oh my God," screamed Austin. "I know how to find her!"

56

Austin was practically bouncing up and down with excitement, a total 180 from where he'd been moments ago. "Tell us", said Kristyn excitedly, hopefully.

"Last year for Christmas I bought all of us Apple AirTags to put on our keys, backpacks, the dog, whatever. I gave Mom one, too."

"Tell me that she has one with her now!" Kristyn said, starting to feel a slight glimmer of hope.

"Mom actually lost hers, if you can believe it. She's not real good with technology...."

"Keep talking!" John practically yelled.

"Even if she had it with her it wouldn't do us any good, because only her iPhone can track her AirTag. Even Apple engineers and the cops can't track it."

"Dammit, Austin, tell us how this is supposed to help us," snapped John, his patience wearing thin.

"I bought a set of four AirTags for myself, so I gave one to Mom. I helped her secure it under the lining of her suitcase. If she took her usual carryon suitcase, then we may be in luck."

"Austin, since it's your AirTag then I'm assuming that only your phone can track it, right?" Kristyn had heard of AirTags but had never used one, so she was relying on Austin at this point. *Thank God for tech-savvy teens!*

"Right. Let me see if I can pull it up. Pray that the suitcase is still with her and it's in an area with cell coverage."

"Is that all you need, cell coverage, to be able to track it?" Kristyn hoped that was the case.

"It's a little bit more complicated than that, but that's a start. We need to have someone, hopefully multiple people, that have iPhones within Bluetooth range. Like within a couple hundred yards." Austin was talking fast, even as his fingers flew over the screen of his phone.

"We know that your mom's phone is turned off or destroyed. We started trying to track her via her phone the second we knew she was taken, but the last hit we had on it was at LAX." Kristyn muted the call momentarily and yelled out, "JJ, get in here! I think we may have found a way to pinpoint Stacey's location!"

JJ practically flew into the room. "What ya got?"

Kristyn briefly updated JJ and she, like all the others, immediately had a reason to be hopeful.

It only took a few minutes and then Austin said excitedly, "I found it! It's still functioning and I've locked-in on the location. We got lucky: apparently this guy has an iPhone, too, and that let us home in on the AirTag via the 'Find My' network."

Kristyn didn't pretend to understand all of that, but what mattered was that Austin had apparently found the location where Williamson was holding Stacey. "Any chance that the app you're using shows their past location history, like to track them from the time he abducted her at the airport?" She didn't really care, per se, but she anticipated the question coming from some members of the task force.

"No, it doesn't store any location history at all. It only helps you find where something is now."

"That's all that really matters," said JJ. "Great thinking, Austin. Send us a screenshot of that and any other information you have so that we can pass it on asap. This is the kind of break we've been hoping for!"

They concluded the call soon after, and everyone's spirits were drastically improved. There were still plans to be made and work to be done, to be sure, but this was the most important breakthrough they'd had in the case. Just before disconnecting, Kristyn added, "Don't forget guys: not a word about this to anyone. NO ONE!"

JJ was ecstatic. "Thank God that Austin thought of this! This is exactly the kind of information we need. Let's get the task force on a call immediately and have them factor this location into the planning."

"Do you think the task force will be prepared to move on it tonight? It's still early and hours before it's even dark. Presumably they'd want to move on this well after sundown, right?"

"Normally, yes, and I assume that would be the case here. Hopefully since the task force is already in place and all their respective commanders are fully supporting this effort, we'll be able to spin-up this operation quickly. I can't imagine a scenario, with Stacey being held hostage and under constant threat of death, that they'd want to delay this another day."

The call with the task force lasted less than an hour, and the relief everyone felt at this point was palpable. There was still work to be done, plans to be developed, and violence to be unleashed, but that concerned them less than the waiting they'd been doing for the nearly 48 hours since Stacey was taken.

"Kristyn, the target location: is it one of the properties that you'd been checking out?" Marshal Astin was curious.

"Yes sir, it is. There were almost a dozen possible target locations up in Topanga Canyon but this one was on our radar. I've already pulled some Google Earth pictures of the property and will share it with you guys, and I'm getting ready to access whatever information is out there regarding blueprints of the inside of the house. Whatever I get, I'll send to you all immediately."

"Great work, Kristyn," added Isaksen. "And great thinking on the part of your nephew, too. The Bureau could use a young man like that."

Kristyn smiled, then said, "Sorry, sir, but he's not even out of high school yet."

He smiled at Kristyn's response, then continued. "So, it's settled then. Everyone meets here at 2100 hours, where we'll run through the plans one last time, load up the gear, and head to Topanga. We'll plan on hitting the house at 0100, after we give the bomb techs 15 minutes to check for booby-traps, trip wires, and other obstacles around the property. I hope it goes without saying that no one leaves this building tonight without their vests and full tactical gear. We are not losing anyone on this operation because they decided to play superhero. Got me?"

Not a single person in the room was in a hurry to die, but to a person, they'd all be happy to ensure that one certain person didn't make it out alive. No one more so than JJ. *This shit ends tonight!*

57

Isaksen was heads down working on plans and considering every possible scenario and contingency when a call came in on his desk video unit. He answered, surprised to see JJ since they'd spoken just a few hours ago. "Hi JJ, what's up?"

"Evening, sir. Just one bit of information to run by you."

"Sure. I'm surprised you're still working. You've been burning the candle at both ends for days. Why don't you take a few hours, try to relax. It's a perfect evening for a walk on the beach."

"It is, sir, but I just heard from one of my contacts that they saw Williamson at a bar down in Huntington Beach. Nothing about seeing a woman with him, but this source has always been reliable, and I think it's worth checking out."

"And you're thinking maybe Williamson has a place down there and that's where he's holding Stacey?"

"Exactly, sir. Not a slam dunk, but worth checking out. At the same time, I was going to have Kristyn check the VRBO and Airbnb listings to see if we can narrow down the possibilities."

"Good idea. She made quick work of finding his rental place a few days ago, hopefully she can get lucky again."

"What do you think about sending some members of the task force down there to canvas the area while I check out the bar and talk to my source? Maybe if we have enough feet on the street, we'll catch a break."

"I like that. I'll get them headed that way. We'll make sure that most units are in unmarked cars so we don't spook him, but we'll have a strong presence and plenty of backup for you if you do get lucky and find him. If you see him or get a good lead on him, call for backup. Don't be a hero."

"Not to worry, sir. I'm leaving the house now and heading south to Huntington Beach. Can you have the lead officer contact me when they make it to the area, and then I'll rendezvous with them."

"Yes, expect to hear from them within the next hour. I just need to brief them and have them gear up."

***

"JJ, it's Isaksen."

"Yes, sir. What can I do for you sir? Oh, by the way – 'Cabernet'. Even though you called me."

"Better safe than sorry. Williamson just contacted me, using his deep fake version of you. I have to admit, the quality of the voice and video was shockingly good."

"But not good enough to fool you...."

"You give me way too much credit. It would have definitely fooled me. But he started right into the conversation without giving the code word. Just in case, though, I immediately worked the challenge question into the conversation, and he had no clue. Thank goodness we added this little bit of spy craft to our planning."

JJ chuckled. "So you threw out the whole challenge question about being a nice evening for a walk on the beach, and he didn't know to say, *'But I hate getting sand between my toes'*. That's hysterical."

"He seems to be under the illusion that he's always the smartest person in the room, apparently. I'm glad that we're able to disabuse him of that notion, though he doesn't know it yet."

And he'll never get a chance to learn it if I have anything to say about it. "Why do you think he reached out to you, sir?"

"I think he was trying to throw us further off his trail. He claimed – as you – to have heard from a source that he was down in Huntington Beach. He wanted me to send the task force down that way, presumably to keep us from looking anywhere near the Topanga Canyon area."

"Poor, clueless bastard. He has no idea the shitstorm that is about to rain down on him tonight." JJ couldn't help but smile in anticipation, even though it was going to be a huge police, FBI, and US Marshal operation with a lot of people putting their lives on the line.

And if there's any justice in this world, this will be the final shitstorm that Brookes Williamson ever sees.

58

WEDNESDAY, JUNE 7

Everyone was assembled in the large conference room and anxious to get started. At just a few minutes after 9pm, Isaksen, Alexander, and Astin walked into the room and got everyone quieted down. JJ and Kristyn were there, too, though their respective roles in the raid were not yet clearly defined.

The task force spent nearly two hours talking through every detail of the plan. At each step they opened it up to questions, concerns, or outright objections. Remarkably, with that much testosterone in the room, to say nothing of that many different agencies, things stayed on track and relatively calm. Normally, you'd expect raised voices, turf war arguments, or even physical violence. After all that this task force had gone through over the past couple of weeks, they had built up a level of trust and respect that precluded that, thankfully.

Isaksen addressed the room. "Kristyn, you've led the efforts researching this area and pinpointing our target for tonight. What more can you tell us?"

Kristyn was surprised to be put on the spot, but she was determined to rise to the occasion. "As was pointed out in the briefing, the target house is near the very top of Topanga Canyon, only about a quarter mile from the Top of Topanga Canyon overlook. That spot is at 3,000 feet elevation, so keep in mind that anyone looking towards the ocean can see damn near to Hawaii, so it's important that we don't look like an invading army for those assigned to approach from the west on South Topanga Canyon Boulevard." About half of the task force would be coming in from the PCH and heading up the mountain on that route.

Kristyn continued, "Also keep in mind that the street where the target house is, Navajo, has cross streets that connect back to Topanga Canyon Boulevard, so if Williamson manages to make a run for it, he can just as easily head over the mountain towards Mulholland Drive as head back down to the PCH. My money would be on heading towards Mulholland or the 101; it's shorter and gives access to a lot more highways. Heading back down towards the PCH has too many possible choke points."

"Makes sense," chimed in LAPD Detective Morgan, who had helped draft the plans for tonight's action. "And your level of confidence that we're targeting the right place?"

She didn't take offense to the question. The task force members were putting their lives on the line, and potentially putting Stacey's at risk, so they had a right to know anything and everything as far as she was concerned. "I'm going to say 90%, detective. We've checked and double-checked that the AirTag pinged from the target location, but I would have liked to have found more confirmation in the way of sightings, maybe records of food or grocery deliveries, or even more interior pictures of the house. I wish we all could leave here with 100% confidence, but we don't live in a perfect world."

Isaksen interjected. "If it were a perfect world, we'd have time for someone to stakeout the house, or maybe fly a drone over the area to see if we could spot Williamson, or at least his car. The best we've managed to do today is have a couple of unmarked cars drive past the house to see if there was any sign of him, but no luck. His car could have been in the garage, but we couldn't take the chance of getting that close to sneak a look. Bottom line, we got what we got, and we'll have to rely on our planning, training, and execution to make this work."

The meeting broke up soon after. As everyone was filing out of the room, Isaksen, Alexander, and Astin asked JJ and Kristyn to hang back for a few minutes.

"What's up, sir?" asked JJ. She hoped that he wasn't about to say that she and Kristyn had to sit this one out and stay here at the FBI office until the raid was over. If that was the case, he was going to have a hell of an argument on his hands.

Isaksen took the question. "We need to discuss your respective roles this evening. Kristyn, I'd like you to ride with me and the task force leaders in the Mobile Command Unit. I want you out of harm's way but close enough that we can have you there the second we free Stacey. She's going to need a friendly and familiar face."

"Thank you, sir. I want to be there, believe me."

"Good. Even though you'll be on the command bus with us, I want you to wear a vest anyway, just in case. I'm not taking any chances on you getting shot again. You've barely had time to heal from the last time you were shot."

"No problem, sir."

Isaksen continued. "JJ, I wish I could tell you to stay here and away from danger, but God knows you'd find a way to sneak out and make your way to Topanga anyway." He gave her a little smirk. "I want you with us but you're to let the task force teams be the first through the door. You're going to be in full body armor, just like the other team members, but I want you there to focus on freeing Stacey and making sure that she's OK. Get her out of there ASAP and we'll have medical personnel close by."

"Will do, sir. And thanks. This is too important, and personal, for me to miss."

"Well for heaven's sake, try not to shoot anybody. Leave that to the team. And try not to get yourself shot in the process. The paperwork would keep me deskbound until I retire. If they didn't fire me first, that is."

"Of course, sir. I have no desire to be shot again. Ever." Her smile showed that she knew that he was busting her chops while still getting his important point across.

"I can second that," added Kristyn.

Astin spoke up. "Dinner just got delivered to the cafeteria, and everyone is assembled down there. We should head downstairs now and grab something before we have to hit the road. It's going to be a long night."

"Agreed. We'll roll out of here in stages starting around 11:45. I don't want the public, or the press, noticing dozens of vehicles all heading out of here at once and ruining our little surprise."

The only person that should be surprised tonight is Brookes Williamson, right before the bullet hits him between the eyes.

59

THURSDAY, JUNE 8

By 12:15am all the teams were at their assigned locations. Vehicles were strategically positioned to be able to block traffic and cut off all possible escape routes should it be necessary. The task force leaders and Kristyn were in the Mobile Command Unit and parked at the Top of Topanga Overlook. Close enough, but not too close. JJ was embedded with a team led by SAC Alexander's Hostage Rescue Team (HRT) leader, Harold McLean, who seemed less than pleased to have a civilian tagging along, even one who was ex-FBI. *Screw him. He'll get over it.*

At 12:30 the bomb squad team, made up of experts from the FBI and LAPD, made their way about 100 yards on foot to check for booby traps. It was tricky going as they moved through the woods and uneven landscape. Fortunately, their night vision goggles helped considerably by lighting the way for them, but still, due to the natural hazards as well as the potential hazards of trip wires or IEDs, they moved gingerly.

The bomb squad took their time and searched thoroughly. They found nothing as they moved through the woods, no signs of trip wires tied between trees, no signs of disturbed ground that might indicate a buried IED, no hazards or booby traps strung from the trees. That was an old trick that the cartels, as well as American pot growers up in the wild hills of Oregon and California used to do: hang sharpened treble fishing hooks at face level. Many a law enforcement member had ended up with a hook in their face, or worse, in an eye, from this simple and cheap 'security'.

Finally reaching the house itself, the team checked for wired doors and windows, as well as any evident security cameras, around the entire perimeter. They also checked for wired explosives attached to the gas meter and outdoor HVAC units and all other utility connections. Nothing. They were surprised, but relieved.

McLean reported in. "This is Boomer 1 calling task force leaders."

"Go ahead Boomer 1. Task force leaders are all present and can hear you."

"Team has searched entire perimeter of the property and the house itself. No indication of bombs or any other type of booby trap. You're clear to proceed."

Isaksen, Alexander, and Astin all exchanged a look that showed their relief.

Alexander responded. "Good work, Boomer 1. Have your team fall back to your secondary positions as backup to primary breach teams."

"Acknowledged, sir. Falling back to our secondary staging position."

"Kristyn, breach is in less than five minutes. Can we get one final confirmation on the AirTag ping?" Isaksen and the others had already asked for this a half dozen times this evening, but Kristyn understood their concerns.

"Standby, sir. My nephew is still online with me. Let me have him check."

"Austin, one final check. Can you ping the AirTag one last time and confirm the location, please."

"I'm looking at it right now, Aunt Kristyn, and it hasn't moved. Confirmed that it's still at the target location." He hesitated for one moment, then added, "Be careful, and don't let anything happen to my mom. Please bring her home to us safely."

Kristyn turned to the team leaders. "We're confirmed, sir."

Astin got on the comms and spoke to the task force. "All teams, we are ready to go in one minute. I repeat, one minute. On my command."

That minute seemed interminable to everyone assembled. Even for grizzled veterans, these 60 seconds felt like a lifetime. Their adrenaline was pouring, their tension off the charts. It took all their training and discipline not to jump the gun and move too early, possibly jeopardizing lives and the mission.

"*Breach! Breach! Go! Go! Go!*"

60

At 1:00am on the dot the FBI HRT team hit the front and back door at the same time while others broke windows on each side of the house. Flashbangs were tossed in from all directions, and only seconds later more than a dozen heavily armed rescue team members crashed through the doors.

Guns drawn, they went from room to room, yelling for anyone inside to get on the ground, hands over their head. With the house filled with smoke from the flashbangs, it was an otherworldly scene with the flashlights attached to their weapons casting an eerie glow as the team worked their way through the house. Half the team moved upstairs, carefully, but within minutes the teams had cleared every single room. No Brookes Williamson. No Stacey.

HRT leader McLean screamed into his radio. "This is team leader. Check every single room, move every single piece of furniture, every carpet, everything, to see if there's a safe room or tunnel leading out of here. Do it now!"

JJ was cleared to enter the house once every room had been checked, and she was confused and stunned that HRT hadn't found anyone inside. Still, she rushed in to do whatever she could to try to determine what had happened to Stacey. She announced herself as she entered, being careful not to startle any of the team members already inside and likely on edge. "This is Jansen, entering the house now."

"Affirmative, Jansen. We've cleared every room, no sign of the targets. We need to find something, anything, to show that they were ever here. Focus there." This from McLean.

"On it," answered JJ. She couldn't wrap her head around the situation and the turmoil was impacting her mind and her body. *No way that Kristyn and Austin were mistaken. There has to be something more to it.* She wanted desperately to talk to Kristyn, to comfort her, but finding evidence that Stacey and Williamson had been here took precedence.

She put on latex gloves and reached for her evidence kit and proceeded to do a quick, cursory search of the kitchen, living room, and other first floor spaces before heading upstairs. She found nothing in the master suite, but finally hit paydirt in the guest bedroom. Stacey's suitcase, still with her ID attached to the handle, was in the closet. Not hidden, just right there in plain sight. "I've got Stacey's suitcase," she announced over the radio for all to hear. I'll bring it up to the Mobile Command Unit as soon as I'm finished processing this room."

She photographed everything, including where the suitcase sat in the closet, everything that was in the dresser and chest of drawers, on the nightstands, everything. As she looked around the walls and pulled back the curtains, she found what she knew was evidence that Stacey had been held here at some point: large holes around the perimeter of each window that indicated that something, likely a piece of plywood, had been bolted over them to keep someone from breaking out or someone outside seeing in. As she looked down at the carpet, she found even more proof that she was on the right track in the form of a few wood splinters and sawdust that had obviously been missed when cleaning up.

"I'm done here, can someone meet me at the house and drive me back to the bus ASAP. We need to process this right away."

"We'll have one of the cars waiting for you as soon as you get outside," responded Alexander.

As JJ turned to leave the room, her phone alerted her to a FaceTime call. Once again, she was shocked to see 'herself' on the distant end of the call. "Bravo, bravo, JJ! Great job finding the house, but how bad for you that Stacey and I aren't there. You should know by now that you shouldn't try to match wits with me. You and the rest of the cretins on the task force are only half-qualified, at best."

"Your luck is quickly running out, you asshole! We're coming to get Stacey, and you."

"Oh, I shudder! How I've enjoyed watching you search the house, especially Stacey's former bedroom. I do admire your thoroughness and professionalism. Not that it's going to matter in the end."

How the hell? JJ looked around, trying to locate the camera that had to have been focused on her.

"Want to make this a game, JJ? Want me to say 'hotter' and 'colder' as you look around the room for the camera? I'm guessing you're in too much of a hurry for that, but I'm happy to play the game if you want."

She didn't want to give him the satisfaction of going along with his taunting, but she was at a bit of a loss. Then she noticed it: a charger plugged into an electrical outlet, but no USB cord plugged in. She'd seen these before in online ads, but never in person. A small camera built directly into the USB charger; not the greatest coverage or resolution, but more than sufficient to get the job done. As she moved to grab the device from the wall, Williamson started to applause on the video.

"Great work, JJ. You are good, I'll give you that. But no matter. I'm better. And Stacey is still mine, at least for as long as I want to have her. Oh, and I do plan to '*have her*'. Bye now!"

JJ wanted to scream, but she couldn't take the time to dwell on it. Grabbing the suitcase, she ran down the stairs and out of the house as fast as she could. Jumping into the waiting car, she immediately got on the radio. "I'll be at the command center in 3 minutes. Williamson just hit me up on FaceTime, and I have an idea on how to track him. I need Kristyn and your top tech people at the command center when I get there."

"We'll be waiting," answered Astin.

JJ's heart was pumping, and the disappointment she'd felt just a few short minutes ago was being replaced by determination and cautious optimism. Optimistic because all indications were that Stacey was still alive. Optimistic because his narcissism and belief in his own superiority may have just led to his undoing. And optimistic because she still believed that Brookes Williamson had zero intention of being taken alive when cornered. *That was perfect because she had zero intention of him being taken alive either.*

61

Kristyn was barely holding it together. She had been hoping and praying that the task force would rescue Stacey and this nightmare would be over, but now she felt like they were back at square one. Austin had been even more upset, feeling like he had failed his mother, but fortunately Kristyn and Isaksen had been able to talk him down and convince him that his information had been spot-on and that they were certain that Stacey had been there at some point. It was hard, but Kristyn convinced him to drop from the call and promised that she'd reach out to him, Amy, and his dad as soon as she knew anything.

Moments later, JJ rushed into the bus. "Guys, gather up. I have an idea for tracking our guy."

"Do you want to fill us in on what Williamson said when he contacted you?", asked Alexander.

"I don't want to waste time with that now, so let me just summarize it by saying that he thinks he's smart, we're dumb, and he still has Stacey. And he thinks he's even smarter because he knew that we were in the house."

"How? Did you see cameras when you went in?" asked Astin.

"No, sir. I don't think anybody did. But it was obvious that he was watching me from our conversation, and he didn't try to hide it. He even challenged me to make it a game of finding them, but before things went too far, I found this in the room where we know that Stacey was being held." She held out the USB spy camera for all to see.

"How is this going to help us find him?" asked Isaksen.

"Because this camera was not connected to Wi-Fi, so he must be accessing the video via cellular or via a mobile hotspot."

"How do you know that it wasn't connected via Wi-Fi?" asked Kristyn.

"Because I did a quick check from my phone and there was no Wi-Fi network in the house. I was able to detect a couple of very weak Wi-Fi signals, but they would have to be from homes down the road from the target house."

The tech guys were listening to the conversation and knew where JJ was going with this. Their fingers were already flying across their keyboards looking for actively pinging cell signals in the area, any hotspot activity they could pinpoint, and any possible traces of the data packets that were probably still being transported from the other cameras in the house to Williamson's computer.

JJ turned to Kristyn. "We need you to do your magic again, too. You and Austin did a great job of finding this house, and you were right on the money. Now we need you to look for another house, probably within a couple of blocks, that would have been rented around the same time. If we're lucky, maybe using the same alias, but I wouldn't count on it."

Isaksen spoke up. "You think he might be that close?"

"Yes, sir. I think it's a virtual certainty. I think he's close enough that he was watching as we raided the wrong house. I know that we can't start a house-to-house search, at least not yet, but my gut tells me that we're going to find that he's right here under our noses. That plays to his narcissism, for sure."

It took almost 20 minutes before the tech team had any answers. "JJ, your hunch was right! Come see!"

Everyone crowded around the monitors while the team leader explained what they'd found. "As you would expect, we're seeing dozens of mobile phones pinging off the cell towers in the area, and we've been able to cross-reference every one of those numbers to an owner and address here in the neighborhood. Except for one."

"So, it's a burner phone then. And it has to be Williamson." Alexander made the leap.

The tech leader continued. "I can't attest to that, sir, but if I had to guess I'd say you're correct. It appears to be a burner phone, and we're trying to see if we can identify where and when it was purchased, but this time of night presents some challenges there. At least if we try to do things the legal way."

"How close can you get to an exact location?", asked JJ.

"Within about 100 yards so far, but at the very least we know that we can eliminate about 75% of the homes in this neighborhood based on proximity and the fact that we identified the legitimate phones belonging to people residing in those homes."

"What about the data packets and the hotspot that you mentioned. Any luck there?" Astin was like everyone, growing more anxious by the minute.

"We're still capturing data packets from the other cameras in the initial target home, and we can identify the IP Address of the computer receiving the data packets, but unfortunately that's not helping us drill down to the exact address. Good for evidence if this case goes to trial, but not much help in the here and now."

JJ kept pushing for more. "And the hotspot? Is that how he's connecting? Wouldn't he have to be within a couple of hundred yards?"

"Less than that in most cases. Usually, it's about 50 feet to maybe 300 feet, but it depends on a number of different factors. In other words, 'your mileage may vary'."

"Still, because of the elevation change in this neighborhood it's possible that there could be some homes within that range that are the next street up or down the hill, right?" JJ was hoping against hope that they could narrow this down quickly.

"I suppose that's possible. If we factor in the hotspot data, I think we can eliminate another dozen or so homes from consideration. Hopefully Kristyn can narrow it down further with her real estate search."

All eyes turned to Kristyn, still head down at her own workstation. Sensing everyone staring at her, she said, "I think I may have it." She was trying not to act overly confident, still feeling the sting of having missed Stacey earlier.

Everyone crowded around Kristyn, and she mirrored her PC onto one of the large monitors for easier viewing. "I found this house that just went under contract last week. We never considered the possibility that Williamson would buy a house; in every other instance, he's been doing short term rentals. The purchase was done under an alias, of course, but it doesn't look like the realty company, or the mortgage company, did much in the way of due diligence on their background checks, because it only took me a few minutes to see that almost everything on his applications was fake."

"Where is this place?" Isaksen was cutting to the chase.

"It's just like JJ guessed, the next block up the hill, and with perfect sightlines to the house that we targeted." Kristyn pulled up a detailed map of the area, followed by a view from Google Earth, and it was evident that she was correct.

"We need to come up with a plan, on the fly, to hit this place quickly before he's able to skate away again." Isaksen was always biased towards action.

Alexander nodded. "I agree. We can't fit the whole task force in here, but let's get the team leaders up here pronto and build a plan, then they can flow it to their guys."

Isaksen turned to the communication specialists. "Get the team leaders up here immediately, and everyone else maintains their current position. From this point forward, let's keep all communications on encrypted protocol only. No analog communications that might be picked up by scanner under any circumstances."

Your time is up, asshole!

62

"Based on the view we have from Google Earth and the realty list-ings that Kristyn found online, it looks like this house is close to its neighbors. We're not going to have to wind our way through the woods and worry about trail cameras and a million places for booby-traps." Astin was speaking.

"True," said HRT leader McLean, "but it means we're totally exposed as we approach the house. Maybe from the moment we pull onto the street. We need to consider that he might take advantage of the higher ground and fire on us from an upstairs window."

"Or, at the very least, see you coming and have time to kill the hos-tage and escape." Morgan felt bad bringing that up in front of Kristyn and JJ, but his point couldn't be ignored.

"Here's the bottom line, as I see it," interjected JJ, growing tired of the back and forth that had been going on for the last 10 minutes. "Just because he didn't set any booby-traps or wire any doors or windows with explosives at the first house doesn't mean that he hasn't done it here. I think it's likely that he has; this is where he's making his last stand. We need the bomb techs to check every possible point of entry for explosives, and once we're inside, it's up to each of us to keep an eye out for trip wires or other traps." JJ was going to be paired-up with the HRT team again on this part of the operation.

Isaksen jumped in. "And this time it's imperative that we do a better job of leveraging our technology, like reconnoitering the area around the house with night vision equipment to detect any security cameras around the perimeter. And let's get that drone up there, neighborhood and privacy concerns be damned, and take advantage of its thermal imaging to see if we can detect the two of them and where they are within the house." He didn't want to point out that he had advocated for use of the drone's thermal imaging capability before approaching the first house, but the idea was rejected by the Assistant DA that had been assigned to accompany them on this operation. *Fucking bureaucrat.*

"Enough talking; we need to roll," said Morgan with obvious irritation in his voice. "If we keep sitting here dicking around, he's going to either harden his position or find a way to escape. He knows we're still in the area and probably planning a house-to-house search. Let's get this show on the road before it's too late."

The teams rolled-out and moved to their staging locations. The drone operator situated himself one block uphill from the new target house and launched it from one of the LAPD SUVs. He guided it in a circuitous route before bringing it close to the target. "Drone up and circling the target. You should have the feed from the onboard cameras and thermal imaging."

"We have your feed coming through now," answered one of the command center techs. The feed was shared on one of the 65" monitors, and it didn't take long to identify that there were two heat signatures – two people – on the first floor of the house.

"This is Isaksen to all teams. Confirmation that we have two people on the first floor, southwest side of the house. One appears to be moving around, the other stationary."

"Sir, based on the floorplan that I was able to access, I'd say that they're in the family room. It appears to be an open floorplan, so the kitchen opens to the family room and formal living room. There are four windows along that side of the house, and it appears to be less than 25 feet from the front entrance." Kristyn was fighting hard to push down her anxiety and nervousness. Keeping busy and contributing to the effort helped.

Isaksen communicated that information to the team, then asked them, "HRT leader, what do you see on the perimeter?"

McLean responded, "So far we've detected four cameras, two in the front and two in the back, and we're prepared to blind them when the boomer team is ready to approach."

"Affirmative. Boomer 1, your team is up. HRT team is clearing the path for you with the cameras." He didn't have to add that he hoped that Williamson wasn't monitoring the cameras closely enough to notice that they'd been effectively disabled.

To everyone's relief, there were no shots fired as the teams approached. They didn't know whether to chalk that up to luck or Williamson's lack of attention, but either way they were relieved to be able to make it safely to their positions around the house. Still, the bomb teams were experienced professionals, and they knew that if a suspect made the approach easy, it's usually because they have a surprise, *or surprises*, waiting elsewhere.

It took longer than they'd hoped, but finally the boomer team had cleared all the points of entry, and as JJ had predicted, they found doors and several windows wired to blow. Finding the traps was not always easy, and never fast, but disarming them and making it safe for the teams to breach was a whole other level of difficulty. One wrong move could detonate the explosives, likely killing the bomb technician and possibly others in the area, including the hostage.

"This is Boomer 1 to command. All planned points of entry have been neutralized and made safe. You are clear to move your teams into position and prepare to breach."

Isaksen, Astin, and Alexander conferred, and then Alexander responded. "HRT team leader, prepare to breach on my command. All other teams, take your positions and prepare for breach. Take every possible precaution to ensure the safety of the hostage. Boomer 1, we'd like your team to follow right behind HRT to look for any traps and explosives inside, help keep them and the hostage safe."

"Affirmative, sir," responded Boomer 1.

Astin added an important point. "The hostage appears to be within

10-15 feet of the windows on the southwest side of the house. Keep that in mind as you breach, and let's not put any flashbangs too close to her position."

Two minutes later Alexander confirmed that everyone was in place and waiting on his command. He looked at Isaksen and Astin to ensure they concurred with the action, and they both nodded their agreement. He looked at Kristyn to reassure her and, maybe in some small way, look for her blessing. She'd been through hell throughout this ordeal but had been an incredibly valuable team member. Without question, she had skin in the game. She nodded and smiled nervously.

"Breach! Breach! Go! Go! Go!"

63

THURSDAY, JUNE 8

The HRT team hit the front and back doors with massive battering rams at the same time, and both doors flew off their hinges. Windows crashed on both sides of the house, and half a dozen flash bangs flew in from the front, back, and east sides. The noise was deafening, and the flashes were so bright it was like the surface of the sun. Anyone inside would have been incapacitated; in Stacey's case, that was true. Her chair had toppled over with her still strapped to the chair's arms and legs, and she was unconscious.

Brookes had noticed the lack of security camera coverage seconds before the teams breached, but it gave him just enough time to dive for cover in the walk-in kitchen pantry. It was still loud, but much less painful than if he'd been on the other side of the door. Most importantly, the darkened pantry, coupled with his eyes being tightly shut, spared him that pain and disorientation. Slowly rising to one knee, he took a moment to regain his balance and coordination and allow his hearing to partially return. Working in the dark, he reached for his holstered Glock 9mm and made sure that he had one in the chamber and ready to go. He felt the pockets on his vest to make sure that he still had spare magazines within reach. *Maybe not enough ammunition to escape, but enough to take down a lot of them before they take me.*

Wanting to strike quickly while his enemies were still fanning out throughout the house and clearing each room, Brookes pushed open the pantry door and burst out with his gun blazing, not bothering to aim

264

but just shooting in the general direction of anyone he saw. Two men in FBI jackets went down, and as he turned to head towards the garage several more men in FBI and LAPD vests and jackets appeared. Shots rang out and missed him by only inches; he ducked behind the large kitchen island. The island provided some cover, but he knew that he'd be surrounded quickly and killed or captured. And, in his mind, being captured was not an option.

He pulled a black box from his vest that had three red buttons on it. He knew that he had only seconds to act before even more cops would descend on him. *This will prove to the world that I am the greatest Slayer of all time.* He pressed the first button on the box and immediately there was a loud, powerful explosion on the second floor at the back of the house. He had no idea if anyone was up there, nor did he care. The violent explosion sent everybody scrambling and provided the diversion he needed. He jumped up from behind the island and fired off four quick rounds and managed to wound one of the LAPD officers.

Brookes pushed the second button and another explosion, this one also upstairs and right across the hallway from the first blast, again caused a massive concussion and more chaos. He could hear the screams coming from upstairs and took satisfaction in knowing that he'd at least taken out many of his pursuers.

Time to make a break for it. Reaching in another vest pocket, he pulled out what looked like two grenades. Pulling the pins, he tossed them towards the family room and a thick fog of purple smoke wafted from the canisters. Using the smoke as cover, he leapt up from behind the island and headed straight towards the door to the garage. Before he'd taken a second step, he felt an intense pain and burning as a bullet hit him in the left bicep and almost took him down. Raising his gun in his right hand, he fired repeatedly and indiscriminately, having no idea where his attacker was positioned. Right now, it wasn't about hitting someone, it was only about having cover fire and time to escape. He fired until he was out of bullets, and by then he was pushing his way through the door into the garage.

He quicky popped another magazine into his gun, despite being slowed by the incredible pain where he'd just been shot. Blood was trailing him and running down his arm, but he couldn't take time to focus on that now. Quickly making his way to the side garage door, he looked quickly to make sure that there was no one hidden there waiting to take him down. Fortunately for him, the explosions had the desired effect and had everyone rushing towards the house to rescue the wounded. *Just like I planned. Now the third explosion will take the whole house to the ground with everyone in it.* The thought made him smile.

Moving quickly outside, he ran to a small fenced-in area that hid the home's HVAC systems and backup generator from view. Behind those there was something large lying on the ground with a dark tarp covering it. Pulling back the tarp revealed a Yamaha YZ250F trail bike which he quickly stood up and rolled out of the fenced area. Jumping on, he kickstarted it in one smooth motion. Wasting no time, he punched the gas and headed for the street.

HRT leader McLean was only a couple of steps behind, but Williamson was accelerating quickly. He made it to the street and took a quick right. Reaching the street only a couple of seconds later, McLean fired nearly 20 rounds at the fleeing bike. Several shots hit the bike, but apparently none hit Williamson since he maintained control and kept going.

Getting on the radio, McLean practically yelled, "Williamson is getting away! He's on a motorcycle heading towards the end of the road, but it's a dead end. We need to move all units that way and try to block him in."

"McLean, this is Jansen. I wounded him before he fled, not sure how badly. I have a trail of blood from the kitchen and out into the garage."

"This is Isaksen. There's a trail at the end of the street that's used for hikers, horses, and BMX-type bikes, and it runs for about a mile and connects to Mulholland Drive. Apparently, this trail is so small and narrow it doesn't even have a name. We need to start moving units up to Mulholland and the surrounding area where dirt roads, fire trails, and hiking trails are shown on the map."

Kristyn couldn't take it any longer. "Please, somebody tell me what's going on with Stacey. Is she safe?" She was almost scared to hear the answer after all the gunfire and explosions coming from the home.

JJ quickly responded. "She's alive, but we need the EMTs in here right now. She's unconscious and has multiple visible injuries, including heavy bruising, abrasions, and what appears to be burns or marks from a stun gun. There might be damage to her jaw and right orbital socket, too. I'll have her ready for the EMTs to take over and transport as soon as they get here."

Kristyn's relief at hearing that Stacey was alive was quickly washed away by hearing JJ's description of her injuries. "I'm riding with the EMTs". She didn't expect anyone to object, and they didn't.

McLean cut in. "We found something on the street that Williamson dropped, likely when one or more of the bullets hit the bike."

"What is it?" asked Alexander.

"It appears to be a detonator, and it has three buttons. Presumably it's one button per explosive, and he already set off two."

Alexander, Isaksen, and Astin looked at each other in horror, totally understanding the implications. Alexander barked into the radio, "Get everyone out of that house immediately. Now! Boomer 1, once everyone has cleared the premises, we'll have your team re-enter and neutralize whatever remaining threat there may be."

"Affirmative, sir." Boomer 1's adrenaline started spiking again, for what seemed like the umpteenth time tonight. *God, what a rush!*

64

THURSDAY, JUNE 8

Even though it was the middle of the night, Kristyn called Stacey's family immediately to report that she was safe. Since she didn't know the extent of Stacey's injuries, she wanted to keep it as non-committal as possible but at least assure them that she was alive and on the way to the hospital.

John picked up on the first ring. "Kristyn, tell me you have some news. We're going crazy here!"

"We recovered Stacey, and we're heading to the hospital once the EMTs have her stabilized."

"Stabilized. What does that mean?" asked Amy, almost scared to hear the answer. "Like from a heart attack?"

"No, not at all. Your mom was unconscious when they raided the house, so they're trying to make sure she's not severely injured. Like a concussion, or a neck or back injury. I'm on my way down to meet the EMTs now and ride with her to the hospital. I'll let you know as soon as I know more."

"What about that bastard Brookes Williamson? Please tell me that you guys killed him," said Austin. He could be forgiven the cursing and the dark thoughts after what they'd been through, and what they imagined Stacey had been through. Even John, generally the disciplinarian in the family, didn't raise any objection.

"He got away, but we know he's injured, and we have dozens of assets out looking for him now. We don't think he'll get very far; he's in some very rugged and steep country, and with his injury, he's going to find it terribly difficult to navigate those trails. Most are barely wide enough for people to hike in the daytime, so he's going to have a hell of a time at night."

"Were any of your people hurt?" asked John.

Kristyn didn't want to go there, especially since she didn't have the facts yet. "There were a few injuries – there almost always are in this kind of operation – but I don't know the extent. This literally just happened in the last five minutes so I don't have all of the details. I just wanted you guys to know that we have your mom and she's safe."

"I want to fly out there to be with my mom," Austin said through his tears and anger.

"I think you all should. Why don't you guys look for flights to-morrow morning and let me know when you're scheduled to arrive. I'll circle back with you tonight as soon as I know which hospital they're taking her to, and of course I'll give you an update on her condition as soon as I know anything."

Kristyn cut the call short so she could ride with Isaksen down to the site. She was already feeling anxiety because she hadn't been there when Stacey was brought out of the house. *I should be the first person she sees, damn it.*

Isaksen keyed his radio with one hand while driving like a mad man with the other. "Boomer 1, this is SAC Isaksen. Has the site been cleared?"

"Yes, sir," responded Boomer 1. "We found a pipe bomb taped to the natural gas line where it comes into the house from the meter and con-nects to the furnace. We've already made it safe and removed it from the premises."

"That sounds like it had the potential to create a pretty massive explosion, right?"

"Yes, sir. The first two explosions, both upstairs, were small by comparison. Basically, it was just something to slow us down without any structural damage, though several of our people were injured, two of them pretty severely. This bomb, if it had gone off, would have likely blown the whole house to hell and back. I think it was his 'you'll never take me alive' plan."

"Affirmative. I'll be onsite in less than two minutes. You can brief me when I get there."

As they approached, there was no doubt which house was involved, as there were more than a dozen police vehicles, several fire engines, and at least seven EMT vehicles. The fire was mostly out and seemed to be confined to the back of the house, a result of the two explosions that Williamson had detonated.

As they pulled up, Kristyn practically leapt from the car before it had even stopped. She was sickened to see several men and women in uniform on stretchers, though she couldn't tell the extent of their injuries. Finally spotting Stacey being wheeled down the sidewalk, she sprinted across the lawn to reach her side. Right away she noticed that Stacey was still unconscious, and that scared the hell out of her. Turning to the EMTs, she started peppering them with questions. "She's my sister, please tell me what's wrong with her. Why is she unconscious? Did she get hurt in the explosions, or as our teams were breaching the house?"

"We won't know anything for certain until we get her to the hospital and get a CT, and maybe an MRI, done. My guess, though, is that she was already unconscious before all of this went down. Based on her pinpoint pupils and a few other telltale signs, I think she may have been drugged. That would actually be a blessing, at least compared to brain trauma from the explosions."

"Anything else you can tell at this early stage, like any injuries that are going to require surgery and long recovery or rehab? I know it's best guess at this point...." She wanted to ask, but resisted, if there was evidence of sexual assault. *Fuck that, call it what it is: rape.* She was terrified of what they might say.

"She's been beaten and abused pretty badly, and I noted at least a dozen spots where she's been burned with what appears to be a stun gun. She's going to need quite a few stitches, and I'd be surprised if she doesn't need surgery on her right cheek and eye socket. Maybe even plastic surgery. She's got to be one tough lady to have lived through this."

The EMTs loaded Stacey in the ambulance and Kristyn climbed in with her. It was all she could do to hold it together. While relieved at rescuing Stacey and finding her alive, she knew that she would never rest until Williamson was either captured or dead. *Preferably dead. Wait....make that definitely dead.*

65

THURSDAY, JUNE 8

SAC Alexander and Marshal Astin were taking point back in the Mobile Command Center, and they were both apoplectic that their teams had suffered numerous injuries and, to make matters worse, Williamson had escaped. The only saving grace, at least so far, is that there had not been any casualties and, per the EMTs, the injuries, though serious, did not appear to be life threatening.

Practically yelling into the radio, Alexander started barking orders. "I need six units moving to Mulholland Drive immediately. Position units where the trail connects back to Mulholland as well as in both directions. Then give me at least four units blocking all entrances to the 101 at Topanga Canyon Boulevard." *God help us if he gets that far out of the containment area at Mulholland. And what about all the back roads leading to the 101?*

Astin was checking the detailed maps of Topanga Canyon. "We need to get every possible air asset we have moving asap."

Alexander nodded and spoke into the radio once more. "Get both of those drones up and moving now. Thermal imaging should be able to lock-in on the motorcycle's heat signature, plus we should be able to zero-in on his headlight out there in the darkness. Let's get the FBI chopper that we staged down off the PCH moving this way right now, and let's get in touch with LAPD and ask them to get a chopper to join the search, too. We need all hands on deck."

Astin spoke to Alexander. "This is a fucking nightmare. There must be 50 miles of trails, maybe more, and our vehicles can't navigate any of them. The smart money says that he'll try to get to Mulholland Drive – it's barely more than a mile away – and from there go balls-to-the-wall for the 101."

"The only things we have going for us at this point is that he's wounded and the trail he's on is narrow and treacherous as hell, even for a dirt bike. It's rated for horses and hikers, primarily. This time of night, he'll be lucky to make it that mile."

"If he sees our cars closing in on the Mulholland end of the trail, he could double back and hit one of the other trails that borders the Caplow Property and reconnects with Mulholland several miles from where we're setting up the blockade." Astin was feeling overwhelmed by all the roads, trails, and rugged terrain they had for a search area.

Alexander considered their predicament. "Bottom line, I think we have to put every possible asset in the air and find him that way, then try to hem him in from all directions. It's not going to be easy; like you said, that's rugged countryside out there and a lot of cover."

"Let's get the HRT team on both of those choppers. I'm going to call in a couple of favors and see if I can get us at least one more copter up here to go with the two we already have."

"Agreed. And if you have any resources that can lend us drones, that would be a huge help." Alexander was sometimes old school and liked to rely on the human element, but he was sure that this operation demanded every bit of technological advantage they could get. "And let's formalize the rules of engagement to everyone in the field: if you have the shot, take the shot."

***

Brookes was hurting. Badly. He always prided himself on his pain tolerance, but this was beyond anything he had experienced before. *My kingdom for a shot of morphine!* The bullet he'd taken in the arm was not a clean through and through, instead shattering some bone and doing considerable damage to the soft tissue. There was a lot of blood, but that was actually the least of his worries. He wasn't going to bleed to death, of that he was certain, but the same couldn't be said about crashing the bike and tumbling down the hillside.

Even in the daylight he knew that he'd have to take it slow on this trail, with its twists and turns, its narrowness, and deep ruts from the recent heavy rains. But at night? It was all but impossible to navigate, especially since he was forced to keep the headlight off. That light would be like a beacon for the cops. More than once he found himself making a wrong turn onto an even smaller side trail. Every bump, every turn, sent excruciating pain through his arm, almost to the point of blacking out. *That would surely be a death sentence out here in this hellish place.*

As he approached the trail's end at Mulholland Drive, he saw the lights from multiple police cars and SUV's approaching from both directions. Slowing to a stop, he looked around and saw more police units than he could count coming from both directions on Mulholland and other roads leading to the 101. Normally, a skilled bike rider could outrun the cops, skirting their roadblocks, cutting through yards and alleys, and making them look like fools. Unfortunately for him, he was a novice rider, at best, and he was injured. He had no illusions of evading so many cops, at least not on the streets. His only chance was the wilderness, following the miles of trails, and hopefully finding a place to connect back to a main road well beyond their roadblocks. *Then the wilderness is where I make my last stand.*

66

JJ jumped into the first copter with McLean and two other members of the HRT. They took off the second everyone was on board and turned straight towards the trail that Williamson had taken. The copter's floodlight lit the way, and it took barely any time to cover the distance from the end of the street up to Mulholland. "No sign of him on this particular trail, so we're going to have to widen our search," said the pilot. "We'll fly a grid pattern to see if we can locate him, and as soon as the other chopper gets here, we'll divide and conquer."

"Do you have the thermal imaging fired-up, too?" asked JJ. "We might have an easier time picking up the heat signature from the motorcycle."

"Yes, ma'am. We have both systems active," he responded.

With every passing minute, the HRT members' tension grew, as did JJ's. The HRT team was beyond pissed because of the injuries sustained by their teammates as well as the LAPD. Add to that the fact that Williamson had rigged the whole house to blow, potentially killing everyone onsite, and they were lusting for blood. They had no intention of letting him escape, and though they may not voice it, not even one of them intended to let him be captured alive. Neither did JJ.

"I didn't think there'd be quite so much cover out here in the canyons. More trees than I expected," said McLean. "Going to make this harder and take longer than I'd hoped."

"That's why I think the thermal imaging is going to be our ace in the hole. He can hide from the spotlight, but nothing he can do about the heat coming off that engine, or his own body heat, for that matter." JJ was cautiously optimistic that one of the thermal imaging units, whether on one of the drones or one of the copters, was going to find him before too much longer. There's only so much terrain he could have covered before we were in the air.

"Chopper 1 and Chopper 2, this is Alexander. One of our drones just picked up Williamson's heat signature, approximately 2 miles southwest of the trail head where we started. His headlight is off and he's moving slowly, but we have a lock on him. Sending you the coordinates now. Chopper 1, converge on him asap. Chopper 2, advise when you're in range."

The pilot relayed the message to the HRT team, and they were ready for action. "He's still got a lot of tree cover, but we have a lock on his position."

McLean spoke to the team. "I want one shooter on each side, and if you have a shot, you take it. JJ, you're with me on this door."

"Do you want me to take the shot?" asked JJ.

"How good are you?"

"Truthfully, I'm only OK."

"I was a sniper with Marine Recon. Mind if I take the shot?"

JJ could only smile. "I think you've earned it."

The pilot announced, "He's getting ready to lose his tree cover for about 75-100 yards. Be ready. And be advised that Chopper 2 and the rest of your team is still at least 10 minutes out."

McLean checked the strap that was securing him to the copter as he stood on the skid and balanced the sniper rifle on his shoulder. *Thank goodness there's no turbulence up here.* As soon as Williamson emerged, slowly, from the tree line, the spotlight locked on him, and half a second later McLean pulled the trigger.

Even at a slow speed, the bike was bouncing and lurching with the rough terrain, and the bullet narrowly missed Williamson but did hit dead center on the bike's engine, shutting it down immediately. Williamson lost control and the bike went down, with him thrown several feet. The bike appeared to crash down on his legs. That was almost as good.

"Suspect is down but still alive, I repeat, suspect is down but still alive. Motorcycle disabled."

The pilot did a good job of keeping the spotlight focused on him, and despite his injuries, Williamson managed to get his gun from his vest and fired several shots at them. All of them missed by a considerable distance. "No place to land anywhere near here, guys. Feel like a little jump instead?"

"Definitely. See if you can put us down near him but not so close where he may get lucky with that pistol. Maybe at the edge of the tree line. And get on the radio to Chopper 2, tell them what we're doing and invite them to the party."

Turning to JJ, McLean asked, "You have any experience rappelling out of a copter? I know you want to be part of this, and that's the only way down."

"I haven't done it since Quantico, but I loved it back then. I'm ready to go. Mind helping hook me up just to make sure I get that part, right? The ride down kinda sucks if you mess that part up."

McLean just smiled and helped her into the harness and double-checked the straps and connection to the copter. "You're all set. I suggest you keep your weapon holstered so you don't drop it, but keep your hands close to it in case you need it."

"OK, team, we're ready to go on the pilot's command. Keep your focus on the suspect because he is armed and seems eager to shoot it out with us. Put down cover fire as needed, but rules of engagement allow for shoot-to-kill. I'm not trading his life for any of yours. I hope that goes without saying."

The pilot came on the intercom. "OK, team, we're near the edge of the clearing, about 100 yards uphill from the suspect. You are cleared to go whenever you're ready."

The chopper was hovering 75 feet from the ground but to JJ it felt like she was looking down from the top of the Empire State Building. *Don't look down. Don't look down.*

Jackson gave the order. "Go! Go!"

JJ muttered a little prayer and stepped out into space. *Am I crazy?*

67

The drop to the ground only took a few seconds, but for JJ it felt interminable and scary as hell. She hadn't admitted to McLean that she almost got booted from the FBI Academy because she had so much trouble rappelling, whether from the stationary towers or from a helicopter. There was no real mystery why she had problems: she was afraid of heights. Not as bad as many people, but still enough to impact her confidence and ability to handle that part of the training. She was able to pass, but barely. She'd worked hard over the years to overcome her fear, using a combination of exposure therapy and a 'just freakin' do it' attitude, and while it was lessened it never entirely went away. *I'm just glad I never had to jump out of a damn plane.*

JJ and McLean quickly unhooked their carabiners and moved for cover. One of the other HRT members that jumped with them, Special Agent Springfield, came under fire from Williamson and, attempting to disconnect quickly and drop for cover, landed awkwardly on the rough and uneven terrain that was made even more treacherous after the rains and flooding that had hit Southern California over the winter.

"This is Springfield to HRT Leader. Taking fire from the suspect but made it down safely. I had a hard landing, nothing broken but pretty sure I have a high ankle sprain. Definitely going to slow me down."

"This is HRT Leader, acknowledged. Hang back and give us cover as needed. We got this."

"What about your other guy, Peters? Did he make it down safely?" JJ was concerned since she hadn't heard him check-in.

McLean shared her concern. "Peters, this is HRT Leader. What's your status?" He waited a moment but got no response. He repeated his call, but still no response.

"Chopper 1, this is HRT Leader. I'm not getting any response from Peters. Do you have eyes on him?"

"This is Chopper 1. No eyes on Peters, but I'm feeling some drag from the starboard side of the aircraft. Maybe he's having trouble unhooking his gear?" What he didn't say, didn't have to say, was that maybe Peters was unable to unhook his gear. Not a pleasant thought, but a real risk with any descent, especially when there is an armed and dangerous suspect shooting wildly at the approaching teams.

Marshal Astin and everyone in the Mobile Command Unit were hearing this and thinking of next steps and how to bring this quickly to an end. "HRT Leader, this is Astin. Chopper 2 and the rest of the team is still about 5 minutes out. We need to get Chopper 1 out of range but still close enough to keep the suspect lit-up. Can you get to Peters and assess the situation?"

Fuck! The whole plan is going to hell! "This is HRT Leader, will do. Jansen and Springfield will provide cover as I make my way over there. It can't be more than 50-100 yards." He turned and signaled to JJ that he was moving downhill to find Peters. She just nodded in acknowledgement.

Several shots rang out and hit within a few yards of his position, and JJ and Springfield responded with heavy fire of their own. Williamson appeared to be in a well-protected position between two large rocks, but he still had to take cover and hold his fire. That was all JJ could hope for at this point.

McLean made it down the hill and was shocked to see Peters sprawled-out on a large boulder, still connected to his rappelling gear. Not good! Before even assessing Peters, he disconnected the gear and informed the pilot so that he could safely clear the area. Turning his attention back to his teammate, he saw a gunshot wound to his right shoulder. Serious, but not fatal, but apparently in this case it was enough to incapacitate Peters and send him hurtling down the rope instead of the controlled descent they've all practiced and performed hundreds of times.

"This is HRT Leader to base. I've located Peters, deceased. Appears to be a hard landing onto a large rock, best guess at this point is that he suffered a broken neck or back. We'll have to evacuate him after this is over." *Now it's down to just the two of us.*

McLean reached out to JJ. "We need to take him now. You circle to the left and close on him from that direction, and I'll move a bit further downhill and come in from the right. And let's try not to shoot each other while we're at it." He hoped that a little bit of levity would cut the tension, though he knew nothing would entirely relieve the stress other than ending this.

JJ moved with as much speed and stealth as the terrain allowed. If she wasn't so focused on Williamson, she would have been concerned about being out here in this wild environment at night knowing that these mountains were home to mountain lions, coyotes, bobcats, and more. As scary as they could be, the human predator she was after was much more of a threat. *But he won't be for much longer.*

The closer she got to his position, the less cover she had available. Hopefully her all-black clothing and protective gear helped to keep her somewhat hidden, otherwise she would be an easy target. As she took the next step, her foot slipped on a rut in the trail and sent a few rocks sliding and bouncing. Immediately three shots rang out and hit within a few yards of her location. *Not that close, but close enough.* She wondered if he even knew who he was shooting at. Not that he probably cared but knowing that it was her would probably excite him to no end. *Maybe even enough to make a mistake?*

"McLean, I'm going to try to draw his fire and give you a chance to get a bit closer. If he knows it's me here and he's got a chance at taking me out, he'll probably lose all focus on you."

"Worth a try, JJ, but be careful. He only has to get lucky once."

JJ took a moment to gather her wits, and before speaking she turned her radio off. *I don't want anyone to hear what I say, not until this is over.* "Brookesy, I told you I'd be the one to get you, the one to end this. And I'm here to keep my promise."

He didn't even bother to respond to her taunt, just rose as far as his injured leg would allow and started firing blindly in her direction. His rage, no doubt coupled with the considerable pain, had his shots wildly scattered.

JJ heard the approach of the second helicopter and saw its sweeping searchlight. Unfortunately, as it approached the light momentarily shined perfectly on McLean as he was struggling to make his way uphill to complete the pincer maneuver. That was all Williamson needed: he swung his gun in that direction and fired two quick shots, one of them hitting McLean in the left thigh and knocking him off his feet.

Rising quickly, JJ fired three shots of her own to send Williamson ducking for cover, and she used that opening to quickly close the gap between them. Coming up behind him, feet planted firmly on a large, flat rock that gave her the perfect high ground advantage, she hissed, "I told you that I'd end this, that I'd end you."

"Go ahead and kill me, bitch! You know that's what you want. Or do you have the guts to do it?"

"Oh, yeah. I have the guts. Now, slowly, pick up your gun. Point it in the general direction of that incoming helicopter." He did as he was told, hoping for a chance to turn the tables and shoot her.

"Now fire three shots, and they better all be way off the mark. You hit that chopper, even once, and I'll make this more painful than you can imagine."

He fired three quick shots. She fired twice in response, one to the chest and one to the head. That was the end of Brookes Williamson.

Quickly turning her radio back on and inserting her earpiece, she called out for McLean. "I'm coming for you now. How badly are you hurt?" She prayed that he was still alive to respond.

"I took one to the leg, bleeding pretty heavily but I'll live. Bullet's still in there, but I don't think it hit anything too vital. Guessing I won't be running any races or doing any ballroom dancing anytime soon."

"I'll be right there. I assume that medics are already on the way, right?"

"Yes, I was able to call it in to the mobile command unit and they're on it now. They're bringing a stretcher from Chopper 1 to ferry me out of here."

It only took a few short minutes to reach him, and JJ immediately started first aid until the medics were able to make their way in. She didn't have a lot to work with, but she was at least able to slow the blood loss and keep pressure on the wound.

"So, JJ, I couldn't hear you on the radio when you caught up to Williamson...."

"Yeah, I think my microphone got knocked loose when I hit the ground earlier...."

"But I did hear him fire three shots......"

"Yeah, he tried one last time to kill me, but luckily he missed....."

"And then I heard you fire twice....."

"Luckily, I didn't miss."

"And that's how it will be recorded in the official report?" he asked with a bit of a knowing smirk.

"Exactly. As they say, 'that's my story, and I'm sticking with it'."

Chapter 69

Thursday, June 8

JJ stayed with McLean and the other HRT team members, both injured and deceased, until they were all evacuated. She then hitched a ride on Chopper 1 back to the Mobile Command Unit and debriefed Isaksen, Alexander, and Astin.

"This was one colossal clusterfuck," Isaksen said by way of kicking things off, "but I'm glad it's finally over. There's going to be a lot of eyes on this, I don't have to tell you, and tons of questions from Washington, the media, and every lawyer that wants his fifteen minutes of fame."

"Way too many innocent people killed, way too many cops killed or injured, and way too much property damage." Astin was still in disbelief that it had taken this long, and this much investment, to bring down one crazed man. Not a good look, in his mind, for the US Marshals.

"And don't forget, an innocent woman dragged into this and beaten, tortured, and used as bait." JJ was referring, of course, to Stacey, and she took that *very* personally.

Isaksen looked at JJ. "Tell me everything about your encounter with Williamson, starting from the time you boarded that helicopter to the moment you walked back in here. Don't leave anything out, and keep in mind that you're probably going to be grilled on this a hundred times by a hundred different people in the coming days." He was saying, without saying it, that she better have her story 100% nailed, including every conceivable detail that might be dissected.. Officially, he cared for the truth. In reality, he knew things weren't always that black and white.

***

JJ finally made it to the hospital after spending what seemed like hours with the task force leadership covering every aspect, every detail, of the operation. She reminded them, more than once, that she was merely a civilian and not in charge of any part of the action. She'd been asked to participate and lend her knowledge and expertise, which she gladly did, but she wouldn't take responsibility for the fallout, including Williamson's death. They had to remind her, conversely, that they weren't trying to throw her under the bus. Anything but. They wanted-

needed - her to be cleared of any wrongdoing and able to stipulate and confirm every step of the operation that they, as leaders, had put into place.

Going straight to Stacey's room, she practically ran into Kristyn's arms, bringing both to tears. "How's Stacey? We've been so worried about her."

"She's regained consciousness, thank God. She's sedated now, which is good because she's in a lot of pain. The doctors say that she's going to need surgery, maybe several, for the injuries to her face and eye socket. Luckily there doesn't appear to be any impact to her vision."

"Thank goodness for that, at least. Did they say how long she'd be here and what she may be facing long-term in the way of rehab?"

"Too soon to tell, but they said early estimates are at least 5-7 days here in the hospital, and tomorrow they'll have some rehabilitation specialists look at her to give us some more information."

"I'm guessing that John and the kids should be arriving this morning?"

"Yes, they get into LAX around 9am. And before they get here, I need to call my parents and Daniel to tell them what has happened. I'm sure they're all going to hate me for keeping it from them. You'll probably be able to hear their screams all the way from Houston and Denver." That drew a bit of a nervous smile from them both.

JJ checked her watch. "I need to check on McLean and Springfield from the HRT team to see how they're doing. Then, if it's OK with you, I'm going to slip home and take a shower, change, and then pick up your family at LAX. I'll bring you a change of clothes, too."

"Are their injuries serious?"

"Springfield probably just has a high-ankle sprain, so he may already be out of here. They probably did a quick X-Ray, taped his ankle, and released him. McLean's is more serious. He took a bullet to the thigh, and they're going to have to extract it and see if there's any damage. He's the kind of guy, though, that they'll probably have to cuff to the bed to keep him here for even 24 hours."

Kristyn smiled. "I don't know about you, but when this is all over, I'd like to be cuffed to the bed so I can sleep for a week straight. No phone calls, no texts, no video, no meetings. Just sleep."

"I think that's something we both need. Hell, something we both deserve."

"Before you go, one question," Kristyn said quietly, almost sheepishly. "How did it feel to kill Brookes Williamson?"

"The politically correct answer is that it's always wrong to take a life, regardless of how big a piece of shit that person is. It's supposed to eat at you, grind you down, totally fuck-up your brain and your life. Maybe that time will come, but today is not that day. Honestly? I couldn't be happier."

68

JJ stayed with McLean and the other HRT team members, both injured and deceased, until they were all evacuated. She then hitched a ride on Chopper 1 back to the Mobile Command Unit and debriefed Isaksen, Alexander, and Astin.

"This was one colossal clusterfuck," Isaksen said by way of kicking things off, "but I'm glad it's finally over. There's going to be a lot of eyes on this, I don't have to tell you, and tons of questions from Washington, the media, and every lawyer that wants his fifteen minutes of fame."

"Way too many innocent people killed, way too many cops killed or injured, and way too much property damage." Astin was still in disbelief that it had taken this long, and this much investment, to bring down one crazed man. Not a good look, in his mind, for the US Marshals.

"And don't forget, an innocent woman dragged into this and beaten, tortured, and used as bait." JJ was referring, of course, to Stacey, and she took that *very* personally.

Isaksen looked at JJ. "Tell me everything about your encounter with Williamson, starting from the time you boarded that helicopter to the moment you walked back in here. Don't leave anything out, and keep in mind that you're probably going to be grilled on this a hundred times by a hundred different people in the coming days." He was saying, without saying it, that she better have her story 100% nailed, including every conceivable detail that might be dissected.. Officially, he cared for the truth. In reality, he knew things weren't always that black and white.

****

JJ finally made it to the hospital after spending what seemed like hours with the task force leadership covering every aspect, every detail, of the operation. She reminded them, more than once, that she was merely a civilian and not in charge of any part of the action. She'd been asked to participate and lend her knowledge and expertise, which she gladly did, but she wouldn't take responsibility for the fallout, including Williamson's death. They had to remind her, conversely, that they weren't trying to throw her under the bus. Anything but. They wanted - *needed* - her to be cleared of any wrongdoing and able to stipulate and confirm every step of the operation that they, as leaders, had put into place.

Going straight to Stacey's room, she practically ran into Kristyn's arms, bringing both to tears. "How's Stacey? We've been so worried about her."

"She's regained consciousness, thank God. She's sedated now, which is good because she's in a lot of pain. The doctors say that she's going to need surgery, maybe several, for the injuries to her face and eye socket. Luckily there doesn't appear to be any impact to her vision."

"Thank goodness for that, at least. Did they say how long she'd be here and what she may be facing long-term in the way of rehab?"

"Too soon to tell, but they said early estimates are at least 5-7 days here in the hospital, and tomorrow they'll have some rehabilitation specialists look at her to give us some more information."

"I'm guessing that John and the kids should be arriving this morning?"

"Yes, they get into LAX around 9am. And before they get here, I need to call my parents and Daniel to tell them what has happened. I'm sure they're all going to hate me for keeping it from them. You'll probably be able to hear their screams all the way from Houston and Denver." That drew a bit of a nervous smile from them both.

JJ checked her watch. "I need to check on McLean and Springfield from the HRT team to see how they're doing. Then, if it's OK with you,

I'm going to slip home and take a shower, change, and then pick up your family at LAX. I'll bring you a change of clothes, too."

"Are their injuries serious?"

"Springfield probably just has a high-ankle sprain, so he may already be out of here. They probably did a quick X-Ray, taped his ankle, and released him. McLean's is more serious. He took a bullet to the thigh, and they're going to have to extract it and see if there's any damage. He's the kind of guy, though, that they'll probably have to cuff to the bed to keep him here for even 24 hours."

Kristyn smiled. "I don't know about you, but when this is all over, I'd like to be cuffed to the bed so I can sleep for a week straight. No phone calls, no texts, no video, no meetings. Just sleep."

"I think that's something we both need. Hell, something we both deserve."

"Before you go, one question," Kristyn said quietly, almost sheepishly. "How did it feel to kill Brookes Williamson?"

"The politically correct answer is that it's always wrong to take a life, regardless of how big a piece of shit that person is. It's supposed to eat at you, grind you down, totally fuck-up your brain and your life. Maybe that time will come, but today is not that day. Honestly? I couldn't be happier."

Epilogue

JJ and Kristyn were both dressed to kill, and while that was not entirely unusual for Kristyn, it was outside of JJ's comfort level. Still, she couldn't deny that she'd enjoyed the day of pampering and primping, having her hair colored and styled by some of the best in the business, and her makeup done to perfection. She had been loaned more than $250,000 worth of jewelry, as had Kristyn, and she was wearing the most beautiful – and painful – pair of strappy Christian Louboutin heels she'd ever seen. For one of the few times she could remember, she looked in the mirror, smiled, and thought to herself, *'Damn, I look good'.* The Christian Siriano dress, which cost more than her FBI annual salary, certainly didn't hurt. It was stunning, with a dramatic neckline cut down to *there*, a side split nearly to her hip, and a clinginess that was like a second skin. While her modesty had her insisting that she had to wear underwear, even if only a dreaded thong, the stylists finally convinced her that underwear wasn't an option by letting her look in the mirror. Regardless of what she tried on, the 'VPL' – Visible Panty Lines – were very evident. She finally relented and agreed to go 'commando'.

Climbing into the limousine provided by the studio, they headed to Grauman's Chinese Theater for the premier of James Cameron's new film starring many of Hollywood's biggest names and with a production budget befitting a James Cameron blockbuster. It was their first premier experience, and they could barely hide their excitement. Most of their team would be attending tonight, too, since their studio was producing both Cameron's picture and *The Murder Game*.

"My God, JJ, you look absolutely stunning tonight." She then leaned-in and whispered in her ear, "I can't even begin to tell you the things

I'm going to do to you tonight when we get home. That dress, those shoes, those jewels, that beautiful hair. Mmmmm." She nuzzled JJ's ear and gave her little butterfly kisses on the neck."

JJ moaned. "Ohhhh....you've got to stop, or I'm not going to make it to the theater. I can't be aroused to the point of being wet when I'm wearing what amounts to a million-dollar silk slip and no panties." She giggled, but deep down she was loving this new experience.

Trying to change the subject to bring the heat down, Kristyn said, "Just think: in less than a year we'll be back here for the premier of our movie! Now that production is back on schedule, we'll probably be done with shooting by Christmas, and then a few months of post-production, and hopefully released for Memorial Day or July 4th. Can you believe it's finally happening?"

"After all that this movie has been challenged with, and all that we've been through, it's incredibly satisfying. I'm proud of what the production and writing teams have accomplished. Heck, I'm proud of us! We've learned a lot, contributed a lot, and deserve to bask in the glow a bit."

Kristyn poured them each a flute of Dom Perignon Champagne from the limo's bar and raised her glass in a toast. "Here's to us! To our first movie production, to the launch of Supersleuth Productions, and our future as Hollywood producers and writers!"

"Cheers!" They clinked glasses and took a sip of the expensive nectar.

"One more toast," said JJ. "Here's to Stacey! She's made it through the surgeries with flying colors, and this Friday marks the last day for her rehabilitation. She's an incredible woman."

"I couldn't agree more, and here's to her and her family. They've been awesome. Even John – he has to get the award for the best, most loyal and comforting ex-husband of all time, to say nothing of a great dad and all-around standup guy."

"He's been a rock for her. So have your parents and Daniel."

"And thankfully, they've finally forgiven me. It was tense there for a while."

"I knew they'd come around. They knew that you were doing

everything you could to ensure that Stacey made it home safely, and in the end that's all that really mattered."

They arrived at the theater soon after, and they had their first red carpet experience. They were practically floating on air, or at least they would have been except that JJ had the constant reminder of being on the ground due to her beautiful but brutally painful shoes. They saw so many movie stars they could barely keep count, and even enjoyed conversations with several of them. They tried to nonchalantly hang around outside to see all the celebrities arriving, and jokingly feigned disappointment that E! News and the other media didn't try to collar them for an on-camera interview.

"That will be next year, when it's our movie!" JJ joked. "We'll have to practice handling all the tough questions, like 'Who are you wearing tonight'."

They went to several of the obligatory after parties, not that they minded at all. More mingling with the beautiful people, more great food, more great champagne. More great industry contacts and people wanting to talk to them about future projects. It was, they both agreed, one of the best evenings of their lives.

Once back home, they didn't waste any time following through on their lust-filled promises made earlier in the evening in the limo. They did, however, at least agree to take their beautiful dresses off, lest they get ruined. The jewels, the killer heels, and the perfect hair and makeup remained in place. Although, a couple of hours later when they were sated and catching their breath, the perfect hair and makeup were long gone, too.

"God, that was amazing. Apparently, dressing you up makes you even more of an animal in bed," Kristyn giggled. "I think we should do this more often."

"I second that," said JJ, lying back with her eyes barely open, totally lost in the afterglow.

As they snuggled, laughed, and just enjoyed the love they shared with one another, Kristyn asked, "When we're done with *The Murder*

Game, what do you see as our next move? Or have you thought that far out yet?"

"Actually, I have thought about it. I'd like us to find our own stories to develop and produce, especially women-centric stories. Not rom-coms, but rich, meaty stories with strong female characters and leads, not stories where the women are just there to support the leading men. Know what I mean?"

"Yeah, I do, and I agree. We should start looking for the next potential project now, start looking at books we might buy the rights to, or screenplays already being shopped around by some of the talented female writers out there."

"There's one other thing I'd like to do when we finish this project, although I'll probably have to invest some time and energy starting soon."

"What's that? You have me curious."

"I want to get my Private Investigator license. It's not the same as being a cop or FBI, for sure, but it keeps me in the game. Maybe I can focus on cases involving the entertainment industry, maybe even uncover cases that we can develop for Supersleuth Productions."

"I totally support you on that. It's part of who you are. I think you should absolutely do it!"

"There's one more thing." Kristyn looked unsure about what was coming. "I'd like you to do it with me. I always said that you'd make a great cop or investigator, and you showed it once again when we were pursuing Brookes Williamson. You're a natural, and such an incredible resource. Will you consider it? I can help you with all the legal and technical stuff. Please?"

"Hmmm, Supersleuth Productions AND Investigations. I kinda like the sound of that. Tell me more."

Acknowledgments

There are so many people that helped make *Glitz. Glamour. Murder.* a reality, from friends, family, coworkers, and especially my long-suffering wife. All writers will tell you that the people in their lives have to hear, *ad nauseum*, about the books we're writing, the books we want to write, and the drama we're experiencing at any given moment trying to write or promote our books. Thankfully most keep a smile and are good sports about it!

To Robert Saxe, for once again stepping-up and volunteering to read the draft manuscript as he was flying all over the world (literally) as the owner and Managing Director of nVision Consulting. He graciously spent hours on video conference calls providing me with valuable feedback.

To Barbara Burgess for her detailed insights and feedback, especially from a 'continuity' perspective since this book was a sequel to *The Murder Game*. Her memory and attention to details were invaluable and kept me from several embarrassing mistakes. As with every book she's ever reviewed for me, the finished product was made considerably better because of her input.

To Jessica Ollinger, for once again making time in her crushing schedule to read the manuscript and provide me with her feedback and insights. She's one of my frequent sounding-boards and someone whose opinions I value highly.

To Fred Zalupski, a man who may not be an editor by trade, but a man whose value as an early reviewer and editor cannot be overstated.

To Renee Cleveland (Instagram: #bookish.human), without whom I'd probably be lost. Her advice, guidance, and support has been invaluable. She has helped to connect me to dozens of book reviewers and important book sites on social media, reviewed this manuscript, and supported me as I scheduled book signings at area bookstores. Any question that comes up about the business side of this crazy book world, Renee is my go-to person.

To Paige Comrie (winewithpaige.com) for her continued support and patience as I try to master the intricacies of managing my website (www.sonnyhudsonauthor.com) and the tools used to manage the mailing list and monthly newsletter. If you're into wine, I HIGHLY recommend that you follow Paige on Instagram (#winewithpaige) and her website. She is knowledgeable, produces beautiful content, and she's just an awesome person. I'm lucky to be her friend.

And finally, I have to thank some of my good friends from Napa, CA that have supported me, inspired me, and graciously allowed me to use their 'names' in *Glitz. Glamour. Murder*. Patrice Breton; Samantha Breton; John Reinert; Stacy Reinert; Carlos Falla; and Paige Comrie.

About the Author

S onny Hudson is the author of crime/murder mysteries and political action thrillers. Readers compared his debut novel, *Let the Truth Be Told*, to such masters as Robert Ludlum, Tom Clancy, and Vince Flynn. *The Murder Game,* the first in the Jessica Jansen Thriller series, debuted in December, 2022 and was an immediate hit with its tight, fast moving story and strong, compelling characters. Reviewers compared it to best-selling authors like David Baldacci, James Patterson, Stuart Woods, and J. D. Robb. *Glitz. Glamour. Murder.* is a sequel to *The Murder Game* and continues to raise the bar for tight, tense, psychological thrillers.

Sonny is a resident of his native Virginia and has spent a long career in the technology world. His writing weaves technology into the action-driven stories, but never lets technology, or any of his characters, become all-powerful or omniscient. He lives by the words, 'Perfection is boring; it's our weaknesses and flaws and capacity to fall short that makes life, and characters, interesting."

To stay up to date on Sonny's work, follow him on www.sonnyhudsonauthor.com. You can sign-up on his website to receive his monthly newsletter and be the first to know when new books are coming down the road. Currently, Book #3 in the Jessica Jansen Thriller series is being written and targeted for a summer, 2024 release.

facebook.com/sonnyhudsonauthor
instagram.com/sonnyhudsonauthor